A Crimson Dawn

Written & illustrated by I A Taylor

To Dylan, we hope
you enjoy the book.
From William Taylor

Olsenton Tales, Book One

To Pippin. You enable me to fly

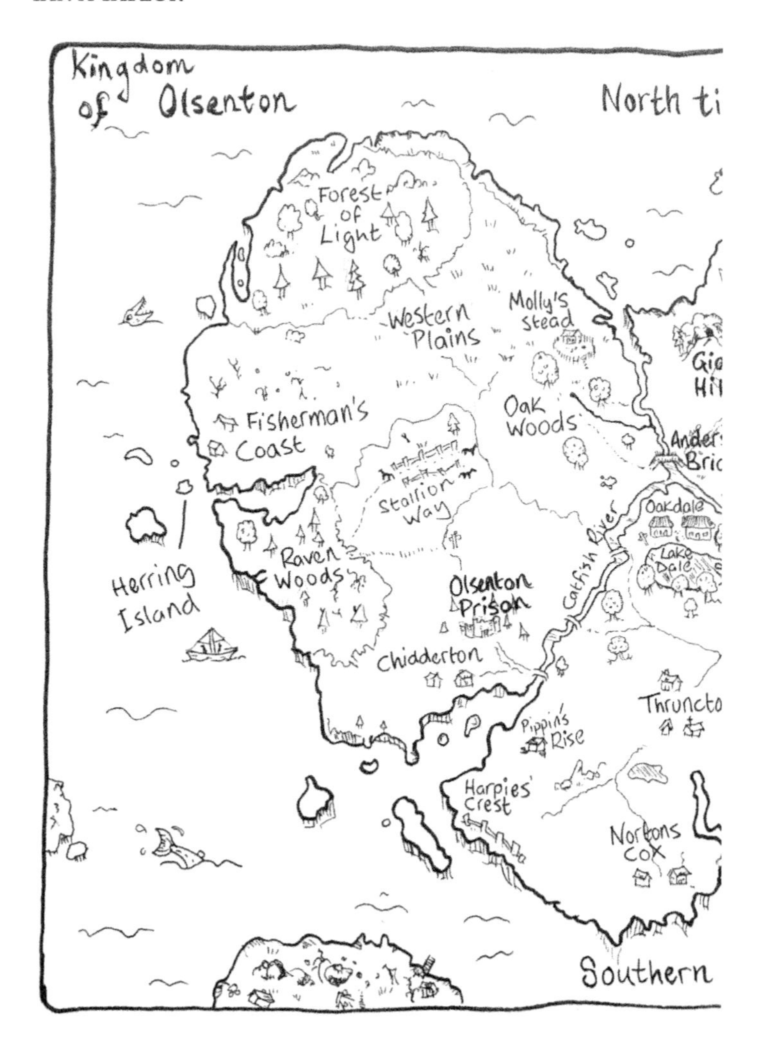
Kingdom of Olsenton
North
Forest of Light
Western Plains
Molly's stead
Fisherman's Coast
Oak Woods
Stallion Way
Oakdale
Lake Dale
Catfish River
Raven Woods
Herring Island
Olsenton Prison
Chidderton
Pippin's Rise
Harpies' Crest
Nortons Cox
Southern

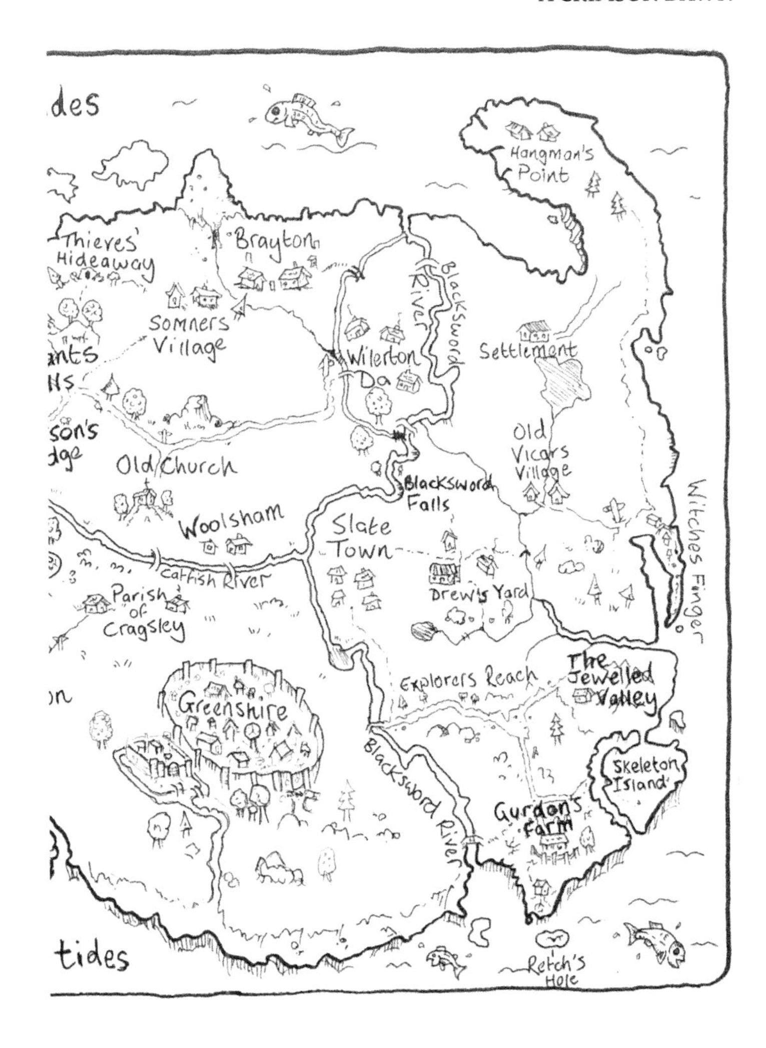
Hangman's Point
Thieves' Hideaway
Brayton
Somners Village
Wilerton Da
River Blacksword
Settlement
Old Church
Old Vicars Village
Blacksword Falls
Woolsham
Slate Town
Drew's Yard
Witches Finger
Catfish River
Parish of Cragsley
Explorers Reach
The Jewelled Valley
Greenshire
Blacksword River
Skeleton Island
Gurdon's Farm
tides
Retch's Hole

Visit my authors page for updates and information on new projects while your feedback is welcomed: ***@Author.Olsentonbooks***

Book cover created by Stardust Book Services.

Illustration designed by Martina of Stardust Book Services

ISBN: 978-1-7392772-0-8

First Edition. version 1.0

Sleeping Puppy Books 2023

'The cruellest villains wear human masks'

- Maximus

It Begins

Winged silhouettes negotiated the treetops while at ground level a cloaked female with feline companion moved parallel. Gazes ahead they clambered through, around and over a myriad of thorny obstructions, moving swift and with purpose. They reached the boundary where, and unwelcoming to them, sunlight filtered the gloom. The female hesitated, stalled in the shadows, for opposite and safe in the light, a figure stood waiting.

A rare visitor to her domain.

There was a tense silence while her eyes narrowed.

"Your bravado carried you here, mister. Naïve I think, as you've a lot to prove. Regardless, move closer."

The individual edged forward, nervous perspiration peppering his skin while she retrieved a wooden box and handful of coins from her cloak. She offered them forth, whereby and with shaking hands, the monies were deposited hastily into a pocket, the box dropped into a satchel.

Observing so vitriol spewed from her lips.

"Carefully, idiot and deliver it to Ms Kryvonis as informed. Don't open it, speak of it, nor tell of your destination."

"You have my word," came the response. "Advise her I shan't fail."

She grimaced.

"Pffft. Ensure you don't. Or she'll see to it you suffer."

Transaction complete they went their separate ways, the duo returning to the shadows, the visitor into the light while a feathered chorus filled the air.

An ear-piercing cacophony indicating events were in motion.

Sinister, and diabolical events with far-reaching consequences...

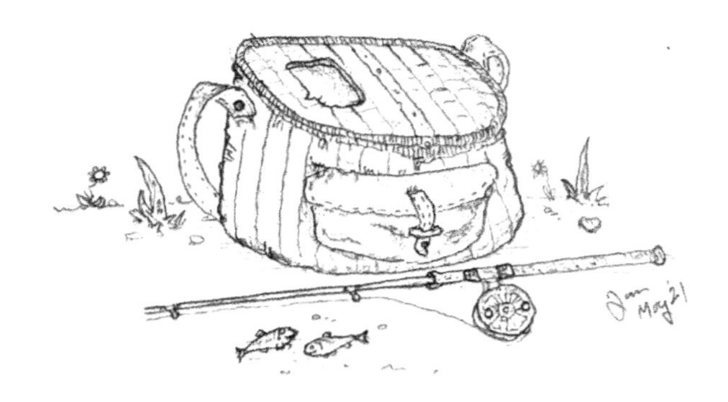

~ *The Mighty Esox* ~

As the sun descended towards the horizon three friends, fishing rods in hands, headed towards lake Dale, a forty-acre body of water located close to their homes in the rural village of Oakdale. They were in high spirits, their sights upon a particular species of fish. As they ambled along observed the waters were calm, only a gentle breeze caressing its glass-like surface; inviting them to explore its depths and, if they were lucky, offer a piscine inhabitant as reward for their efforts. They each carried a satchel stuffed with supplies as well as essential hook baits for the day. The oldest was fifteen and named Brenton Walker – though preferred others address him as 'Bren.' Of medium height, dark hair, chestnut eyes, and handsome in appearance. A considerate and sensitive young man who respected those he deemed worthy while avoiding those he didn't. The second boy was named Charlie Wilson. Fourteen years old with blonde hair. A cautious lad, always anticipating a 'worst case scenario' should they encounter anything unexpected during their adventures. That said he was loyal and would fight their corner should trouble rear its head. He'd ensure justice prevailed no matter how long it took.

The third in the trio's name was Hawk Critchley. Twelve years' old, perpetually mischievous and open-minded.

The topic of conversation was about the Biggest Pike Competition; an ongoing, and year-long angling challenge between them. The previous winner was Charlie. An achievement that thrilled him. Fuelling their obsession was the supposed existence of an exceptionally large specimen; a fish they'd named 'Lucifer'.

As they stopped bankside, eager to set their hooks Charlie scanned the expanse, a thoughtful smile upon his face.

"So, is today the day he shows himself?"

"I hope so," replied Bren optimistically. "I want revenge."

His friends exchanged cynical glances while he diverted his gaze to the rippled surface, his thoughts returning to an encounter he'd never forget.

It was several weeks before but remained forefront in his mind. He was lakeside and alone, the first time he'd hunted a razor-toothed predator unassisted; with the idea of having friends nearby should he encounter difficulties being of minimum concern.

He cast a frantically wriggling lobworm into the margins, hoping to catch a perch. If that. However, with his gaze defocussed, his thoughts anywhere but waterside, felt the rod's butt slam against his thigh, an unpleasant thud returning him to reality. He grabbed the object and clambered to his feet, his pulse accelerating rapidly. He watched in amazement as the line zipped across the surface and away, the handle of his centre-pin reel spinning uncontrollably backwards; too fast to take a hold of. Instead he pressed his thumb firm against the spool, risking severe friction burns; but knew he must apply pressure, or he'd soon run out of line.

He gritted his teeth; sensed he'd hooked into something special. Something memorable. Was it *HIM?*

It couldn't have been, could it?

A protracted tug of war began, while he glanced left then right, desperate to catch the attention of any passer-by. There wasn't anybody.

His destiny was to fight alone.

He made progress, but briefly. For the fish was strong. Incredibly strong and living up to its earned moniker, making sudden, and powerful surges before holding stubbornly in place; tricking him into believing the hooks had come loose and lodged on the hard bottom. Which they hadn't. To say it was a mental, as well as physical contest was never truer. There were instances where he were rooted to the spot, rod doubled over, fearing the blank might crack under the strain. An unthinkable proposition.

Then, with aching arms, and back, and with sweat cascading between his shoulder blades he gradually gained line. Inch by inch. Yard by yard. Every millimetre earned with spent perspiration. His eyes widened the instant he observed the beast as it bore an unmissable scar running diagonally across the rear of its olive-green skull. He observed in amazement as it arched clear of the waters; offering a tantalising first glimpse, before rising majestic, surface spray sent in all directions.

He remembered the mixture of fear and elation: intimidated by it, as well as a building excitement should he bring it to land; and how he might cope with the monumental task of unhooking it without having his fingers bitten. No. He couldn't allow such thoughts. He needed to remain composed. However he did visualise himself parading victorious through the village, waving his hands in celebration with his friends, neighbours, *everybody* in awe of his achievement. If briefly.

Unfortunately the tussle ended abruptly and in bitter disappointment. As following one particularly powerful run the hooks came free; inexplicably so; with the rod suddenly straightening, any tension loosening, causing his body to fall limp also; and in turn informing him he'd suffered the terrible 'one-that-got-away' scenario.

An occurrence all anglers dread.

That was his. And it hurt. And to make matters worse, none of his friends believed he'd ever hooked it. Even his announcement of the tell-tale scar did little to convince them.

They were, and remained, sceptical.

Hawk's exuberant words tore him from his daydream.

"I've got a special bait today. So if anyone's going to hook him it's going to be me."

His friends peered into the tub while Bren regained his bearings.

"Huh? Roach. Your secret bait is a roach? There's nothing special about that."

He gestured to Charlie, who was wearing a similar expression.

"But lots of people use those as bait. What's so special about yours?"

He rotated it, inspecting its milky-white eyes.

"Well, uh, nothing really. It's just a...a regular fish. But I *know* it'll catch me a big one!"

***

A little later, with their floats bobbing gently upon the surface and the trio fishless, the topic of conversation had shifted to something much more serious. A major bone of contention for one of them in particular. Hawk shook his head apathetically as he addressed Bren.

"You need to stand up to him then, fight back for once."

He sighed, staring forlorn at the ground.

"I can't. You know that. Even though he's fourteen he's built like a man. His face is hairy and everything."

Charlie raised a hand and caressed his own smooth chin.

"Yeah. He shaves too. He's a freak."

Now is a suitable time to enlighten you about whom they were referring to. The individual in question was a boy named Kieron Chudley - the village bully who, frustratingly, lived along the same lane as Bren and Charlie.

For reasons unknown to Bren, he'd targeted him for an ongoing campaign of abuse, though according to Charlie and Hawk the real reason he disliked him so much was because of his handsome appearance and keen eye for Grace. Hawk's older sister. He were jealous to the core. He had a crush on her too, but she found him repulsive; insisting he were a 'troll hidden beneath human skin.' He'd chosen him to become his regular 'punchbag'; were an unfortunate victim of the thug's frustration.

So with that explained let's return to the conversation with Hawk offering his opinion.

"Maybe he'll direct his hate towards somebody else soon. Charlie perhaps."

His eyes widened in response, the thought causing him anxiety.

"Not me! I haven't done anything wrong."

Hawk laughed uneasily, sensing he may have overstepped the mark.

"I'm joking. Why would he turn against you?"

It was too late though. He'd planted a seed of doubt in his mind. Bren stepped in to placate him.

"Don't worry. He's made it clear it's me he hates. Nothing's going to change that."

He visualised the bully's freckled face, mop

of ginger hair.

"He's so mean. I *hate* him. So...bloody much."

At that moment Hawk's float bobbed up and down, indicating a presence below. He lunged instinctively froward, grabbing the rod in excitement.

"Shall I strike?"

His two companions replied at the same time, their experience greater.

"No – it's too early."

There – again! The float dipped briefly below the surface before popping back into view, causing him, who couldn't wait any longer, to yank the rod high into...nothing. The line slackened disappointingly. Having observed the event Charlie made eye contact.

"Ugh! You were too quick. We told you to wait!"

The wind knocked cleaned from his sails; he sighed.

"But my dad said if I leave it too long the fish might swallow the hooks, and that would be bad."

"Well that can happen, I know," added Bren. "But you need to wait a bit longer - but not *too* long."

With the remark confusing to his ears he threw the rod to the ground.

"Gah! Stupid pike. Stupid fishing, and stupid waste of time!"

Always considerate, Bren placed a hand on his shoulder.

"Hey, no need to do that. Pick it up and try again. You can do it."

He shook his head in response, the empty feeling of failure yet to subside.

"But...Urgh! That could have been him, and...and I missed!"

Charlie didn't help matters either, rubbing salt into the already sore wound. He whispered into his ear.

"I know. Imagine if you caught him. But you didn't."

Bren glared in response.

"Stop! There's no need to say that. It probably wasn't him; likely a smaller one. And if it was it means we've both missed him now – and it also means he's out there still."

Hawk sighed, wishing to move on.

"It doesn't matter. We'll never know."

He picked up his rod and reeled the line in.

"Fine. I'll try again. Do any of you have a

gudgeon?"

The two returned surprised gazes with Bren commenting.

"What!? You only had ONE bit of bait, why didn't you bring plenty like us?"

He held up his empty tub, an embarrassed look about him.

"No. I uh, had others, too but I lost them. I knocked the tub over, and they, um they fell in the water."

Regardless, they soon had their hooks baited and lines recast but remained bite less and fishless. Therefore it wasn't long before Charlie and Hawk's attention waned, agreeing they'd missed the opportunity to catch. They wore fatigued expressions while they packed away their tackle before wandering off to explore the nearby woods. Bren meanwhile were content to be alone. He knew he wouldn't encounter Lucifer again. How did he know? Simple. He had a gut feeling. Like most of us, he relied on instinct, and chose to trust it. However he persevered as he loved the atmosphere of being lakeside, as well as the opportunity to observe the abundant wildlife. However it wasn't long before the duo returned, both bored.

"Any more bites?" enquired Charlie.

He shrugged indifferently

"Nope. I don't think I'm going to catch either."

Hawk peered in the direction of the village.

"Us too. We've had enough and we're going home."

Charlie gestured to his left.

"But we did see smoke over there."

He pointed to an area of woodland in the distance.

"Either somebody's lit a campfire or there's one burning out-of-control somewhere."

Bren glanced in the same direction spying a trail of smoke rising above the treetops, the breeze wafting it in their direction. Therefore it wasn't long before he were alone again. So feeling perpetually curious as well as fed up with waiting for a fish that wasn't likely to bite, packed away his gear and headed in the same direction.

After treading carefully through and around the undergrowth he'd soon reached his destination: as there, beyond a wall of hedgerows he spied smoke spiralling into the atmosphere, but not vast plumes as anticipated. Instead heard the gentle crackling of wood burning upon an organised campfire. So opting to peer discreetly through the vegetation spied a lone figure – a man sitting down amongst a clearing, providing cover from the wind and prying eyes perhaps.

He was occupied with cooking something upon the end of a lengthy stick. Appearance wise he had shoulder length chestnut hair, parted in the middle. A full beard covering a strong, square jaw; no nonsense expression upon his face. He was dressed in a beige long-sleeved tunic, cotton trousers and calf length leather boots. Age wise in his mid-to-late twenties. He kept watch curious as to who the stranger might be and how long he'd been there. However it wasn't long before his sneaky presence was detected with the individual turning in his direction, a scornful look about him.

"Who goes there? Show yourself before I come and find you."

He froze, wondering how the stranger knew he were there. He continued.

"Step forward immediately. I can *smell* you. Don't make me say it again."

Sensing if he were to make a run for it the stranger would easily catch him, he declared himself.

"I will. I'm...I'm coming out."

He pushed through the undergrowth and into view, causing him to chuckle with delight.

"Oh, it's just a nosy boy. Why were you watching me, and how can I help?"

He hesitated, with it being a critical moment. The individual. Who was he, and what were his intentions good, bad, indifferent? His mind raced while he leant forward, eying him head to toe.

"Well, are you going to answer?"

He inspected the tidy and organised space and did. Choosing honesty.

"My name is Brenton. I'm alone. I er, I saw the smoke."

The stranger chuckled.

"So you came to investigate, yes."

"Yes. I thought there might be a forest fire or something."

"Well Brenton, as you can see there is no forest fire. Merely a man cooking supper. So what now, are you going to continue on your way or hoping to stay and talk? It's your choice."

He considered his options, knew it wasn't late in the day and darkness wouldn't descend for a while. Added to that his home wasn't too far away; but also, there was *something* about the stranger. He had honest eyes; their blue shade displaying a hint of mischief.

He stepped forward.

"If you don't mind, I can be your company for a bit."

The man smiled.

"Excellent. And as good manners dictate, you're due an introduction."

He tapped two fingers against his chest.

"I'm known as Maximus. And I guarantee you've nothing to fear. It so happens you've stumbled upon me whilst I'm eating supper. Roasted squirrel in fact and recently caught. Sparse of meat to be truthful but after sprinkling with seasoning, tasty none the less. Would you like some?"

He inspected the offering which, to his untrained eyes, appeared undercooked though he needn't have worried as he knew what he were doing. Regardless he arrived at a sensible decision.

"No thank you. I'll eat later with my family.

He nodded nonplussed.

"Fine. More for me then."

A short silence followed broken by Maximus with another question.

"I assume you live local. So what brought you here today other than the smoke?"

He observed the teen clutching his angling gear.

"Was it fishing, hunting, or both things perchance?"

Feeling at ease in his presence, he smiled.

"Yep. In the village over there. I've been fishing with friends. At the lake-."

The man interjected, eager to share his appreciation of the surroundings.

"Indeed. The vast and magnificent lake Dale. Did you catch anything?"

He shook his head in return.

"Not today. We were trying to catch pike. A competition thingy. There's a really big one in there. We've been trying to catch it for a long time. We call it 'Lucifer'."

Curious Maximus glanced briefly to his own nearby rod and reel.

"Competition? Interesting. And Lucifer, eh? I guess it must be big then. And fierce?"

Bren nodded enthusiastically.

"Yes. I hooked it once. Um, recently, but it escaped the hooks and got away. We think it's a thirty pounder. Maybe bigger. Everyone says it's uncatchable, but not me. I'll catch it one day."

Maximus smiled.

"Well I hope you succeed. But be mindful of the sharp teeth if you do. They'll slice through your soft skin in no time."

Bren held up his left hand and pointed to his index finger.

"I know. This one has a scar from a bite once. Look."

He acknowledged the story.

"Ah, you bare the mark of a predator hunter. You're part of a special club then. You should be proud."

He bit into the meat before continuing.

"So I guess you'd like to know more about me?"

Bren smiled in return.

"If you like."

He nodded while gesturing to the space around them.

"Yes. I am enjoying a short break here before returning home with my horse."

He gestured towards his steed nearby, tethered to the trunk of an evergreen. A fine-looking animal with a white coat and eyes full of life, its mane a light shade of grey, build muscular, and capable of moving at great speed if it wished.

"Rapscallion's his name. A fine horse to be sure, though mischievous."

Bren held his gaze upon it.

"That's an unusual name but a nice one."

He diverted his attention to a magnificent

looking sword hanging from a branch within reach of Maximus' location. He observed as such.

"Oh, you've spied my blade - an essential weapon for any traveller. A good sword is worth its weight in gold."

He grabbed hold of the weapon, unsheathed it carefully before offering it forth.

"Have a look if you're willing, as you'll need a weapon of your own one day. The kingdom is a dangerous place you know."

He took possession, were surprised by its unexpected heft, but appreciated its elegant design and craftsmanship, its potential for causing great harm or defending one's self. He spied the razor-sharp edge, peppered with dents and chips as well as the overall artistry; the hilt wrapped in soft leather. Curious he moved his thumb along its length but was soon interrupted.

"STOP! I wouldn't do that if I were you. You'll find your thumb on the ground and blood everywhere."

His skin flushed an embarrassed shade of red as he handed the object back.

"Sorry. That's the nicest sword I've ever seen, but heavier than I thought it'd be. Thank you for letting me hold it."

Maximus smiled, appreciating his

manners.

"That's decent of you. You're one of only a few to have held it. I'd consider yourself lucky."

He nodded in appreciation.

"I...I do."

Following that he rose to his feet and wiped the dust from his trousers, feeling the encounter had run its course. He glanced at Rapscallion and smiled before gesturing in the direction of the village.

"It's um, it's time for me to go now. I've been out for ages so my parents will be wondering where I am."

Maximus nodded, as he had other tasks to complete.

"Yes. You head home to a tasty dinner. I must tend Rapscallion anyway. I don't want him sulking, which he sometimes does."

He rose to his feet too and offered a parting wave.

"It's been a pleasure meeting you today, young man. Be sure to tread carefully and get home safe."

~ A DAZZLING ENTRANCE ~

Bren opened the front door and trudged inside. A cosy property adorned with sparse and simple furniture. A two-seater couch, pair of leather armchairs, the cushions showing signs of heavy wear. A bookcase along with clay ornaments, nothing extravagant or expensive but enough to add a decorative flourish. The flooring was typical timber boards illustrating heavy use with dents, scratches, and unsightly gouges. The walls were a cream render with cracks here and there.

He spied his mother in the living room, occupied with mundane tasks. Her name was Alexandra, thirty-four years' old, long brown hair tied in a ponytail, her dress patterned with a flower design. She doted on her family: in particular her only child Brenton, and loving husband Clayton. A sincere and caring individual not at all wise when it came to the outside world, having originated from a secluded village elsewhere; with the notion of anything bad happening to them filling her with dread.

Bren paced towards the diner while his rod tip scraped against the wall giving away his presence. Hearing such, she spun around her gaze penetrating his.

"Where have you been, and what have you been up to? I saw Charlie and Hawk pass by a long time ago."

He was taken aback.

"Nothing. Um, fishing was rubbish, so I ended up talking to a man."

She stepped forward; unsure she'd heard him correctly.

"You what, a man you say? Someone from the village, or a stranger?"

He pleaded innocence, a confused frown creasing his forehead.

"Huh. No. Not from around here but a nice man. He's um, passing through, and camping by the lake."

Having heard the conversation his father Clayton appeared, dark hair, and looking remarkably similar to his son. He looked to them in turn.

"OK, this fella. Tell us more."

He complied.

"Yes. His name is Maximus. Said he's heading home following time away. He's camping by the lake for a bit, to er, rest and recover. That's all."

"To recover from what exactly, and what else did he ask, did he wonder where you live, anything like that?" questioned Clayton.

"No. I, uh, I don't know. Nothing like that. Only my name. We uh, talked about fishing and stuff. Oh, and his white horse. He wasn't threatening at all," answered the lad wondering why the interrogation.

Alexandra crossed her arms.

"Strangers indeed. You know how I feel about you talking those you don't know. What if he were a sinister man, a murderer, what then? I'll tell you what then – you could be dead, floating face down in the lake – with your throat slit!"

Clayton interrupted, believing she'd overreacted.

"Steady on love. There's no need to frighten him. He assessed the situation. He's old enough to make certain decisions."

She remained unconvinced.

"Certain decisions? Hmpf. Like what? Like placing his meal plate in the washing bowl which he never does. I'm not so sure. He's a lot to learn still. I don't want anything to happen to him. He's more than precious."

Bren's gaze switched between them, held out his open palms.

"Child? No. And dad's right. I could have chosen not to speak to him, but he seemed friendly. Nothing happened."

She glared, needing more reassurance.

"You're regarded as a child until you're sixteen whether you like it or not. It'd be eighteen if I had my way. And do you intend to speak with him again?"

"Huh, eighteen? But I'll be a man at sixteen. Like dad was. And I don't think so. He's only stopping for a few days then he'll be on his way."

Clayton had the final word wishing to put an end to the, as he saw it, storm in a tea cup.

"There you go. No harm done. And you *do* know it's good to meet a new face once in a while, right?"

She yielded.

"Hmpf. As long as it's a friendly face I don't mind. We don't get many visitors to these parts which is why I worry when we do. He's our only child. And extremely precious."

She turned to him.

"The only one to continue your bloodline. A fact you know *too* well."

***

The next day arrived and there was a commotion in the village square with several residents congregated in a large group: excited chatter heard too. Reacting to that Bren peered from an upstairs window, curious as to what was taking place. It were clear something was occurring, but he needed more information. He called out curious.

"Hey, what's going on?"

A woman hollered in return.

"I can't believe it. We've a visitor."

She beckoned him down as she joined the ever-expanding congregation. So wasting no time and worried he'd miss out on something exciting he slipped on his boots and rushed into the street. As he approached the group – a throng of curious locals – he spied Hawk and Charlie, their backs to him. He drew level and tapped Hawk on the shoulder, who spun around, eyes gleaming.

"This is amazing!"

He nudged through the crowd to witness what the fuss was about. And there, stood centre stage was a rare visitor to the town; tall, thin, and clothed in a well-worn black pin-striped suit along with winkle-picker boots; jet-black hair, parted in the middle; a long, wavy moustache – curled up at the corners, certainly unique in appearance when compared to a typical resident. His dark eyes flitted rapidly from person to person trying his utmost to make eye contact with each and every one.

Located near was a wooden-wheeled folding trolley of sorts stocked with strange bottles and other assorted items. It were a work of admiration; constructed of the finest timbers and carved with patterns and swirls and strange foreign texts; the wheels spoked with whitened wood. High end carpentry for sure.

Behind those items stood an ornate display box similar in appearance to the main stand; again constructed of the best materials; its myriad of compartments and drawers containing something or other. The individual had commanded the attentions of all in attendance. The trio in particular. But as the crowd continued to swell and the excited cacophony with it he realised his words had been lost to the masses; required a different approach to aid his presentation. He dug two fingers into his breast pocket and retrieved something; held that same something into the air between forefinger and thumb.

He cleared his throat before shouting at the top of his voice. A faux, aristocratic accent.

"Ladies and gentlemen, boys and girls; may I have your attention? For I hold here a valuable welcome gift. A gift to somebody. BUT only the one."

Silence followed, an anticipatory pause as he continued.

"Oh yes. I'm holding a golden coin. A genuine one, which as you know is worth much indeed."

He hesitated, increasing the tension further.

"This coin. THIS precious object shall belong to one of you very soon."

The audience murmured, exchanged joyous glances while he continued.

"But before any transactions take place, I must introduce myself first. A necessary and proper introduction."

He bowed.

"Indeed. I am Kapernicus Weezle, esteemed purveyor of rarities, and I am at your service!"

Gasps followed while he paced back and forth, confident and self-assured; his agenda: to convince as many of them as possible to purchase his wares.

~ Weezle by Name ~

The merchant's dark eyes scanned the interested faces, many open mouthed and eager to open their purses.

"Yes. The one and only Kapernicus Weezle Esquire; purveyor of the finest potions and most interesting of curiosities!"

He spread his arms wide and gestured to his products.

"None of these items are available anywhere else other than here, in my possession. For I have travelled far and wide, high, and low, to search for and acquire the most interesting and diverse range of goods you see; their quality high, the prices perpetually low."

An impatient voice called out.

"But what about the gold coin then?"

He waved a forefinger rapidly.

"I'll return to that in a moment. But now you must exercise patience. As amongst my wares you'll find the most essential of high-end goods, from potions to medicines, ointments, to food stuffs. With many purloined from lands across the seas. You name it and I might just have it!"

Meanwhile, enveloped in the performance Bren felt a tug on his tunic diverting his attention from the pedlar. It was Clayton. He'd heard the commotion and wasn't impressed. He didn't want his kin ripped off; assuming he'd waste any coins on junk.

"Come away."

He shook his head failing to understand the interruption.

"What, why?"

Clayton's gaze penetrated his own.

"Come home with me. That *thing* is a conman, a hustler. He's here to rip us off. You included."

But I haven't got any...urgh. Leave me alone."

He pulled away from him. As far as he were concerned the fun was just beginning.

"But I want to stay. Like everyone else."

Conceding defeat Clayton shrugged indifferently, unwilling to engage in a messy and public confrontation. He raised his palms into the 'surrender' position.

"Fine. Do what you like but don't say I never warned you."

He turned and headed away while Bren dug deep into his pockets, checking for funds. They were empty as expected so returned his attention to the visitor who was mid-pitch.

"I'd like a volunteer. Just the one."

He scanned the observing faces.

"I need someone with a...ahem, spotty complexion. Anybody?"

Following a short delay a young girl stepped gingerly forward, her face speckled with teenage spots, her auburn hair in need of a good brush. She glanced about nervously while several folks cheered her bravery. Reacting appropriately Kapernicus moved in and took a gentle hold of her hand while she looked submissively to the ground. Observing so he adopted a sympathetic tone.

"No, no, my dear, you must hold your head high. Stand tall and proud. I admire you for stepping forward. And as reward for your bravery I have something to help you; help reveal the beauty hidden behind your mask of unsightly pimples!"

She smiled a cautious smile, while a round of applause echoed around the space. Meanwhile he grabbed a small bottle containing a luminous green substance which he held the aloft.

"Behold the *cure!*"

Most cheered in response while others remained stone-faced, adopting suspicious expressions instead, their attitudes that of cynicism. He observed as such and narrowed his eyes, felt displeased but turned his attention to the youngster. He shook the bottle enticingly before removing the cork stopper. Following that he took a sniff, as did she whereby an interested smile appeared on her face. The merchant was in his element, creating drama from nothing. He popped the cork and poured three small drops onto his fingertips before placing the bottle on the table. He crouched low, took a deep breath before leaning close to the girl, making firm eye contact.

"Young lady do I have permission to apply some to your skin?"

She didn't answer, instead peered over her left shoulder as a woman emerged from the crowd; serious faced, staring down her nose, her attitude one of suspicion.

"That's my daughter you 'ave there. First 'ow much will this 'cure' cost me, and will it work? I'll 'ave you know she is conscious of 'er complexion. That green stuff you're 'oldin' better not cause 'er any 'arm."

He took a dramatic step back.

"What!? Oh no my dear. I assure you this is a tried-and-tested formula. Essential for the aid and removal of teenage spots and blemishes. Created by royal physicians no less. An ointment fit for a Princess. You have my *word* on that!"

She took stock of his statement,

approached her daughter making eye contact with her.

"Royalty, eh? Well, what do you want my darlin,' wanna try it?"

She nodded eagerly while the woman turned her attentions to the merchant.

"Alright mister you 'ave our trust. Please 'elp 'er. It would mean so much."

He moved to the youngster, stopping suddenly.

"But first! And before I apply the ointment you need to know it's effects aren't instant. Oh no. It will take several applications over a period of many days to even begin to see the results."

He drew a deep breath.

"And to further enhance its effects you'll need to help it along by eating only food stuffs of good quality; fruits vegetables and to drink plenty of water. That is of utmost importance. You must *work* with the ointment if you know what I mean."

He positioned his hands and fingers into a 'steepled' position illustrating supreme self-confidence – arrogance even. Then whilst switching his gaze between daughter and mother.

"So... do you wish to proceed?"

She replied, unconvinced.

"I assume I'll need to purchase the 'ole bottle, yeah?"

He nodded eagerly while she continued.

"'Hmm. 'Ow much will it cost me then?"

He snatched a scroll of yellowed paper from a drawer then began to unroll it, his thin fingers moving rapidly; the object unfurling to approximately three feet in length. He placed his spectacles upon the end of his nose and scanned the text, his gaze moving slowly left to right. Seconds later he emitted a tiny, forced cough.

"Here we are. The lowest amount I can accept is... let's see... *five* coins. How does that sound? A mere five as the price for your daughter's radiance to shine through; her innocent beauty to become once more apparent."

There followed a momentary pause while she considered the proposal. At the same time, the sound of murmuring prevailed, indicating some found the price acceptable while others grumbled in discontent. Meanwhile he waited patiently switching his gaze between the masses, the girl, and her mother. Finally, and to put them out of their collective misery she arrived at a decision.

"Yeah. We fink it's a fair deal."

Whoops and hollering followed, further

validating her decision to buy while Kapernicus' smile spread from ear to ear. He bowed, one arm placed across his chest, the other held horizontal.

"And for that I say a huge thank you."

He stroked his chin, glancing back and forth between them while the crowd fell silent.

"Hmm. Listen well, for I haven't finished...as you are the first customers of the day, I have decided to accept a loss of profit for your benefit and therefore chosen to deduct ONE coin from the selling price. Meaning it will cost you *four* instead."

He winked at the girl then continued.

"And with the spare one you might treat yourselves to some honey cakes. If you so wish."

She smiled gleefully in response as did her mother. A bargain indeed. She opened her drawstring purse while he stepped eagerly forward, his heart pounding beneath his chest. Selling were what he lived for. And that simple negotiation was only the beginning. He narrowed his eyes, holding out an open palm in anticipation. It's then the random voice sounded again.

"But what about the gold coin, where is it?"

With a nod of the head and flick of the wrist he held it aloft.

"Of course. And excellent timing, ma'am. I hadn't forgotten about it, oh no. Let me complete this transaction first then I'll explain what's going to happen next."

A short silence followed while the goods were exchanged. Finally after pocketing payment he moved a wooden crate in front of himself before turning it upside down. He stepped atop it before addressing the crowd.

"Regarding this then. I have a proposition for you. I can either throw it amongst you whereby ONE lucky person will have the opportunity to catch it. OR I can throw TWENTY-FIVE coins worth only HALF its value, ensuring MANY will have coins to collect."

He scanned the excited faces.

"What will it be?"

Predictably shouting and debate ensued with nobody able to produce a definitive answer to the conundrum. Some attempted quick calculation, double-checking his information were correct. Regardless he observed as a few residents argued, with some coming close to blows. He grinned knowingly; aware he were manipulating them all. Finally having seen and heard enough, he spread his arms wide.

"Everyone listen. Pay attention please."

The crowd fell silent.

"I know it can't be easy trying to agree on this matter, so I'll choose an individual to decide instead."

He pointed towards them, moving a finger slowly while excited children – and adults alike - jumped up and down, vying for his attention.

Finally he'd made his choice, pointed to a ginger-haired youth; a serious, chubby, freckle-faced youth, dressed in brown dungarees, short-sleeved mustard colour tunic and well-worn boots; the mean face of a bully. Yep, Kieron the village bully of all people. Bren and friends looked at each other in disgust. Others felt the same judging by their reactions; with a collective grumble heard.

Regardless the choice had been made. His gaze remained fixed upon the youth.

"Boy what is your name?"

"Kieron mister, and I ain't a boy. I'm a young man," came the curt response.

He raised a single eyebrow.

"Okay *young man*...you are the chosen one. What do you say?"

He glanced left then right, an arrogant smirk upon his face.

"I say throw the fing. I'm gonna catch it."

Dissenting voices followed, but it mattered

not. He had final say.

Kapernicus placed the coin atop his thumbnail before flicking it high into the air. At the same time some in attendance, including adults, jumped up and down trying to gain as much leverage as they could whilst attempting to stop others doing the same. In moments and amid the commotion the coin had disappeared, fallen somewhere between them all; become invisible amongst the dirt, grass, and weeds. A few dropped to their knees scrambling to part the vegetation, desperate to catch sight of the glorious, golden shine but amongst the many feet, the dirt, as well as dust the object was lost.

Meanwhile Kapernicus had once more become the centre of attention. He'd opened wide the doors to his stall, and as a result, the majority forgot about the coin; had become distracted by his other wares instead. They gathered around, jostling for space; their numbers including Bren, Charlie, and Hawk. The trio stood side by side transfixed by the sights.

He adjusted hair.

"So ladies and gentlemen as is custom I shall now read to you a selection of items in my ever-expanding inventory."

He took a deep breath.

"In no particular order I have: *Love potions, healing oils, opposite-sex-attracting balms, anti-*

hair-loss potions, eating disorder pills, bowel-relaxants, muscle-enhancing cremes, stink bombs, itching powder, anti-itching powder powder..."

He took a further breath before continuing.

"And for the keen cooks amongst you I have: *the finest crushed garlic paste, paprika powder, flavour enhancing cubes, dried oxen strips and much, much more.*"

He shifted his focus to the display case at the rear of the table widening his eyes as he sought to catch the attention of the younger members of the audience including the three friends.

"Now for the children here - and young at heart of course - I will display some of my other curiosities; for your personal viewing pleasures. HOWEVER you must understand most of these items are one of a kind. You will NOT find them ANYWHERE else in the known world so therefore can carry a most *expensive* of price tags and I'm talking a price far out of the range of your average pocket monies."

Kieron, his tolerance always low, called out, having heard enough waffle.

"Get on wiv it, mate!"

He glared at the youth, muttering under his breath.

"Mate? I'm no 'mate' of yours. Ahem."

He plucked a small, angular wooden box carved with ornate patterns from a drawer, the object no bigger than a matchbox say. He held it proudly aloft.

"This is a mystery box - a puzzle box. Witness as I place another gold coin inside."

He quickly and discreetly switched the object with a single penny before closing the drawer, but it was done so quick that none could tell. He shook the object, the rattling noise indicating the 'gold' were inside before continuing.

"Now and for the meagre sum of ten coins you may purchase this item safe in the knowledge you have a valuable gold piece to find. But be mindful that in order to solve the puzzle and therefore open the drawer, you will need to solve the intricate design and fiendish nature of this wooden curio. Succeed and the grand reward will be yours. However fail and frustration will be your only company. Indeed, you might try to force it, but I assure you it has been constructed to resist such attempts. Now any takers?"

There came an instant response from a gentleman in the group. A thickset individual fancying his chances.

"Me. I'll take it. I'll open it easily!"

He stepped forward and the transaction was soon completed. Then as the various assorted and mostly useless items were shown and snapped up by some in attendance, the three friends, all penniless began to lose interest. That is until Charlie pointed to a glass bottle, the object bathed in shade and located not-quite-out-of-sight at the rear of the case. He informed his friends of his observation whereby they too were curious causing Bren to request the merchant's attention.

"Mister. That bottle at the back. What's in it, please?"

Appreciating the manners he gasped in delight, cupping his hands together and pacing over to the trio.

"Ah, yes, very observant young man. Incredibly observant in fact. Would you, ah, would you like to *see* it?"

All three nodded excitedly. Even Kieron stood behind and to one side was intrigued. In moments he had taken hold of the object and placed it across his open palm. Following that he moved slowly and dramatically closer to them. Several adults were mesmerised by the presentation too: their eyes transfixed; their interest levels through the roof. The bottle in question was of exquisite design; a colour of smoky grey glass, with decorative runes etched across the front centre. The base rectangular, rounded corners, about seven inches in height, four wide, and two deep. The top secured with a cork stopper with reinforcing wire wrapped tightly around it ensuring all contents remained within.

He cradled the object, displaying as much of it and its contents as possible. Then as he paced enticingly back and forth he opened his mouth.

"Now, *this* is the *pièce de résistance* – but unfortunately NOT for sale! However I am willing to impart some interesting facts about it."

He cleared his throat, adjusted his footing.

"Now THIS item is truly and most certainly ONE-OF-A-KIND. The only one in existence, no less. For it is a creature of..."

He narrowed his eyes, scanned the enthralled faces, building the tension further,

"*unknown identification...*"

Everyone exchanged marvelled glances while the sounds of unintelligible whispering was heard.

He continued.

"It's claimed this...creature once belonged to a powerful and mysterious wizard – nay, warlock! It's said it has...powers, dangerous and *supernatural* powers, is savage, voracious and unrelenting when free. But when finally captured and contained by a fearless mage countless years ago it was placed in this glass prison where it remains, *to its absolute resentment...*dormant."

A voice called out, interrupting him.

"I want to buy it! How much is it?"

He rolled his eyes in resignation while glancing to the guilty party.

"As previously stated, it is NOT for sale."

Undeterred the voice continued.

"Yeah, but how much if it was?"

He nibbled his bottom lip.

"Urgh...you're insistent. That much is clear. So *if* it were for sale I would accept no less than one thousand coins. But to repeat my previous statement it is certainly NOT for sale. To you nor anybody else. Not even the king of Olsenton himself!"

That of course made everybody without exception want to know more about the item and its mysterious contents. Or at the very least get a closer look at what lurked inside. Bren leant in; his curiosity piqued. He reached forward oh-so desperate to at least touch it, but no, the merchant held it close and tight, ensuring overly interested fingers remained at a safe distance. Undeterred he pleaded.

"Can I take a closer look please?"

The merchant yielded, sensing to sate the customers' appetite would be good P.R.

"But of course, you may *all* take a closer look. BUT it shall remain in my possession at all times. No…touching!"

He moved closer to Bren, the three friends jostling to obtain the best view. However due to a combination of darkened glass and the creature appearing curled up tight at the bottom couldn't see much. Charlie was the first to comment, disappointment in his voice.

"Oh, is that it? It looks just like a newt…and so small."

Hawk agreed.

"It does, but with a different shaped head."

Bren leant closer still, saddened at how little he could see. He focused his gaze, eyes straining before he gasped in horror.

Did it open an eye, did it wink at him? He stood open-mouthed.

"*Did you see that?* Did anybody else see it?"

All in attendance shook their heads having witnessed nothing unusual. However he knew what he saw and repeated his statement.

"It did. It…it winked at me!"

Charlie returned a suspicious look as did Hawk.

Why would you say that? It definitely didn't."

Undeterred he repeated his remark.

"But it did. Why would I lie?"

He glanced around the vicinity observing others shaking their heads, indicating they hadn't either.

Kapernicus reactions were swift. He'd felt similar, taken a sharp intake of breath and withdrawn the object. He stepped back concealing it in the folds of his blazer.

"Okay everyone I think you've seen enough

for today. It's time for me to pack away and retire for the evening. However I am most grateful for your attendance and attentions."

Suddenly, and seemingly from nowhere Bren felt a terrible pain in his lower back which caused him to crumple to the ground. His friends, as well as a few other villagers, rushed to his aid, all shocked by what might have occurred. However in no time at all he was sitting up, but in a state of shock. He'd never felt anything like it before. His mind was in turmoil. Was he sick? Might he have a hidden illness waiting to claim him? Regardless his friends gathered close, questioned him with Charlie the most concerned for his welfare.

"What, uh, what happened to you?"

He shook his head, taking deep, recovering breaths.

"I'm not sure. There was a pain in my back. Like I'd been...I don't know. Hit by something."

It was then he spied Kieron in the vicinity, walking slowly backwards yet staring in his direction, a vile, and guilty smirk upon his face, causing him to realise a horrible truth: he'd been assaulted from behind.

Punched in the kidneys by a cowardly bully.

He looked to the ground as tears formed in his eyes, a sickening feeling in the pit of his stomach. Neither of his friends observed his presence though. Instead their concerns were with him. His mood dropped further; a crushing tidal wave of depression washing over him.

Moments later his parents appeared on the scene, having heard of his turmoil. Clayton helped him to his feet while Alexandra made a fuss over his welfare. He though, he chose not to speak; were too distraught. He stood in place eyes fixed upon his enemy, feeling as though the weight of the kingdom was on his shoulders; and once more wondering why him, and not somebody else for once.

However leaving it all behind, he headed home to recover, his loving parents either side offering support while Kapernicus having packed up for the day wheeled his stall towards the village guest house. Meanwhile, still in place was the thug, satisfied he'd caused yet more misery for his nemesis.

For all he cared, and along with the gold coin he'd found amongst the grasses, *and* having caused Bren more anguish, believed he'd sleep soundly that night.

Very soundly indeed.

~ Moonlit Shenanigans ~

The next morning arrived, and Bren and Charlie were at the village square seated upon a wooden bench. Facility wise there was little of note; a few other wooden benches, a noticeboard, nothing to occupy them *or* adults for that matter They were discussing recent events, with Bren having put the previous day's woes to rest. For the time being anyway.

Charlie was buzzing still. The merchant's presence of great interest to him.

"That seller is great. Don't you think?"

Bren agreed, a joyful smile upon his face.

"Of course. But weren't we the only ones without any coins? It seemed everybody bought something except for us."

"Well if we want money I guess we'll need to earn it," replied Charlie.

He nodded in support.

"True. Anyway hasn't he left the village now?"

Charlie glanced to his right.

"No. He's here still. Staying at the guesthouse I think."

He changed the subject, his thoughts returning to darker times.

"How's your back now, and what happened yesterday?"

Bren gritted his teeth and relayed the facts.

"It was Kieron. He punched me from behind. I knew it was him when I saw him staring at me over there."

He pointed to the spot where the thug had been standing at the time. Charlie shook his head piteously.

"He's a nasty piece-of-work. He really hates you. I hope something bad happens to him one day. I really do"

"Me too," sighed Bren.

Charlie continued his views.

"I hate Troll and Rat just like you two. Oh, and I told Grace about the merchant."

Bren's ears pricked up while he continued.

"I saw her earlier. She said he sounded bizarre. And also said the creature in the bottle was lies; said it was too small to be real. What do you think?"

He processed the statement.

"Lies? Too small? Some creatures are even smaller. To say they were lies sounds like something she'd say. She's suspicious like that. But I know what she means, it *did* look like a newt, but didn't the merchant say it belonged to a wizard or something?"

"A warlock," confirmed Charlie.

"That's right," agreed Bren. "A warlock. So maybe it can change its size or something, otherwise you could, you know kill it by stepping on it!"

"Actually..." commented Charlie, "what *is* the difference between a wizard and a warlock, does anybody know?"

Suddenly a third voice sounded, coming from behind them and evoking a surprised reaction. It was Grace, dressed in a knee length white dress patterned with mauve swirls. Long hair draped over her shoulders; freckles dotted across her pale skin. Her eyes were a sparkling blue grey, footwear simple slip-on pumps. She stood with her arms tightly folded.

"The difference between a wizard and a warlock is this: one practices magic and is seen as good, helpful even. And a warlock is evil. Like a witch. But a man instead. I can't believe you didn't know that."

Bren replied defensively.

"Not everybody is as smart as you, but thanks for telling us anyway."

Charlie glanced over her shoulder.

"Where's Hawk, will we see him today?"

She sneered.

"How should I know? I'm not his keeper. He was indoors helping with chores when I left."

Bren shook his head, annoyed at yet more conflict, though mild. She observed his expression and inspected him top to bottom.

"I saw what happened yesterday you know."

He replied curious as to her meaning.

"What, the merchant?"

"No, in the square. I saw Troll hit you. He was watching you for a while before he walked up and punched you right in the back. I can't believe nobody else saw him. It was cowardly and cheap, and he wonders why I hate him."

She visualised him in her mind's eye.

"He's a coward and a bully and picks on people because he can. He's the size of his dad yet attacks others because he's stronger than them."

"And nasty!" added Bren.

"Yes," confirmed the girl. "Just because someone's stronger than other people, it doesn't give them reason to be mean."

"Yep," agreed Bren. "And because his home life is bad, he takes out his frustrations on me. Why not someone else?"

Interrupting them all Hawk's voice

suddenly sounded, but with mischievous intent.

"It's because he loves Grace like you do!"

Bren's face turned a bright shade of red – highly embarrassed by the remark. If he could, he would have clicked his fingers and disappeared. But he couldn't. Even Charlie felt embarrassed. Everyone knew how he felt about Grace. Even his parents who opted to keep it to themselves. But it shouldn't have been broadcast like that. Should NEVER have been called in public.

And Grace usually so self-assured felt the pressure. She reached to grab her sibling - to teach him a lesson. But Hawk, being fleet of foot, evaded her, laughing as he did. She retorted, her cheeks a fiery shade of red.

"No he doesn't. Shut up!"

He didn't care, considered his remark hilarious. Luckily, it was Charlie who saved the day, changing the subject and putting an end to the awkwardness.

"Urgh. It doesn't matter who loves who. What we all want to know is whether the merchant will be selling again today?"

Bren acknowledged the intervention.

"Good question. Hopefully he is. I want to see what else he has."

Grace moved to the front of the trio, placing

both hands upon her hips.

"Stupid Merchant. Skinny idiot. Hmpf. I know you don't have any money so why go to see him? Still, you DO know he's selling lies, right?"

Charlie replied, a confused sneer upon his face.

"What? We want to see what stuff he has. Plus, you said 'lies' again. What does it even *mean?*"

"It means dummy, he's selling fake things. Tricks and stuff. Things that don't work or have no value."

The trio exchanged curious glances while Bren commented, disagreeing with the statement.

"Not true. We saw what he had for sale. You weren't even there."

She saw things differently.

"I was close enough to hear most of what he was saying. But it doesn't matter. He sold loads of stuff anyway. And it's not as if affects me either. He'll go to Cragsley tomorrow – to rip *them* off. Well, they're meanies. So who cares? Yeah. I heard your dad mention it to someone. He knows he's a fraud too."

She turned and headed off before making one final comment.

"See you later children."

Unaffected by the remark they exchanged wry smiles. Bren shook his head, his feelings similar to his pals.

"Hmpf. She's wrong for once. Like he said: he only sells good things."

Later that day with Charlie and Hawk occupied elsewhere, Bren sought Maximus' company again. He arrived at the campsite mid-afternoon and fortunately for him he were present, contentedly tending the campfire, its warmth and distinct odour welcoming to the teen. He spied the youngster and smiled in recognition.

"Ah, my curious friend. Good to see you again. Take a seat."

He acknowledged, sat upon the grass opposite him who continued.

"How can I help you today, what would you like to talk about?"

He smiled, eager to resume conversation.

"Do you know much about travelling merchants, and are they really vagabonds?"

Maximus chuckled under his breath, unsurprised at the observation.

"Merchants eh? I'd say yes AND no. But mostly yes. By that I mean they are a common presence nowadays; and regarded as pests by some. I have encountered several on my travels. First and foremost you need to know they are an organised bunch and out to make as much profit as they can. They don't care who they sell to, young old, rich, or poor. Nobody is off limits."

He stared into the distance reminiscing.

"However, with that said bargains *can*

be had. But only occasionally. Heh. Wily and persistent sorts."

Bren listened intently while he continued.

"To clarify: travelling merchants, salespersons, entertainers or whatever you'd like to call them are out for one thing: to make money at your expense. Who was the one in your village, what was his, or her, name?"

"Uh, Kepen... Karper, er, Kapernicus Weezle," the name brand new to him as well as its tricky pronunciation. "And he's still there. He's stopping at the guesthouse."

Maximus plucked at his beard.

"Can't say I've met that one before. Interesting choice of name. Merchants are also 'performers' or 'actors'. They wander the kingdom as colourful, extravagant types, dazzling and bewitching people with bizarre and unusual wares, taking advantage of their naivety. To say they are clever, cunning types might be an understatement. But they also come with zero conscience."

Such information was revelatory, and he believed every word regaled. Maximus continued; his gaze held upon the flames.

"Also they can be devious; sometimes working in pairs with an accomplice hiding amongst the crowd; helping to create a frenzy of excitement if you will. Did you by chance purchase anything?"

He emitted a mournful sigh.

"No. I never have money. But most did, and they seemed incredibly happy-"

"To part with their cash," finished the man.

"Yes."

He chuckled.

"Oh well. A harsh lesson learned for them then."

There followed a brief silence while he stoked the campfire, poking the embers into life, the boy mesmerised by the action. He observed as he stared into the flames, wondering what might have been going through his mind. He thought back to his own younger years, and whether he'd have been brave enough to befriend a stranger. He didn't know. He was a believer, to an extent, that all things happened for a reason, whether immediately apparent or in hindsight. One thing was certain: he wouldn't have minded being young again. He considered if the lad was lonely, and if his arrival had meant more to him than he might have realised. Further to that he wondered whether he knew of his identity. His status of being the so-called saviour of Olsenton. However putting those thoughts to one side he engaged him further.

"So your friends, do they live near?"

He rubbed his eyes.

"Uh, yes, in the village. My two best friends live uh, close to me."

"And their names?"

"Oh, Charlie and Hawk."

Maximus raised his eyebrows.

"Hawk? That's a…uh *original* name. It's up there with Rapscallion and Kapernicus. Well, nearly."

Bren smiled.

"Yes. Hawk, named by his parents who… uh, aren't like most other parents I guess. They are very…uh, they believe in nature and the um, bond between humans and the world. Things like that."

"Hm. Interesting, is there a special someone, a girl, or do you consider yourself too young for that sort of thing?"

He mulled the question.

"Well…there *is* a girl."

Maximus coaxed him further.

"And?"

"But I don't think she likes me the same way."

"Oh, really?"

"Well, she might but I annoy her more than anything. And I don't think her parents are keen on me either. She's Hawk's older sister. Sixteen years old and really smart."

"And you are?"

"Er, fifteen. And not as clever."

Maximus chuckled, found the conversation interesting.

"Perhaps not, but I bet you possess skills she'll never have. So, what is it about her you find so intriguing?"

He pictured her in his mind's eye.

"Um, she's really pretty and smart. Oh I said that already. I like her hair. It's a nice colour, like blonde but with some brown bits in."

"Mousey, you mean?" returned Maximus. "They call that shade 'mousey'."

"Yeah. A bit like yours but not as dark. And um, her nose is cute."

Maximus tipped his head back and chuckled.

"Cute nose, eh? Well I never...they say the course of true love never runs smoothly, but if it's meant to be between you, it WILL happen, and the bit about you annoying her more than anything? It might be she expects you to act a certain way perhaps. Though don't change the way you naturally act. That would be wrong. You're an energetic teen after all, with plenty of time to mature. She'll either accept you for who you are and learn to live with it or you'll go your separate ways."

Bren nodded in agreement.

"I suppose."

Maximus continued.

"Is there anything else on your mind? I have lots of time on my hands and offering free advice. A promotion of sorts."

The lad rubbed the back of his neck – a gesture he picked up on.

"What is it, something bothering you though you don't have to discuss it if you don't want to."

He fidgeted uncomfortably causing Maximus to lower his voice.

"I am willing to listen. I wouldn't have suggested it otherwise."

He took an anticipatory deep breath.

"Well there's this boy. Fourteen. Though he looks much older."

Maximus knew what was to come.

"And he's a bully, yes?"

He nodded in affirmation while Maximus

continued.

"Tell me about him. Has he hurt you?"

Bren directed his gaze towards the ground while he probed further.

"How often, recently?"

Unable to speak and knowing if he did he'll burst into unstoppable floods of tears, the teen bit his lip. Observing so Maximus rose to his feet and moved nearer; crouched to the same level but knew not to invade his personal space. He lowered his tone.

"I can help you with this if you want me to. But I'll understand if you'd rather I didn't."

Bren took a preparatory deep breath.

"Only yesterday he hurt me. When I was watching the merchant. He punched me in the back. I, I did nothing wrong, and he hurt me. Really hurt me. I never knew he was there."

Maximus shook his head in pity. Such news riled him. Nobody likes bullies. You, me, most others. And though he'd never been unfortunate enough to suffer at the hands of one, had witnessed the damaging effects of such behaviour during his time. He knew he must help. It was his duty.

He sighed.

"So a bully *and* a coward. That is often the

way. Do you know of any reason he dislikes you?"

"Yes. Because of Grace."

"The girl you spoke of?"

He nodded while Maximus continued

"He has eyes for her too, correct?"

He nodded again while the hero scratched at his scalp.

"Hm. We need to solve this problem of yours – and quickly. What of your parents, your father, for instance, what did he say?"

"He, um, er *they* don't know. I don't speak about it."

"And why is that?"

"I don't want my mum to worry, and my dad, he might overreact."

"Overreact how?"

"He might hurt them both. Kieron AND his father."

"Really, he'd hurt them both?"

"Yes. Everyone in the village knows how mean his father is. There is no mother, she left a long time ago. He only has one leg. The other had to be um, chopped after an infection. Well most of it. There's a bit of a stump left but he takes out his anger out on Kieron who-"

Maximus finished the sentence.

"Takes out his frustrations upon you, correct?"

Bren looked mournfully to the ground.

"It seems that way."

"And he sees the girl as the ideal excuse to do so."

He nodded.

"Probably."

Maximus rose to his feet, began pacing back and forth.

"Correct me if I'm wrong but, apart from his hate campaign against you, he appears happy in your company, right?"

"Yep. Why then..."

"Because a smile masks his sadness," interrupted the man. "A sly and clever tactic. His aim is to cause you suffering and misery; so pretends to be 'happy' to make you feel worse. Hmm. You probably don't understand my point as it's a psychological ploy used by such types. Anyway, how to deal with this problem quickly and efficiently..."

He plucked at his beard while the cogs in his mind sprung to life.

"Indeed, there are many ways to go about this but hear me out. Sometimes to achieve initial peace of mind it pays to take the stealthier route. Not a direct attack, but something more discreet which will cause *him* suffering for once."

Bren listened intently while he continued.

"Yes, there are multiple options available, and I have a few ideas at my disposal. But how about this for starters; you know where he lives, correct?"

"I do," confirmed the teen.

"Do you...uh, will you have access to an open window, ground level, ideally his bedroom quarters?"

Bren felt his spirits lifting.

"I think so. He...he lives in a house with no upstairs. A bungalow, dad said."

"Great, just what we need," smiled the hero. "How about this, to get warmed up?"

He retrieved a glass bottle from his backpack causing the boy to lean forward. Next he removed the cork stopper then headed to a nearby bush, gesturing to an insect flying back and forth.

"See this wasp? This angry thing could be our weapon of choice this time. What do you think?"

Bren adopted a confused demeanour while he continued keenly.

"Observe..."

He headed to the campfire and dipped a little finger into a pot of something. He placed the same finger into the neck of the bottle, wiping the substance as best he could into the vessel. Next, he placed the bottle carefully in an upright position to ensure it wouldn't topple over. He moved to the boy's side while a mischievous glint appeared in his eyes.

"Now we wait."

He licked the fingertip clean of residue.

"Honey – as you know - is irresistible to those things."

It took a minute or two for a wasp to investigate the object; attracted by the irresistable aroma. It hovered around the neck, weighing up its options before clambering inside.

Maximus grinned while the cogs whirred in his pal's mind. A few seconds later a second one appeared. It too hovered momentarily before cautiously entering the neck of the bottle. Maximus' reacted speedily, pushing the stopper in place. He held the object high.

"What do you think, are you game?"

Bren pondered the question before the penny dropped.

"Oh. Let them go in his room. So they can...uh, hmm. I'm not sure. What if I get caught?"

"Well, you'll need your wits about you then; be cunning like a fox and choose the right moment," replied the hero, inspecting the fruits of his labour.

Bren took the object and examined it closely too, observing the small amount of honey had dripped down the inside of the glass towards the bottom. Meanwhile the ever curious, and hungry insects had homed in on it and become trapped, equalling two highly agitated, mini-monsters, ready to attack the next thing they crossed paths with.

***

Later that day Bren was at home, leaning out of an upstairs window, drumming his fingers impatiently upon the glass pane.

Waiting.

The streets below had become quiet as the impending darkness and the opportunity for stealthy sneaking was upon the village. So filled with trepidation, he glanced at the object in his grip and took a deep breath. He squinted, rotated it nervously. Would the plan *really* work, would the wasps really assume attack mode once the cork were removed? They'd head for the nearest exit, wouldn't they? He sighed, sceptical of the whole idea. Regardless, there was only one way to find out: get on with the task, quite literally, at hand. He peered one final time into the darkened streets. Empty.

The time to prove his mettle was upon him.

So avoiding his parents' gazes he slipped stealthily out the front door and made his way towards the home of the enemy, and it wasn't long before he was in position, pulse racing; crouched near to the chosen window.

The property and surrounding gardens stood out amongst the others in the village as that one showed obvious neglect. The grasses long and weed-filled, nettles and brambles growing out of control, and the glass panes in need of a good clean. As luck would have it, and deservedly so, the window was ajar – open just enough for the plan to commence. He shook his head in disbelief, unable to believe his good fortune before he froze. He'd heard a voice from inside the property – sounding close too. He bit his lip, held his breath, his heart pounding furiously beneath his chest. So much so, he could feel it pulsing in his ears.

"NO! *You* shut up!"

Came a sudden loud voice. It was Kieron and he were engaged in an argument. Of course he was. That's what he excelled at thought Bren. Moments later a second voice sounded - his father.

"You what? What did you say?"

"Nuffink. I didn't say nuffink."

"Well you're a liar. If I hear you talk back anytime soon, I'll thrash your hide!" retorted the man.

Having had a moment to consider a response, Kieron had the final word but spoke in a hushed tone ensuring his father didn't hear.

"Idiot."

Bren listened intently as he heard his nemesis milling around metres away, grumbling, sniffing and sighing; a depressing thug's chorus with only a dividing wall and cautious crouch between them. However the peace was shattered once more by the father's booming voice.

"Come 'ere. Now!"

He emitted a disgruntled huff before exiting the room, the sound of his feet thumping upon the wooden floorboards easy to follow.

So with the coast finally clear and the ideal opportunity to strike before him Bren took a deep breath. And with severely shaking hands he moved into position offering the bottle to the opening. Then with increasingly sweaty fingers he popped the cork and pushed the neck inside the space. He observed intently, desperate for the insects to exit as quickly as possible and in moments, the first was free.

The second though took its time. He tapped the glass expectantly, wishing it free. Then as the seconds...ticked...by...feeling like an eternity it had reached the exit. Looked left then right before taking to the air. He emitted a sigh of relief as the unmistakeable buzzing of its wings headed further into the room, growing dimmer as they did. Finally he pushed the window closed, his mind in a state of stressed euphoria, concerned the creatures might turn around and come for him instead.

Impossible of course but to an irrational mind it wasn't.

Then as he scurried away from the scene, you'd have expected him to be wearing the biggest of satisfied grins. After all the torment he'd endured, he believed his actions were justified. But with all said and done, those nerve-wracking minutes below the bully's window had been the most terrifying of his life so far.

~ *The Day's Takings* ~

Tucked away in a first-floor room at the village guest house Kapernicus was counting the profits from his earlier and extraordinarily successful sales presentation. The room was plain to say the least. But it didn't matter. It were only home for a few days and fit for purpose. Sparsely decorated with a few items of furniture and accessories. A single bed, with him seated comfortably upon it, a small, bedside table with lit candle. A token painting of a goose hung high, while the walls were painted in neutral cream. So, counting completed and satisfied with the day's takings, he sauntered over to the bedroom window before peering out and breathing in the evening air. To say he was in a wonderful place mentally was an understatement. He felt untouchable. He'd been on the road for what seemed like months with barely a break. But he didn't care. For, in his humble opinion, he, the one and only Kapernicus Weezle Esquire, was one of, if not THE top seller for his organisation. An expert in his art. He believed he could sell salt to the sea such was his confidence. He inspected his hands, his long fingers, the skin as soft as a baby's bottom. You see, he'd never worked a hard days graft in his life. Physically at least. But if he were to argue that being a wily wordsmith were graft, then he'd be crowned Prince of Grafters for sure. If such a title existed of course. He possessed more than a silver tongue. That said, the few who knew him well would regard him as an exceedingly capable individual (in his chosen field).

He ran his fingers through his locks, inspecting the candle-lit cottages inhabited by his customers. Each one going about their business.

"Heh, gullible puppets. How much will I swindle from you tomorrow?"

He turned to his right, spying his reflection in the mirror and afforded himself a cheeky wink. Full head of black hair? Yes. Gorgeous, and well-groomed moustache? Yes. Goatee beard without a bristle out of place? Oh yes. Even better he had all his teeth still. And they were nowhere near as yellow as many others he'd observed. Devilishly handsome in appearance? According to himself, yes. Tall, lithe, fleet of foot and willing to travel wherever necessary for the keen pursuit of profit? If his itinerary dictated he must. However his solitude and period of self-reverence was broken by an unexpected knock at the door. He spun on his heels aggrieved at the intrusion.

"Ugh. Ridiculous timing. Who is it?"

"It is I, the landlady, do you have a moment?" came the reply.

He opened the door and adopted a 'friendly' face, his PR face for standing there, hands clasped together, and wearing the cheesiest of grins was the guest house owner, Ms Barnes. A middle-aged woman, wavy hair and round face. He eyed her top to bottom, intent on keeping conversation to a minimum.

"How may I help you?"

"Do you…are you intending to stop here for very long?"

Confirming his suspicions she were there to be nosy he snapped an abrupt reply.

"No."

The remark caught her off guard. However she retorted immediately; she'd asked a simple question, nothing more. And besides it were her property, HER territory.

"Have I said anything to upset you mister Weezle?"

Remembering his place, and indeed his act, he back peddled.

"Oh, I'm sorry Ms Barnes. Truly I am. If I sounded short it was because I've been thinking of a dear friend; one recently departed from this plane."

She fell for his lie. Accepted it without question or further thought.

"I'm sad to hear that. However I'm curious. Do you intend to depart tomorrow morning or uh, later in the day?"

"Oh no. I intend to depart the day after, following lunch. I'd like the opportunity to offer my wares to the residents here one more time and maybe have a proper look around. My impressions are this a wonderful village with a thrifty community. I'd like to take it in at my leisure and perhaps spread the word."

She rubbed her hands together.

"Great. Fabulous news. We don't get many passers-by, and I've plenty of rooms at good rates. So for you to do so will be gentlemanly. Oh and you must take a dip in the lake. Clean water and not too chilly at this time of year. Uh, will you be requiring a breakfast in the morning?"

He mulled the question.

"Unfortunately I haven't packed my trunks. A shame. But the breakfast? Not sure. I'll let you know in due course. But right now I'm in need of rest. I'm in a melancholy mood as it's been a long, exciting, and tiring day tinged with sadness. But I'm sure you can see that."

She stepped back, bowing subconsciously.

"Perfect, sir. I'll leave you in peace. But if you need anything you know where to find me."

She turned away and headed down the

stairs while his nostrils flared.

"Pffft. I'll arrange my own breakfast thank you."

***

Further along the lane Bren had managed to sneak into his home undetected; was in bed and unable to sleep, his mind in turmoil. He was wondering whether:

A: he should have released the wasps into Kieron's room.

B: would they really do as he and Maximus hoped?

C: if so would Kieron seek violent retribution? And what if his father was attacked?

D: even know they were planted there in the first instance?

And then what if he did get stung but had an allergic reaction? He could die! Would that be good or bad? He didn't know. So many potential outcomes and worries on his mind. He tossed and turned beneath the blankets, annoyed that his clothing was twisting this way and that, uncomfortable to say the least. He stared out the window, the moon catching his eye and sighed further. Stupid moon. Why of all nights was it a full one tonight, and why was he unlucky enough to have it beaming into his room of all things? He huffed and puffed in annoyance. It seemed as something was always out to aggravate him. Truth is he were highly stressed. What with the bully problem, the fact he hadn't managed to successfully land Lucifer, constantly tiffing with the girl of his dreams. He considered whether the torment would ever end? He thought about Charlie and Hawk. Two good friends. Especially Charlie who he never gave enough attention to. He expected they were sleeping comfortably. Each one in a softer bed. A warmer bed. And with NO moonlight disturbing them. Urgh!

Following a poor night's sleep he'd risen with the village cockerel; spent many depressing hours deep in thought. His new plan was to seek out Maximus to inform him the wasp idea may have been a bad idea after all. But what if he disagreed and saw him as weak - a failure, *cowardly* even? Or what if he were to send him away saying he didn't want to see him again? So many stresses. He paced back and forth in the kitchen, choosing to avoid breakfast; normally one of his favourite meals of the day. He so wished he never let the wasps loose.

Or was he glad he did?

Soon enough his parents were up and about with morning pleasantries exchanged before they sensed something was worrying him. His lack of appetite, unusual fidgeting but more importantly his evasiveness spoke volumes. Wishing to confront the problem head-on Clayton pulled him to one side. To clear the air.

"What's on your mind, my son, anything bothering you?"

The boy made brief eye contact, attempted to appear convincing.

"Nothing. Nothing's wrong. The owls, they er, kept me awake again."

Now Clayton knew the owl excuse was a lie as the birds had *always* been a nightly presence.

And knew they'd never bothered him before. So expecting his stubbornness wouldn't yield to his questioning opted to put an end to the matter. For the time being at least.

He sighed in resignation.

"Fair enough I suppose. They *can* grate. But if you need to speak to anyone, know that me or your mother are here for you."

He nodded in return, feeling his lies had been convincing and his father easily placated.

"I will. Now do you mind if I go outside?"

"Sure," came the response. "But be home before dark."

He exited the room, pleased with a victorious outcome while Clayton turned to Alexandra, who'd been listening closely. She grinned thoughtfully choosing to remain optimistic.

"I think girl problems again - that what's her name around the corner. Always squabbling they are. Throw raging hormones into the mix and you've got a recipe for disaster. Hmm. But I'm sure he'll tell us about it eventually."

Clayton peered out of the kitchen window, observing him head down, deep in thought. He bit his lip, knowing he had a hormonal teen with much on his mind, and was finding growing up difficult to cope with.

“Hmm. Maybe. But you know what he’s like.”

Back at the bully's residence Kieron and his father had each suffered a bad night. An awfully bad night. They had, as anticipated by Bren and Maximus, suffered attack by the insects whilst sleeping. Kieron's face was swollen and red, having been stung under the right eye. His father meanwhile had been twice victim. Once on the chest, the other on the stump. As a result both were in a foul mood with only each other to blame AND take out their frustrations on. Kieron was in the family bathroom, standing at the wash basin staring at his almost-unrecognisable reflection in the mirror. He muttered under his breath, disgusted with his appearance.

"Urgh. I look like an ugly pig - and it hurts when I talk."

Burt, meanwhile, an exact replica appearance wise, was confined to bed, with his chest reddened and painful while his stump was glowing a luminous shade of pink. He shouted to his son who heard but didn't care.

"How did TWO of those things get into the house? How!? I'll tell you how, YOU must have left the windows open again. You know it's your job to close everyfin'. You know I struggle to do it!"

Reacting to the accusation Kieron slammed his fists into the basin, causing water to spray here, there and everywhere.

"No I didn't. I closed everyfin' like I always do. It's not my fault."

Uneducated and uninterested when it came to fauna or florae the man replied.

"Bumble bees! *Stoopid* bumble bees. I thought they were the friendly ones."

Now fortunately *and* amazingly for Bren he'd heard every word of the argument. He happened to be passing by on his way to seek Maximus' counsel. He were in the right place at precisely the right time. A huge weight had been lifted from his shoulders; all the worrying and stressing had been for nothing. A jovial skip appeared in his step. A beaming smile spread across his face. He processed their conversation, amazed at the father's ignorance.

"Stupid man. They weren't bumble bees. They were wasps. And they stung you good and proper."

He marched onwards, whistling happily, believing the day was going to be a pleasant one after all.

The short distance to Maximus' camp flew by for the lad who observed he were nowhere to be seen. Only Rapscallion was present, his head down, munching contentedly upon the grass, tail swaying from side to side. He smiled and approached the animal, who raised its head in recognition.

"Hello mister Rapscallion. How are you today? Do you really bite people, and may I stroke your fur?"

The horse stared in return, causing him to halt. He weighed up his options. Should he advance or retreat? The morning had been going better than expected. So for Maximus to find out he'd been chomped by his steed wouldn't be in his interests; would hurt immensely and certainly sour proceedings. But what if he were friendly and wanted to be stroked? He glanced at his hands and fingers, spying the healed scar. The area was perhaps two centimetres in length. But to suffer a bite from an angry horse? That might take a chunk of flesh. A horrifying notion. He nibbled his bottom lip nervously, imagining various scenarios. Overanalysing the situation like he always did. He scolded himself, knew he'd experienced another period of self-doubt. He clenched a fist in frustration, realising he should have known better. He were fifteen after all.

Putting an end to the conundrum he chose to be brave, maintained eye contact with and strode boldly forward. And....moments later was successfully stroking him. He'd done it. A small victory for his lacklustre confidence. And the act was of mutual benefit to the pair. He got to experience the incredibly soft and warm coat while Rapscallion received some overdue attention. Yet, further to that, little did they know but a bond was beginning to form. A bond between man. Well, *boy* and beast. Rapscallion was an intelligent steed after all. Smarter and more capable than the average horse. Maximus knew and appreciated the fact. They were inseparable. Best friends is one way to put it. And to anyone who loves animals knows, such a bond is precious.

After a few fantastic minutes, the encounter had run its course. Bren wished to converse with Maximus while Rapscallion was hungry for more grass. However, in a cautious frame of mind he opted to keep the encounter secret. If only for the reason he might not have approved.

Curious he scoured the area, and it wasn't long before he found him, who was lakeside, bare feet dangling in the water, a line cast with yellow-topped float bobbing gently on the surface. He spied Bren and called out interested in an update.

"How did it go; did you do it?"

The beaming smile said it all with the same expression spreading across his own face.

"Well, are you going to tell me?"

Bren quickened his pace.

"Can I sit near you?"

He pointed to a patch to the left of him, who

patted the ground expectantly.

"Of course."

He took a seat and did. He regaled the whole tale, from beginning to end, his body animated, with Maximus happy to observe he were finally in a positive mood. He chuckled aloud, a relieved and sincere response.

"Do you feel better now?"

He nodded in affirmation, only temporarily placated as he bore further worries.

"Yes. But er, what about next time he attacks, what then?"

Maximus recast his bait affording himself thinking time.

"Hmm. You've made a good point. A very good one in fact. It seems we must take further action; think of something to stop him targeting you at all."

He adjusted his float's position while pondering the situation.

"Hmm. We've established he's bigger and stronger than you, so fisticuffs won't solve this. More sneaky tactics won't stop him either as the idea of that approach is he will have no idea it's you so therefore see no reason to stop. I knew that with the wasp caper but was curious to know if it'd work. Which fortunately it did. Hm. We need to think more...I know - your two friends - can you not join forces to teach him a good lesson, issue him a solid beating for once, make him truly regretful?"

Bren shook his head wishing he could say the opposite of what he were about to reply.

"No. They'll never agree to that. They are frightened of him so er, won't want to stand by my side."

Maximus continued, disappointment in his voice.

"Right, so we need to do *something* that frightens him; to know it was caused by you and any retribution wouldn't be in his interests to pursue."

Bren looked him up and down, spying his strong and capable arms. Large hands which would transform into tight fists when clenched. He pictured the same fists pummelling Kieron's nose flat. Boxing his ears 'til they were swollen and red. He imagined him on his knees begging for mercy with none shown. Finally he pictured Maximus' hefty boot kicking him repeatedly up the backside, chasing him around the village square and into the sticky pig's mud at old Percy's property. Finally he'd had an idea. A fabulous, torment-ending idea but was afraid to ask. Maximus sensed his trepidation, locked gazes with him.

"Well, spit it out."

He did, his words coy.

"Couldn't you, uh, couldn't *you* threaten him?"

Maximus' mood changed, adopted a dour tone.

"Oh no. That wouldn't be proper. That isn't the way to go about this unfortunately. For instance when I move on what's stopping him from finding someone to threaten you, what then?"

Bren nodded, knew he was speaking sense, and forgot he was soon to leave the area.

"Ugh, so when *are* you leaving?"

Maximus drew a deep breath, gazing around the space.

"My plan was to leave tomorrow, but there's no rush, and you need my help still. After all you feel unable to approach your own parents for advice, so I'm content to hang around for a while longer. If you agree that is."

Bren smiled in response, appreciating the positive attitude. He replied graciously.

"Of course I agree. I really am thankful mister Maximus. You don't have to help me but I'm glad you are."

He chuckled.

"It's my pleasure, and you don't need

to address me as mister Maximus either. It's unnecessary. But I believe in helping those in *need* of help. In my experience that doesn't happen enough. Besides, if I'm there for you then one day you might help someone else in need."

He raised his rod high as the float dipped below the surface. However he'd been distracted and reacted poorly.

"Curses. Now why don't you head back while I consider our next move. Return tomorrow and hopefully I'll have something figured out."

The boy rose to his feet.

"I will. And I hope you catch something. But not *him!*"

"I shan't," replied the hero. "Lucifer is your nemesis. Yours to battle and no one else."

Bren smiled in appreciation.

"Thanks again. See you next time."

He looked ahead, spying chimney smoke rising from his home, thoughts of his mother's cooking something to look forward to, while Maximus' attention switched to Rapscallion, the animal having wandered into view. Then as the teen moved out of ear shot he addressed him, a mischievous glint in his eye, the words cryptic.

"Everything alright mister popular? You should know I never miss a trick."

The horse held his gaze for a few seconds before continuing to munch on the grass. Either it were oblivious to the remark or didn't care to hear it.

~ Interested Parties ~

Returning to the village square Kapernicus was setting out his stall, eager for another opportunity to 'entertain' the locals. He scanned the area, observing there were fewer interested parties. He hesitated, grabbed his intricately carved cane from the side of his stall before waving it high in the air; the silver bells at the end emitting their distinct ringing sound. The act elicited an immediate response, with a woman appearing at her front door. She'd heard the chorus and felt the need to investigate. However upon spying him she shook her head apathetically before heading back inside. Observing the snub he emitted a derisory snort.

"Bah. Offal-eating cretin. I wouldn't want your coin anyway."

Following that all was quiet with him tending his fingernails, a displacement activity, serving no real purpose other than to kill time. Suddenly, from his blindside a voice caught him off guard, causing him a mild fright.

"Oy mister!"

He spun on his heels and stood close were two of the most unwelcome of 'shoppers'. It was Kieron, red-faced and with a shinier, tighter complexion than earlier, and thoroughly unpleasant. His side-kick Albert accompanied him, a boy not yet seen. He was Kieron's understudy, right-hand boy if you will. He was fifteen - a year older than Kieron but immature and easily led. Appearance wise he possessed a 'ratty' face, and coincidentally, was known as 'The Rat' by the villagers. An offensive label for an unlikeable individual. He had a spotty complexion, overly large nostrils, affording his face an imbalanced look. He too was wearing dungarees, a light shade of brown and soiled bleached tunic. His footwear were brown leather boots, clunky in appearance. Too big for his feet. His aim it seemed was to please his younger friend. Volunteering often to conduct his 'dirty' work.

Kapernicus inspected them top to bottom, his top lip curled in disdain.

"Can I help you?"

The two craned their necks, looked past him.

"We wanna see what you've got for sale again," came the reply. "We missed some of the fings yesterday."

"But do you have funds," he snorted, "either of you?"

Both dipped their mitts into their dungarees pockets, rummaging for coins.

"Yeah."

He acknowledged and grinned. But something had piqued his interest. He moved closer to Kieron, eyeing him with a laser-focused stare.

"Are you the one from yesterday, the pushy one, and if so what happened to your face?"

He replied sheepishly, inflated lips squeezing out painful words.

"I got…stung…bee..."

Kapernicus raised his eyebrows with delight.

"Hmph. So you did. And I don't mind saying but you look hilarious. As if your face has suffered a good spanking."

Albert interrupted him, protective of his pal.

"That's rude talk, mister. Adults should be respectful to young 'uns like us."

He scoffed.

"Respectful? Pfft. Respect for others no longer exists, I'm afraid. It's every man for himself now."

Albert spied his right foot tapping impatiently.

"Why's your foot movin' like that?"

He inspected their faces, their individual complexions and features.

"It's a habit. We all have them. Yours must be picking your nose and his must be squeezing pus from boils."

He directed his gaze to Kieron who seemed ignorant of his remark. His focus was on the open storage unit. Albert continued uncaring of the comment.

"So, what you sellin' then? I wanna spend my money on somethin'."

He replied in a similar fashion.

"Well what type of *thing* are you looking for, playthings, amusements, doodads?"

Kieron stepped forward, emitting a single world.

"Potions."

"I see," returned the merchant. He eyed his goods, a finger moving along each item in turn.

"Lots to choose from then. Hmm. Let's see. We have bad luck…appetite-reducing… flatulence-creating…love…"

Kieron stopped him in his tracks.

"That one!"

Kapernicus' finger hovered next to the 'love' potion while Albert stared in bemusement. On the spot and highly embarrassed Kieron gestured for him to move away.

"Go."

He moved to one side while Kapernicus collected a small glass bottle, offered it forth, but stopping short of handing it over.

"Love. A fine choice. An exceptionally fine choice. Is there a special…someone, do you wish to tell?"

Kieron attempted to grab the bottle, but his reactions were speedier.

"Oh, no. Not until you've paid. I require five coins first."

Kieron opened a grubby hand, was clutching nine or ten.

"Take."

Kapernicus offered a mischievous smile.

"Oh I will."

He helped himself to six though saying five out loud. He pocketed the objects before handing the item over.

He steepled his fingers and peered down his nose, his gaze switching between them.

"Now the all-important instructions which you must abide by. Indeed, for the potion to be effective you must convince the object of your desires to drink it. Consume a healthy dose. That can be willingly or otherwise; easy or tricky, depending on your relationship with them. Or you can use your cunning. The choice is yours."

Kieron hesitated, never having heard the word 'cunning' before and subsequently had no idea what he meant. Regardless he placed the bottle into his tunic pocket before requesting Albert re-join them. Which he did. So feeling it was his turn to buy, he inspected the remaining items before his gaze settled upon two items. The first being a labelled container of 'vomit pills' - harmless, but foul-tasting prank items for children or the young at heart. The second, the smoky glass bottle – the one containing the mysterious sleeping creature.

"I'm gonna buy the vomit fings so I can put one in my mum's cup o' tea. Then I wanna see that one."

The pills were purchased before Kapernicus held the bottle up to show them. He cradled it carefully, maintaining a safe distance.

"I'm tired of repeating the following phrase but this is still not for sale and never will be. You may look but no fondling and don't take too long."

He peered over their shoulders, spying a villager ambling in their direction.

"I have other customers you know."

They ignored him, opting to take their time instead. They stretched their necks, eying the contents in minute detail, each seeing something different. However after a moment they gasped in surprise, their movements in perfect synch. They took a cautious step back with their eyes agog. Kapernicus reacted also, ushering them quickly away.

"Be gone. Both of you!"

They did as instructed but stopped to confer with their previously bold demeanours dented.

It was Albert who broke the silence.

"Did...did you hear it? It spoke to me."

He nodded in affirmation, his palms sticky with perspiration. Whatever he saw, or thought he saw, had rocked him to the core. He stood open mouthed while his accomplice continued.

"What did it say to you? It said to me 'free me. Release me'."

He returned a bewildered stare.

"Yeah. Same."

As they separated to digest the experience, Kieron considered Bren's comment the previous day. He realised he weren't attention-seeking at all. So the punch to the kidneys he gave him needed to be justified by his annoying good looks instead. Ultimately though, what he claimed to have seen was true, and were right there, in the merchant's possession and available to take ownership of if they wanted it.

But only with the sneakiest of minds and quickest of hands.

Meanwhile Bren had returned home and was in the kitchen with his parents. The pair were busy with their daily tasks, in that instance preparing a home-made dish; and glad to witness he'd finally perked up. Clayton wiped his hands upon his apron and offered a welcoming smile.

"Here he is, fisher boy extraordinaire. Heh. Seriously, it's good to see you your old self again."

"Yes. We worry about you my boy," confirmed Alexandra. "So what was this morning about, are you ready to tell us?"

He shook his head.

"No. Everything's fine. I was just uh, feeling a bit down. That's all."

Clayton winked discreetly at her, opting to maintain the status quo.

"And you needed some fresh air, something like that?"

"Yes, something like that," confirmed the boy. "Dinner smells nice, and I know it won't be ready until later so I'm going out again if it's okay. It's clouded over and there's a monster to catch!"

Alexandra raised her eyebrows. A statement she'd heard several times in the past.

"Oh, you mean Lucifer. Going out already, and with your friends again I suppose? Just be careful he doesn't pull you in!"

His gaze switched to Clayton.

"No. Just me this time. And he won't. Dad reckons I'm good enough to get him in now, don't you dad?"

The two smiled in recognition with the man acknowledging the remark.

"I do. I know you learnt loads from your last battle. But don't underestimate him. He's big for a reason: that fish is a wily old bugger and will take some effort to catch."

"I know," confirmed the boy. "But I'm ready

this time."

He turned on his heels, feeling a renewed vigour. Things were looking up it seemed. Shortly, and with him on his way, Clayton and Alexandra were in discussion, the topic of his social life on the agenda once more.

She was airing her feelings.

"Should we be worried about him, I mean *really* be concerned?"

He sighed, mulling over possible replies.

"I don't think so. We were young too, remember. He's gonna have weightier worries one day. The bully problem will fizzle out eventually. And the issue with the girl we're worried about? We shouldn't be. She's a fiery one for sure but their tit for tat relationship is a life lesson for them both. They're well matched I think. Hmm. Did you see his expression as he left? He seemed happy for once; even smiled at me. Yes, we should give him valuable space instead of smothering him. He needs it more than ever right now."

Further along the lane there was a knock at the guest house' front door. Ms Barnes answered to find Kieron and Albert her audience, their arms folded tight across their chests. She was familiar with both as well as their 'reputation' amongst the villagers and hadn't anticipated their company. She adopted a similar, defensive posture as well as a suitably negative attitude.

"What is it, and how can I help you?"

Albert took the lead.

"We 'eard the merchant is staying 'ere. Is that true?"

Her gaze intensified.

"Why do you ask?"

"Cos we'd like to buy some more fings from 'im. Can we come in and see 'im?"

"No. He's out," declared the woman. "Try the village square."

She eyed Kieron closely.

"You're quiet, master Chudley. Cat got your tongue?"

Embarrassed of his appearance he directed his gaze to the floor.

"No. Face hurts."

She stifled a chuckle, glad to see him suffering.

"Oh I see."

Albert continued.

"What room is 'e staying in then?"

"Oh, on the first..." replied the woman before hesitating. "Why do you ask?"

He shrugged nonchalantly.

"Um. Dunno. Just wondered."

"Well. I've no more to tell you and I'm busy. Goodbye."

And just like that the door was slammed in their faces as they diverted their attentions to the first floor. Albert grinned knowingly while Kieron attempted to but couldn't.

It hurt too much.

***

That evening, under cover of darkness the duo were at the rear of the guest house, a discreet location lined with overhanging trees, somewhere nefarious activity could take place. If one were that way inclined of course. Both were dressed in black, their tunic hoods raised over their heads.

They had crime on their minds. They'd been intrigued by the merchant's wares and discussed their first 'job' together: a domestic burglary. They'd marvelled over the 'fing in the bottle'. Its intriguing appearance. Its apparent ability to 'speak' and what it might look like if held in the palm of a hand. They'd progressed from stealing produce from the local store to nabbing the odd item from residents. Nothing big or expensive, but they were finding their criminal feet, so to speak. They'd discussed taking ownership of the merchant's goods. Or as many of them as they could get. And with that in mind had reconvened in the shadows to commence proceedings. They moved into position, looked up to one of the rear windows, spying a familiar, candle-lit shadow moving back and forth. Kieron grinned in his accomplice' direction, who nodded the affirmative.

Reacting accordingly Albert moved to a silver birch, looked the tree up and down, assessing its suitability for climbing. He nodded at Kieron who grinned in return, the pair in agreement. He took a deep breath, readying himself, proceeded to cautiously climb the object, ensuring he remained as silent and as careful as he could; hesitating occasionally, checking with Kieron it were safe to continue. It wasn't long before he reached a suitably thick branch, the same level with the first-floor window; the one they'd been observing. As anticipated it was Kapernicus' room. Other than the occupant being present, it was so far, so good.

Albert raised a thumb to Kieron who returned the gesture. Now they knew the outcome of their scheme relied on resilience and good fortune. Albert waited patiently as the man inside went about his bedtime preparations. His beady gaze followed the individual who'd occasionally pick at his nose, mutter under his breath. In other words function as though he were in a private space. Which he should have been. Below, Kieron had been mulling over the fallout – *if* their escapades bore fruit. He knew his father must remain ignorant at all times. Should never know. He'd considered where to stash any goods - *if* acquired. In truth he'd throw any useless tat in the bushes, while anything of value could be hidden until he were ready to dispose of it. He pictured his father's frequently furious face. The worn-in, angered expression and the often-repeated speech about his wife betraying them both. He wondered where she was, and why she left them. Was it something HE did wrong, or was it because of his grumpy father's actions? He might never know.

Suddenly something brushed against his shins, frightening the wind out of him. A cat had wandered close. Too close in fact. He hated cats. Actually he hated most animals, pets included, believing if it couldn't be eaten, what were the point of its existence. He swung a leg and delivered a swift and (vicious) kick to it, sending it spiralling through the air. It smashed into the stone wall, screeching loud and in pain.

Having heard the commotion, Albert froze while the merchant moved to investigate. He leant out of the window, inspecting the darkness below, observing as the animal sped away into the night while Kieron stood rooted to the spot, his heart racing furiously beneath his chest. There was a tense silence while his eyes gradually accustomed to the conditions, fingers tapping impatiently upon the ledge

Albert held his breath, was less than seven feet away, his heart racing even faster, so to be seen would ensure disaster for him *and* his accomplice. Kapernicus though emitted a disgruntled snort having seen nothing of concern so leant back inside and stood in place. He snapped two fingers together having remembered something which caused him to mutter under his breath.

"Of course. I need to speak with her."

He exited the room, closing the door behind him.

Albert couldn't believe his luck. He wasted no time, shimmied along the branch towards the window ledge. Then with the agility of a squirrel sprung from his perch and into the room. He nailed the landing – not too heavy and looked to his feet observing thick socks covering the OUTSIDE of his boots and thought to himself a wise and clever decision made. He scanned the room, spying the display case. He grabbed it. It was weighty, but importantly locked! Pondering his next move and knowing time were of the essence he became aware of heavy footsteps as they made their way back up the staircase and in his direction. No time to waste. He needed to think quickly. He dashed over to the window and spied Kieron below, eyes glistening expectantly.

In the relative peace he'd heard the bootsteps too, gesturing 'hurry up'. Albert, his expression one of immense panic leant out of the window and reached down as far as he could; holding the case at arm's length while Kieron manoeuvred into position. He stood on his tiptoes, reaching as far as *he* could; the resulting space between them about eight feet. He spoke with urgency, encouraging his friend to be decisive.

"Drop it then."

Albert complied, gradually releasing his grip while Kieron readied himself. He caught the object but didn't anticipate its cumbersome nature which caused him to lose his balance. He stumbled backwards towards the tree trunk but luckily remained on his feet. Albert, meanwhile, had opted to exit the room the same way he entered; by manoeuvring out of the window and were hanging precariously by his fingertips. He peered gingerly below, estimating the drop to be about five or so feet, a potentially dangerous and damaging distance if he were to land awkwardly. Then as Kieron beckoned him down, heard the merchant re-enter the room, the 'clunk' sound of the door closing unmistakeable. The thug panicked further, his breathing becoming erratic. His gaze flitted between room above and ground below. He shook his head indecisively, deeming the drop too far and too dangerous to attempt. He muttered words of self-pity under his breath, wishing he were anywhere but there.

Several seconds passed with the tense atmosphere unbearable for the duo.

Kieron knew what were at stake too, moved to the side of the house, remaining hidden in shadow. Albert meanwhile was feeling the strain, his grip weakening, slipping even. He grimaced because of the strain, while sweat ran down his forehead and into his eyes. He suddenly heard the merchant gasp; noticing he'd been robbed.

He instinctively let go and crashed to the ground before looking up as Kapernicus leant out the window peering down at him. His eyes were bulbous and filled with anger. Fortunately for the thief his hood was still up, disguising his identity. Kapernicus though spied his silhouette, shouting furiously as he did.

"Stay where you are, villain!"

Meanwhile, self-preservation had kicked in

for Kieron who'd dashed away with the prize. Albert clambered to his feet but felt an intense pain in his ankle – a shock sensation that travelled along his calf. He'd landed awkwardly after all and hurt himself but could run, though much slower and tellingly. He steadied himself, rose to his feet, then, while grimacing through the pain made his way towards freedom as the merchants' screams echoed through the property.

He struggled onwards, knowing if he were caught he'd be due the most severe of thrashings, a stint in the stocks even. He pushed forward each painful step taking him further away from his potential pursuer. Finally and with a huge sigh of relief he disappeared amongst a cluster of bushes as the door to the guesthouse flung open.

Kapernicus appeared, dashing back and forth, side to side, arms flailing, gesticulating wildly, unsure in which direction to head, shouting the most offensive profanities. He were beyond livid.

Albert meanwhile knew how lucky he'd been. He peered discreetly through the bushes, observing as Ms Barnes appeared. She joined the merchant's side, dashing about like the proverbial headless chicken in a pointless yet well-meaning gesture of solidarity. He though, his silhouette obscured by overhanging vegetation took a painful step back and knew he and his accomplice must lie low for a few days or suffer the consequences if found out.

~ *The Unthinkable* ~

Kieron approached his bedroom window severely out of breath and in possession of stolen goods. He may have been a local hoodlum and cowardly bully, but the evening's events had propelled him into much more serious territory - he was an accomplice to theft, a burglary; the first of many perhaps. He crouched below the window, his mind racing. First things first he considered. He needed to hide the wooden case. He peered into his bedroom before gently pulling the window open. Some good news at last: as usual his father hadn't secured it and were nowhere to be seen. He slipped the weighty object through the opening and managed to place it gently and most importantly, *quietly* upon the bedroom floor.

Next: stage two. To enter the house without causing suspicion. He hesitated, composed himself, needed to act like everything was fine. Because it was, right? He took a preparatory deep breath, his nostrils flared as he made his way to the front door before turning the brass handle; the sound of which, though minimal was greeted by a booming voice.

"And where have you been? Do you know what the time is?"

He headed to his father's bedroom,

observed him bedridden as usual. He replied, rehearsed lies spewing forth.

"With Albert. Exploring."

"In the dark, in the pitch black?" questioned the man. "What do you take me for, an idiot or summink?"

He threw his hands into the air.

"You know what? I don't care. Do what ya like. But don't bring trouble to my front door or I'll beat you black and blue."

"But, uh..."

He abandoned his reply, instead turned his back and exited the room; taking the short walk to his own bedroom while his father's continued vitriol rained on deaf ears.

He grinned to himself, emitted a relieved sigh. He didn't care what his father thought, in the same way his father didn't seem to care about him. He slid onto his bed and kicked off his boots believing it had been a good night after all.

Albert meanwhile had returned home too; and fortunately for him his parents were sleeping and oblivious to his criminal capers. He crept along the hallway, stepping gingerly around and over the few known creaky floorboards before entering his sanctuary. He closed the bedroom door and climbed atop his bed while his eyes glistened with salty relief. A tear of self-pity ran down his cheek as he pondered events, his brain a mass of pulsing activity. He was never going to fall asleep as he had far too much on his mind. As well as a throbbing ankle. He picked nervously at his nose while reliving the events. Did the merchant identify him, and if so, would he come beating at the front door? That'd do much more than startle his parents. He knew his father had a mean streak which he rarely witnessed. But his mother? He believed she were a soft touch. He rationalised if he were to be found out he'd rush to her for protection and deny any wrong doing. After all, and as far as he were concerned she had her husband wrapped around her little finger.

***

The next day arrived, and word had spread about the theft and with no other inhabitants as suspects, fingers were pointed in the hoodlums' direction. They weren't in the village though. As previously agreed they'd risen early and were situated on the bank of lake Dale. A temporary refuge for the pair. They had the stolen case with them; their plan to inspect the spoils inside. As predicted, neither had slept well the previous night, with Kieron's excitement of a 'successful job' fresh on his mind while Albert's throbbing ankle and the adrenalin of their first 'real' crime in his thoughts. That as well as a few other nagging issues...

His facial swelling subsided, Kieron dropped to his knees and grabbed the case. He inspected it from all angles while appreciating the unusual detailing. He'd never seen anything like it. High end, and worth-stealing goods for certain. His mind was filled with excitement. He wondered if it might contain quantities of gold, silver or jewels even. His gaze switched to Albert momentarily and was surprised to observe his expression wasn't as intense. He held his gaze.

"It went well, yeah?"

He raised his eyebrows in return.

"Yeah. All right I s'pose. But I been finkin'. We're gonna share the stuff, right?"

"Of course. We'll split it: half for you, half for me."

"Oh," came the response. "Good. But before we open it, wot 'appened at the square the uvver day, with you and Brenton?"

"Didn't I tell you?"

"No."

"Heh," chuckled the bully. "I gave him a good old fump because I'm sick of seeing 'im going about all 'appy and stuff. My next plan is to make 'im bleed."

"Bleed, really?"

"Uh-huh. 'urt 'im good an' proper. Dunno 'ow, but I will."

Albert pictured him stabbing the teen in the back, the thought unsavoury. He wasn't keen on Bren *or* his friends either but didn't wish to be accomplice to bloodletting. That'd be a step too far. Being a spoilt and only child, and with his facial features unique, he never mixed in social circles. He'd considered himself awkward and vulnerable to verbal assault so opted to stand on the periphery of gatherings. His parents weren't 'mixers' either. They opted to remain private, and in truth, were seen as quirky. They all were. So, feeling he had nowhere else to turn for company, chose Kieron, an outcast of a similar kind as his only friend with the duo bearing a constant grudge against the villagers.

Kieron grinned gleefully while he slid the blade between the centre joins. He held both objects firm as he ran the object along its length.

"Urgh. It's stuck."

He pushed, twisted, forced the blade, finally it pinched the skin.

"For crap's sake. Open stoopid fing!"

He threw it down in frustration and glared at his friend.

"Why ya' askin' anyway?"

He adopted a coy expression. In his mind Kieron were jealous of Bren. Obviously so.

"Er, cos you're always talkin' about 'im that's all. And what about Grace, you fink she'll ever be your, uh, girlfriend?"

He visualised her contemptuous stare. She'd never choose to be his partner. In that life or the next while he couldn't recall a single instance where she offered him a polite smile. Derisory and mocking insults, yes. But never a compliment. She were out of his league and knew a bad seed when she saw one. Her fearless interactions riled him but, and though she'd leave him seething on occasion, especially if there were witnesses to her many verbal assaults, never lashed out. Not even the once. And bearing in mind his father used to frequently inflict the same upon his mother, it were of credit to him.

Still, hiding his true feelings he 'loved' her, he replied.

"Nah. I don't want 'er to be anyway. She's an idiot like 'er mate Brenton.

Albert grabbed the blade and poked it below

the mechanism, choosing a different angle. He slid the object upwards which instigated a positive click. Feeling the lock had been breached, Kieron retook possession of the case. He slid his fingertips between the centre and tugged hard, causing the object to pop open, some of its contents falling onto the grass or rolling into the water. Both scrambled frantically to collect the goods. Albert though, still had an axe to grind about the previous evening's shenanigans, with further views and events playing on his mind as much as his aching ankle. He held his tongue while his accomplice sorted through the spoils; finally plucking up the courage to mention his concerns.

"You, uh, left me be'ind last night. What if I was caught?"

He returned a derisory snort.

"I 'ad no choice. You were 'anging there. We could 'ave both been done. That...that wouldn't make sense, yeah."

"Yeah, but my ankle still 'urts."

He offered the affected area a gentle rub while Kieron glanced at his him, his attitude one of 'couldn't-give-a-damn.'

"And? It'll get better soon enough. Look what we got. It was worth the risk. And you, would you 'ave stayed be'ind to 'elp me?"

He nodded, though unconvinced at the haul before them.

"You know I would."

Regardless, amongst the many items Kieron was first to take hold of the main prize: the bottled creature. As first seen it was curled at the bottom of the object, to all intents and purposes sleeping. He stared into the murky liquid as a feeling of disappointment washed over him. In his mind the thing would have been lively and eager to be set free. He held the object up and squinted.

"Ugh. Is it dead?"

He moved it to eye level, inspecting it further before giving it a good shake. Which he shouldn't have.

He *really* shouldn't have.

It awoke, and though no more than two inches in length, began to spin around furiously. Faster and faster it moved, creating a spinning whirlpool of sorts. The bottle vibrated violently in his grip, taking him by surprise. He instinctively offered it to Albert who took a brief hold but didn't want it either. They exchanged horrified glances, with the continued, and fierce resistance, he felt the urge to let go. Which he did. He dropped it at their feet while it landed on the grass. They observed in silence while the object spun unpredictably this way and that, flattening the grass as it did

Unsure of their next move they took a cautious step away. It was then they heard the eery voice which caused the hairs on the back of their necks to stand on end.

Repeated, sinister, and demanding of them.

"Release me. Set me freeee..."

A feeling of unimaginable terror consumed them, causing Kieron to panic.

"KILL IT!"

Reacting to the command Albert grabbed a rock and raised it above his head while his gaze rested on the object. Kieron though couldn't fathom the hesitation.

"What are you waiting for? KILL IT!"

Albert reacted, threw the rock onto the bottle, smashing it in the process, but to their joint horror it didn't perish. Quite the opposite in fact. It spun and writhed in a frenzied manner – as if experiencing a seizure. Kieron stepped forward and raised a boot to squash it flat but lacked accuracy. He begged Albert to assist.

"Help me then!"

Albert raised his leg in the air too, but as he stamped his boot down, squealed in pain.

"Oof! My ankle!"

Having evaded their attacks the mini beast

writhed, flipped while its tiny jaws snapped furiously. Meanwhile the duo had become rooted to the spot in fear, their naïve curiosity having

got the better of them. However, Kieron opted for the sensible first option: lunged and raised another boot. But missed again.

And then...disaster struck.

The grass was damp affording the creature opportunity to head towards the water it craved. It wriggled, flipped, and gyrated once more, desperate to find sanctuary. Kieron tried a third time to squash it but lost his footing instead, tumbled head first into the lake; the resulting splash wave helping it immensely. It slid along the grass and into the murky depths, disappearing immediately from sight. Kieron meanwhile splashed his arms frantically, struggling to keep his head above water.

"I can't flippin' swim. 'elp me!"

Albert dropped to his knees and following an immense effort pulled him to safety. Mentally and physically exhausted the duo rolled onto their backs, staring forlorn at the sky, hearts thumping frantically. Their beleaguered minds were spinning with assorted questions as well as regrets. Regardless they held the same position for several minutes, observing as the clouds thickened, becoming inexplicably darker. Albert was first to regain his composure, sat up and commented, already knowing the answer to the question he were about to ask.

"Do you uh...do you fink it's dead?"

He ran a hand along his drenched attire and replied.

"Of course not. It wanted to get into the water. Wasn't it obvious?"

Albert returned a bewildered gaze.

"I dunno. I fink so. But what do we do now? It's uh, it's gone."

Kieron rose wearily to his feet, a regretful grimace upon his face, and the merchant's words ringing in his ears.

"Supernatural powers…savage and unrelenting!"

"This is bad you know. Really bad."

They exchanged mournful shakes of the head before beginning the trudge homewards while in the lake beyond something new and unnatural stirred – with vicious intent and a voracious appetite.

~ *Accusing Fingers* ~

In the village, Clayton responded to a heavy banging at his front door, the sound unpleasant as well as unwelcoming. He thundered down the hallway before opening it and was surprised to observe Kapernicus, red-faced and accusing.

"Do you know anything about my stolen property?"

To say the home owner was taken aback was an understatement. He was furious.

"Wait a second mister. What gives you the right to disturb my family time with your shouting and accusing?"

He didn't care, feeling his question must be answered.

"Well do you, do you know who stole my goods?"

Before Clayton could reply however he spied Bren and Alexandra standing along the hallway. He pointed a bony finger.

"Do YOU know who took my goods?"

They didn't respond, didn't know and didn't care. So having heard more than enough Clayton exited the house, grabbing him by the shirt and shoving him forcefully backwards.

"How dare you knock here accusing us of

something we know nothing about. Get lost before I break your nose!"

He shoved him yet again and pointed past him.

"Get off my property and back to the sewers you rat."

The merchant weren't in the mood to hear such talk. He were determined and on the warpath . He sneered while straightening his crumpled clothes.

"Rat? How dare you. As for you, commoner, I'll find out who took them and there'll be hell to pay. Just you see!"

Clayton stepped forward, clenching a tight fist.

"We don't know, and we don't *care* who took your rubbish. NOBODY DOES!"

He turned his back and entered his home before slamming the door closed. Undeterred Kapernicus dusted himself down and headed straight for the next property to continue his rant. He wanted answers. Urgently.

***

Meanwhile at the village community centre an emergency meeting had been called. Several locals had congregated, all furious at not only the accusing and angry merchant loose but the fact a theft had occurred: not only shattering the calm of the village but causing immense anxiety. Stood front and centre was the committee spokesperson, Stanley Purser, sixty-eight years old, tall with thick, grey hair, dulling blue eyes and dressed in comfortable attire of grey trousers and knitted cardigan. He'd lived in the village all his life and was respected by the majority of the locals. So much so he bore the interesting title: *Honourable Chief Executive of the Committee for the Residents of Oakdale Village Community Centre.* Or: H.C.E.C.R.O.V.C.C for short. A convoluted, and silly honour for the village elder. But not according to him. He cherished the moniker. Especially as it were created by his wife.

He addressed the assembly, indicating they remain composed. Few were.

"Yes, yes. I understand your frustrations, but we need to deal with these issues one at a time, in an orderly fashion and NOT make rash decisions."

Several shouts followed his statement. All unintelligible. He called again.

"Order! Order!"

Silence. He continued.

"Let's hear you one at a time, please."

The guesthouse owner raised her hand and he acknowledged.

"Yes, Ms Barnes. What do you have to say?"

She crossed her arms.

"It concerns the theft. I believe the two village idiots are to blame. The bully and his cohort. They knocked at my door yesterday asking to speak to Mister Weezle; curious which room he was staying in, which I thought was strange."

A random voice interrupted her. "Yeah, it must have been them." Another voice overlapped. "Yes. To the stocks. Thieving toe rags!"

He shouted above them all, his gaze switching between the attendees.

"Order, I say! Right, thank you Ms Barnes. That's valuable information. I'll look into it."

Upon hearing his statement another voice sounded, a further point to add.

"And who's gonna stop him bangin' on everyone's doors?"

***

Moving locations to the village square Kapernicus had exhausted himself, had intruded on every household and was none the wiser. However he'd earned himself a black eye for his actions and was seated upon a wooden bench, wallowing in self-pity.

"This is bad. Extremely bad."

He could hear passing locals, their vitriol aimed in his direction.

"Why don't he get lost?"

"Conniving conman."

"Junk pedlar."

But chose to keep his head down, fearing any eye contact might instigate violence. Suddenly a hand grabbed him by the shoulder causing him to spin around in surprise. It was Maximus. He'd wandered into the village, curious to have a look around. However in a simple twist of fate, had spied him, his unique garb standing out.

Feeling violated he struggled in vain to break free.

"Get your hands off me. How dare you!?"

Maximus relaxed his grip and took a step back, eying him top to bottom.

"Steady on chap. I'd like a word that's all."

He scowled.

"Chap, and what kind of word? Who are you, and what do you want? Do *you* know who took my wares?"

He raised his eyebrows in response, feeling none the wiser .

"Stolen wares? No. I don't know that. However, it's clear you're upset."

He cracked his knuckles, assuming a serious demeanour.

"On that basis I have question. One you will answer. What exactly *were* you selling, and why so anxious, don't you people peddle junk?"

He gasped at the gall of the stranger.

"Junk? How dare you? I've never been so insulted in my li..."

Maximus' voice boomed over him.

"ENOUGH! Drop the performance."

He moved in closer.

"I never came looking but happened across you. Your garments are a giveaway. I know all about your type, and don't want to ask again. So, what were you selling that's got you so enraged, or is it concerned?"

Sensing he was no fool and physically superior he took a deep breath, scanned the vicinity for any locals who might be observing. Spying none he leant forward while his gaze penetrated Maximus' own.

"But I need to know who you are first. I can tell you're not from around here. And how do you know so much about me? Tell me or my lips will remain sealed."

He shrugged his shoulders indifferently.

"Fair enough. I've no need for secrets. I am

a passing traveller, and been made aware of your presence here as well as your stock of goods…"

Kapernicus looked him up and down, observing his muscular frame, serious expression.

"But your name, *WHAT* is your *NAME?*"

His gaze penetrated the merchant's own.

"Maximus."

Kapernicus' eyes narrowed, the wheels in his mind spinning furiously.

"Hmm. Maximus, eh? Not *THE* Maximus surely?"

He grinned in return, confirming his suspicions. Witnessing so the pedlar leapt excitedly into the air.

"Magnificent! Incredible!"

He gripped a hold of his forearm, stopping him in his tracks.

"Stop this. I wish to remain discreet."

Kapernicus giggled, tried desperately to subdue his excitement but failed to do so causing him to question further.

"Why the celebrations, do I know you?"

He looked to the ground, eyes flitting left to right, hands clasped tightly together, his demeanour that of a giddy school boy.

"No, we have never met before. But I cannot believe it. You, the one-and-only, bona-fide hero. In the right place at precisely the wrong time."

Maximus leant in close; his blue eyes narrowed.

"And what's that supposed to mean?"

The merchant hesitated; his triumphant attitude reversed. He adopted a hurried, worried disposition.

"Ah, but we must move from here first. Somewhere out of sight to converse."

Maximus crossed his arms.

"Why the sudden urgency?"

The merchant's facial expression became that of stone.

"Because the lives of the village population could depend on it!"

Meanwhile, there was trouble at the bully's house. Big trouble. Kieron had returned and was facing a torrent of abuse. He cowered upon his bed as his father, propped up by a walking sticked bawled at him.

"I'm going to ask you ONE MORE TIME. Did you, or did you not steal that bloke's stuff?"

Kieron cupped his hands over his face.

"No. I didn't. Why would I? How many more times do I need to say?"

The man raised a tight fist, preparing to strike, but held it in place while adrenalin coursed through his veins.

"I've 'ad that bloke at my door shouting, cursing, and threatening me. I gave 'im a wallop for his troubles, so if you're lying I'll beat you so much worse."

Kieron's bottom lip quivered.

"But I didn't. Honest."

There was a momentary silence with them frozen in place. Kieron expected an imminent assault while his father held back. He'd been in the same position many times past: beaten his long-absent wife. He stared down his nose at his offspring. He KNEW he was lying and was desperate to take out his frustrations on him. But was secretly glad he had. He had nothing but contempt for the villagers too. He were embittered. There were many reasons for this, but the main ones being his disability and his wife leaving him. Being unable to move freely about had damaged his mental health. Freedom of movement was crucial to him. He was once a proud and confident individual. But the process, and after effects, of having one leg surgically removed had eaten him away. There was a reason for this, one of his own doing. But remaining in denial he opted to focus his negativity on everybody else instead. Hold them unjustly to account. His eyes flitted about the room and spied nothing untoward. However he did observe an empty ale bottle stood against the skirting board which reminded him he were due another.

He lowered his arm and relaxed his fist.

"Outta my sight. I'll deal with you later."

Further along the lane Albert had returned home too. His parents had led him to the kitchen where they stood, arms tightly folded, a serious mood pervading. The father, black brushed-back hair, chubby frame sneered.

"So, you want us to believe you had nothing to do with the burglary, right?"

Albert nodded, inched towards his mother, who gestured he move closer. Which he did. She switched glances between the two before offering her verdict.

"I think we can consider the matter closed and for what it's worth I believe him when he said Kieron did it. That boy is a worthless good-for-nothing after all."

She looked her son up and down.

"From now on you steer clear of him OK?"

He nodded in affirmation.

"I will."

His father, feeling he had more to say, chose to stand down. He, similar to most parents 'knew' their children; knew their motivations and capabilities. Or so he thought. He believed Albert and his thuggish accomplice had ripped off the merchant but chose, at that moment anyway, to keep the peace. His thoughts were if she wanted to live in denial; were happy to brush his actions under the carpet, it was her choice. As were the consequences. He had better things to do with his time. However, he did have one comment to make, a final opinion on the matter.

"Regardless in everyone's' eyes they believe you and yer mate did it. So for you and *all* our sakes keep a low profile 'til the truth comes out. You hear me?"

Albert nodded once more, an uneasy sensation rumbling through his gut.

"Yeah. He, uh, he's not my friend anymore. He's nuffink but a trouble maker."

***

Meanwhile Maximus and Kapernicus had found somewhere quiet to have their conference with the merchant pacing back and forth, 'enlightening' our hero.

"It is known as 'Morgrae' in fact. And I was scheduled to deliver it to a client. I made clear it wasn't for sale. I made it clear many times over."

The hero snorted in derision.

"But in somebody's eyes the temptation to steal it was too much."

"So it seems," confirmed the pedlar. "It, along with my entire stock, was stolen from my lodgings last evening. A bare-faced robbery by who-knows-who."

He shook his head mournfully.

"But we need to find it and take possession of it as soon as we can. If it's freed from its vessel – and we must assume it is, it will grow bigger, stronger it's appetite for flesh unquenching."

Maximus sighed knowingly.

"Flesh-eating, eh? Hm. This is serious. Where did you obtain it and who tasked you with its delivery?"

The man hesitated causing him to raise his voice.

"WELL? If you want the thing stopped, you

MUST tell me!"

He looked submissively to the ground; felt he had no choice but to speak the truth.

"Szrania. Her name is Szrania" *(pronounced Shrarn-yer)*

Maximus wracked his brain but was unfamiliar with the individual.

"And who is this 'Szrania' and where will I find her?"

Kapernicus hesitated initially then quickened his pace. Finally he looked Maximus out the corner of his eye, his words tumbling from his lips.

"The, uh, Woods. You'll need to venture into Raven Woods..."

Upon hearing such, Maximus threw his head back in frustration, a sour grimace spread across his face. He turned to the merchant; steely gaze fixed upon him.

"Really? This 'Szrania' is not only a witch but resides there of all places!"

He thrust his open palms skywards.

"Of course she does. *All* witches live there.

Kapernicus returned a meek response.

"Uh, yes. I'm uh, I'm afraid so."

Maximus clenched his fists, unwilling and

unable to hide his frustration. He took a few steps and kicked a clump of grass which seemed pointless but was a slight release of anger.

"I *hate* dealing with those things; vile abominations."

He locked eyes with the merchant.

"Have you any idea how dangerous those Woods are? I'll tell you. It's a sinful location inhabited by demons and monsters too. I should drag you there and leave you. No, beat you silly, *then* leave you there!"

He grabbed a rock; threw it with force into the distance before cracking his knuckles.

"Urgh. Never mind. In the meantime your job, whether you like it or not, is to placate the locals; bear the brunt of their frustrations if you have to. And you're not going to like this, bearing in mind you have a black eye already, but take a beating if they see fit."

Kapernicus raised a forefinger to the tender area, imagined a flurry of furious fists pounding his head. And the suffering he'd endure. He was no fighter that's for sure, with the notion of an angry mob descending upon him unpalatable.

Maximus continued.

"Right. No time to waste. I'll gather my belongings and set forth."

He headed away but spun on his heels and

cast him an icy glare.

"And should you abandon them; leave them to suffer I'll hunt you down and bring you to justice my way...and believe me you do not want that."

Kapernicus shook his head in return. And though feeling aggrieved wanted to retort but knew his place. He knew of the hero's revered reputation and knew to argue back would end in a verbal battering at best.

"I... I won't..."

Having packed his gear away and mentally preparing for the journey ahead, Maximus glanced towards the lake as something had caught his eye. He moved cautiously to the waters' edge spying as he did several objects bobbing gently upon the surface, their silhouettes swaying amongst the ripples. He stood intrigued as the breeze caused them to move towards him and soon had a clearer view. He emitted a deep sigh, and felt instantly disheartened as, upon closer inspection, observed discarded bottles, balsa trinket boxes, ointment containers, all of novel design, as well as pieces of sodden paper. He grabbed one of the bottles while the label peeled away at his touch. It read: 'Love Potion'. He sighed again, rose to his feet, approached Rapscallion who's attention, as always, was on his master. He spoke addressed the animal softly though his words were never more serious.

"You're not going to like this my friend, but we've a hell of a journey ahead."

It snorted with displeasure, shook its head in disagreement even. However he placed a protective palm upon its flank and emitted a prolonged sigh. One from deep inside.

"But we'll come through. We always do."

It was then he felt a chill wind blow; the same causing the hairs on the back of his neck to stand on end. He turned to face the lake, taking a moment to consider what might be lurking there, while out of sight, with the previously gentle waves taking on a choppier, disturbed appearance, they were harbouring something unseen and deadly which moved purposely beneath the surface.

~ Wheels in Motion ~

Back at the village, Bren, Charlie, Hawk and Grace were in conversation with the girl imparting her wisdom.

"I have zero pity for him. He rips people off for a living and finally had his comeuppance. And if he knows what's good for him, he'll leave as soon as possible."

Bren nodded in agreement.

"Yes. He's made loads of enemies today and they won't forgive him either. People here never forgive. They bear grudges."

Having been listening closely Charlie uttered his opinion.

"Kieron."

The others glared in confusion. He clarified his statement.

"*He* took the stuff. I hate the merchant too and glad he was robbed. He's a horrible man. But who else could it have been?"

Hearing such, Hawk chipped in, reinforcing the claim.

"Yep. Probably had help from 'The Rat' too. I reckon they did it and will stay out of sight for a while."

"Or suffer everybody's wrath," added Grace.

It was at that moment Bren spied Kieron in the distance. He was skulking alongside a hedgerow at the end of the lane but appeared cautious and mindful of who might spy him. He pointed in his direction.

"Look. There he is now."

Grace called out, happily exposing his cover.

"Troll! What have you been up to?"

He glanced in her direction but hurried on his way, while Charlie offered his verdict.

"See. He IS guilty. There's no way he'd let you get away with that."

"Yes, especially as I'm here too," opined Bren.

In moments he'd moved from their line of sight. Hawk commented without thinking, the potential for an interesting sequence of events forefront in his mind.

"Let's follow him, to see where he's going."

The others pondered his request with Bren responding first.

"I'm not sure. What if he sees us?"

"We make sure he doesn't," returned Grace.

Having had second thoughts, and considering Bren's ongoing woes, Hawk changed his tune, the notion of future conflict unappealing.

"Actually I don't know."

She turned to him, unsurprised by his change of mind.

"Fine. You return home. But don't even think about telling mum and dad what's going on."

Hawk gulped, knew the consequences of snitching would be a damn good hair-pulling. A painful and unforgettable lesson he'd suffered many times past. And didn't wish to experience again. With the stern look in his sister's eyes that meant business. As it happened conflict was a common occurrence between them as it is most siblings. Earlier that day they'd come close to blows over a plum of all things. To a pair with nothing better to do, squabbling over a piece of fruit was a worthwhile cause. A valid reason to argue. Much to their parents frustration of course. Hawk was fond of issuing a bruising thump to her upper arm while she always went for the hair. She'd grab a clump and tug him to the ground; them fighting like proverbial cat and dog.

He looked to Charlie and Bren hoping for their input, their approval perhaps. Instead Charlie had thought along similar lines.

"I er, don't think it's a good idea either."

Grace shrugged nonplussed.

“You stop here too. Keep him company while we go.”

Bren was surprised by the comment. Genuinely surprised. He never imagined she’d consider such a move. He glanced in her direction where she returned a perplexed expression.

“What, are you afraid too?”

He snapped back.

“Not at all.”

She assumed control of the situation.

“It’s settled then. You wimps stay and hug each other while we follow the troll. But if you see The Rat, don’t be afraid to question him. There’s two of you remember.”

Meanwhile Kapernicus was at a loose end and unsure what to do next. There was nothing for him outside, nowhere to go and in a dreadful state having lost his gear. As he knew, like all merchants of the Order did, to lose possession of their goods was unthinkable. A situation worthy of investigation. How could he return to headquarters empty handed and explain himself to Master Prendeghast? He wouldn't dare dream it, let alone attempt it. He'd stashed his quarterly profits in one of the drawers too. An unpalatable situation for sure. No. He mustn't leave the area until he'd at least tried to reclaim his goods.

Further to that, the missing cargo. He *was* transporting plenty of worthless tat, but a few valuable items too. What of them? Were they lost forever, being sold on, lying somewhere waiting to be discovered? Most importantly, the Morgrae. For that to be on the loose was too dreadful a supposition to contemplate. How would he explain that to the customer? He couldn't. She'd never understand, let alone forgive. The deal struck between them was his first, and he knew how important it was to fulfil his end of the bargain; yet through his choices had allowed everything to fall apart.

A pickle indeed.

Added to his self-inflicted woes he feared if he returned to the village he'd, at best, be picked out and harassed. Likely beaten. He chewed nervously at his fingernails, muttered under his breath.

"Foolish man. What have you done?"

He had though observed which direction Maximus went as he returned to his camp. So, feeling he'd nothing more to lose, headed in the same direction. Usually, and instead of keeping to the beaten track he opted to make his way through the undergrowth; cursing under his breath as his well-worn, yet prized suit snagged on the myriad of protruding brambles.

"Bah. Stupid vegetation. Stupid cobwebs."

He eventually entered a clearing, the same one where Maximus had been and spied the flattened grass, still-smoking campfire remains before placing his hands upon his hips. The truth was he were hungry and thirsty having spent so much energy harassing the villagers. He spied a pile of discarded bones and fruit remains, those deposited by the hero. He cursed under his breath as a chill wind blew causing him to shudder uncomfortably. He shook his head, peeved at his predicament. He scanned the area feeling unnerved, listening intently, while his ears strained to pick out any unusual sound, his eyes: anything unusual.

Suddenly there! Right there. Through the bushes he spied a silhouette moving cautiously along the lake's banks, a hundred yards away perhaps. The individual keen to remain discreet. He crouched low and moved in the same direction, treading carefully so as not give away his presence. Soon enough he obtained a clear view of the person causing him to gasp.

It was Kieron. The ruffian from the village. He narrowed his eyes, while words of contempt rolled off his tongue.

"Greasy snake. What *are* you up to?"

He continued onwards stepping in time with the youth, his gaze fixed upon him. Finally Kieron disappeared behind a clump of trees near to the lake's edge. He quickened his pace afraid of losing him, dashed carefully along a thin strip of embankment – an unwelcome bath should he had lost his footing. Meanwhile his unfit nature illustrated itself by his laboured breathing. He pulled a handkerchief from his breast pocket which he used to wipe a glistening brow.

Unknown to him however was the fact that Bren and Grace were following *him*. They'd been tailing Kieron for a while, remaining far enough behind as to not get caught and had only spied him moments before and were as surprised by his appearance as he were by Kieron's random appearance.

Grace glanced to Bren, her mind spinning at the unfolding events.

"What's going on, are they meeting

somewhere?"

He shrugged in response.

"I don't know. But keep up"

She tutted under her breath, feeling her pace was adequate under the circumstances.

"Huh? This is fine."

Ahead of them Kieron were settled and rifling through the remains of the display case, his plan being to return a few items back to the village, the idea to feel vindicated with his recent activities. He were absorbed in his work, sifting through the goods, tossing bits and bobs this way and that, pocketing the occasional item. Suddenly he emitted a surprised howl, as he were caught red-handed by the merchant. Furious the man lunged forward and grabbed his tunic.

"So it WAS you, you vile piece of turd."

Kieron shrugged off his grip, scrambled to his feet and locked eyes.

"Yeah. So what? What are...?"

He didn't finish though as Kapernicus, seething with rage, made a bony fist and punched him square on the nose. He rocked on his heels. And though the strike was tame in its delivery, the accuracy was spot on with him having been taken by surprise stumbled backwards, a trickle of blood pooling above his top lip. He sneezed once, then twice in quick succession, wiping the blood away then lunged towards the enemy, his face contorted with rage and demanding immediate payback.

"I'm gonna finish you old man!"

They crashed to the ground with Kieron on top. He issued a flurry of rapid punches while Kapernicus held firm; raised his arms to shield his face. That in itself irritated the youth as his bony fore arms caused hurt to his fists as they caught on the solid surface. Next they rolled comically about the ground, neither causing the other harm in the process, instead coating their already dirty clothing in more filth. That continued for several more seconds until Bren and Grace appeared on the scene. The pair having heard the commotion. Bren stared in amazement at what he were witnessing while Grace's instincts were to bellow at the top of her voice.

"What's going on?"

She moved towards them, with the intention of separating them but Bren intervened. He grabbed her left arm stopping her in her tracks. She glared in response.

"What are you doing?"

"No. Leave them to it," insisted the boy.

He were happy to observe them fight. And the more they hurt each other, the better.

Kapernicus was first to observe their arrival. He spun frantically on the ground, desperate to escape the bully's grip. His gaze switched between the two.

"Help me!"

Upon hearing so Kieron looked up and gasped, his nemesis' appearance having riled him further.

"Huh? It's you!"

Bren took an instinctive and cautious step back while the thug realised he had TWO targets to contend with. He cursed through gritted teeth.

"You're…dead too…Brenton."

But no sooner had he finished his threat when Kapernicus' swinging elbow smashed him in the mouth causing a split top lip. He pushed his tongue forward realising his two front teeth had been knocked loose also. That infuriated him further, knowing he'd lose them both and in turn affect his appearance for the rest of his life.

He screamed aloud, smashing *his* elbow onto Kapernicus' back causing the merchant to wail in agony. Then as he writhed in pain the bully scrambled to his feet, keen to take out his anger on Bren, but unfortunately for him, and fortunately for Bren, the bank was wet from the soaking received the previous day. Instead he lost his footing, crashed onto his back, winding himself before sliding into the lake again. Observing so, Grace called in anguish.

"Oh, no! He could drown!"

Bren's instinct was to rush to his aid and looked at the grounded merchant who shook his head in disagreement finding the idea preposterous.

In that moment he was torn, he was certain the bully couldn't swim. He knew because his father, following his own misfortune in the water, wouldn't teach him to. But after all he'd put him through, and still might, he was expected to help him. Really? His conflicted mind raced; his heart rate rose exponentially. He were in turmoil.

He looked to Grace, hoping for her input but she was running in panicked circles. Kieron's head broke surface, his arms splashing furiously, his voice spluttering.

"Somebody...help!"

It was then he thought of Maximus – and what he would do. He knew he'd intervene. And though he still had no idea as to his real identity, knew he'd save the day; because it were the right thing to do. That caused his humane instincts to kick in.

"I'll...I'll get something to pull you out."

He rushed to the nearest tree and attempted to break off a length of branch. However the limb was firm; attached to a healthy trunk. He looked for another, but they were all the same: fixed stubbornly in place. He looked to Kapernicus, for his advice, but he'd risen to his feet and was moving in a similar manner to Grace. He called out again.

"Merchant! Help me!"

Meanwhile Kieron splashed and spluttered some more, attempted, and failed, to make landfall while Bren's hands had become sore. He looked up and spied an unexpected sight; the waters beyond the bully had many rings upon its surface, spreading outwards and expanding; his thoughts being something had spooked the entire fish population.

He pointed in the same direction.

"Look."

Grace and Kapernicus diverted their attention to the lake too, swapping concerned glances. Then as Bren continued to tug hopelessly on the stubborn branch, Kieron peered into the depths and bellowed again.

"Aargh! Something's BITING ME!"

His head bobbed briefly below the water before breaking surface again whereby he held his right arm aloft revealing his HAND was

MISSING leaving the jagged stump of a blood-oozing wrist visible. He screamed a third time, the waters around him severely disturbed.

"And again!"

Witnessing so Kapernicus dashed to Bren's aid, the pair pulling in tandem, twisting, bending the object but to no avail. Then after what seemed an eternity they managed to break the branch free. A thin but capable looking length. Reacting to that Bren raced to the water's edge and fell to his knees, fed the object towards the stricken boy, its leaf-covered limbs obscuring his view of the individual. Meanwhile, sensing salvation Kieron's outstretched left-hand clawed at the tip of the object desperate to take a hold. He screamed again his eyes tightly closed.

"It hurts so much!"

Grace screeched a panicked reply, her gaze switching between the bully and the two bankside saviours.

"Grab it!"

Kapernicus moved into position behind the boy, gripping onto his tunic.

"Lean forward. A bit more..."

Bren complied. Reached forward. Every tendon in his body straining under the tension. He spied the bully in a terrible state, splashing furiously, red-tinged water spraying everywhere. He gritted his teeth while Grace preyed under her breath; the trio wishing him safe passage home. He adjusted his grip, fed the object a...little...further enabling him to grab the tip with his left hand. Unable to sigh in relief the duo pulled him closer while the water around him was a bubbling cauldron of activity; fizzing, gurgling, pieces of something or other swirling before them.

Finally and following a mammoth effort he was on dry land. But as they afforded him a visual inspection were witness to an extremely disturbing sight: He was minus his RIGHT FOOT as well as his right hand. His jagged and blood-drenched shin bone visible through his torn trousers.

He rolled onto his back and observed the true damage; for as well as the missing appendages there were bite marks on his legs, torso, everywhere in fact. He cried out in anguish, a desperate, knowing scream causing all in attendance to feel his pain.

At the same time, at the waters' edge a mysterious shape moved in, just below the surface; winding, turning, mopping up stray morsels. The four observed in stunned silence while it swam effortlessly in a large, circular motion propelled forward by tiny, fingered arms before emitting a cluster of large bubbles which broke surface. A show of gratitude perhaps. All except Grace realised it must have been the escaped creature. However it was larger than when released.

At least three feet larger.

They observed astounded for a while longer as it belched, releasing more bubbles but with small chunks of Kieron's skin and muscle fibres rising to the surface.

Witnessing such caused Kapernicus to become enraged, confirming his worst fears; that the creature really was on the loose and not only that but was hungry for human flesh too. He bawled at the victim, zero pity in his voice or words.

"YOU RELEASED IT didn't you?"

He sputtered an agonised, confused response while Bren and Grace stood by in horror.

"Released what, where? Did we? We, we didn't mean to."

Kapernicus jumped up and down, seething and in dire straits.

"Fool! YOU caused this. Now we're ALL going to die!"

As mature as she thought she was the events had become too much for Grace. She dropped to her knees, bawling her eyes out with Bren also in distress. He wasn't sure what to do either. He wondered whether he should comfort her, or try to help his nemesis? It was all too much. He suffered a panic attack, his breathing became erratic, his mind was in turmoil.

Kapernicus meanwhile was far from his comfort zone too. It was a desperate situation to have found himself in. He'd have typically fled the scene; self-preservation would have kicked in. But even he knew that wasn't an option. He assessed the situation, gathered what little composure he had left. He didn't know first aid. Even simple practice, never mind the aftermath of limb amputation. He'd never had children either but being the only adult present felt obliged to take charge; choosing to assist the youngsters. He rushed in and grabbed them each by the wrist.

"Come with me. We'll find help..."

~ *A Reluctant Journey* ~

It was mid-morning as Maximus astride his trusty steed Rapscallion entered the dreaded location known as 'Raven Woods'. For as far back as he could remember the Woods, located west of the kingdom, were used to assist in the discipline of unruly children. They'd be scolded and informed that if their 'behaviour didn't improve they'd be taken to Raven Woods and left there'. Yes, that grim of a place; said to be the preferred residence of witches and other foul manifestations; able to live their lives safe in the knowledge the Woods, along with resident ravens, would warn them should any intruders arrive.

As he crossed the boundary, and moved below the first of many twisting, gnarled trees he peered over his shoulder at the disappearing sun;

appreciating its warm glow while considering he might not have the opportunity to do so again. He shook his head solemnly, stomach feeling inexplicably hollow. Meanwhile, and in tune, Rapscallion fidgeted, knew they'd entered dangerous and unwelcoming territory, his white shade in contrast to the pervading grimness.

The pair were shocked when the calls of many ravens sounded, shrieking, penetrating as if to send them a warning. Rapscallion reacted with surprise, attempted to bolt but Maximus gripped the reins and held firm. Unperturbed he leant forward and whispered softly in his ear.

"Everything's fine, lad. There's nothing to fear."

He was lying. He were dreading the journey too.

As they moved forward his gaze flitted from side-to-side attempting to penetrate the murkiness, felt there were a thousand eyes watching them – all with hateful intent. He heard the fluttering of wings amongst the canopy, many pairs, moving unseen, keeping pace. He took a deep breath and placed one hand on the hilt of his sword.

It wasn't long before the first threat appeared.

A thin, thorn-encrusted branch moved over head, slithering silent and with wicked purpose. Rapscallion sensed it, shook his head nervously, his large eyes opened wider than ever. He unsheathed his sword and went into action; struck rapid and accurate, chopping the object in two. At that moment he observed all others in the vicinity retract, surrender perhaps, clearing his path. If slightly.

He looked further ahead but couldn't see much; for the vegetation was thick and shimmering, alive to his eyes; could read his thoughts, sense his fears even. He shook his head believing the woods cursed, serving evil mistresses. He glanced over his right shoulder; the exterior daylight had diminished leaving them disadvantaged to incoming threats. However he relied on his senses more, his hearing, eyes straining to 'see' but continued onwards, knowing he must.

It was then he heard the familiar purring of a cat, detected it moving alongside at a safe distance yet unable to pinpoint its location. He scanned the vicinity expecting an imminent assault, but none was forthcoming. However all fell silent as he continued onwards making slow but steady progress, nervous perspiration peppering his brow.

Suddenly a shape appeared on a branch ahead. A cat indeed – a definite feline shape; it's almond-shaped eyes staring hard into his own, its claws glistening. Rapscallion hesitated, took a precautionary step back, his equine senses in full effect.

He pointed his sword at it causing it to hiss in response, it's lean body a silky black, its stare piercing. There was a momentary stalemate before it bounded along the path ahead. It stopped and turned to face him, who sensed it was requesting he follow it.

Which he did. He stroked Rapscallion's mane once more attempting to offer reassurance, comfort even. Trusting its master the horse obliged and moved forward. He knew it to be a witch's familiar, a malevolent guardian if you will, and hoped it might belong to the one he were seeking: Szrania.

The process continued for a while longer with the cat occasionally stopping, indicating the route he should take. Finally they drew near to a secluded cottage, its chimney spewing thick smoke, illuminated by a misty red glow, being strongest behind and fading as it spread further afield. Initial inspection revealed the outside was encased in a thick covering of ivy, brambles, and moss, with little brick work showing; its few wood framed windows affected by the same vegetation.

The path leading to the slightly ajar front door was overgrown with nettles and hadn't been used as access for some time. Near to it was an unmissable pile of small bones. All of various shapes, sizes and condition, newer ones white, older ones dark and infested with mould.

The cat issued one final hiss before leaping onto a branch and disappearing amongst the florae. He scanned the vicinity, ponderous, planning his next move. This must be Szrania's residence, he considered. *It needed to be*. Either that or he'd been led astray.

It wasn't long before he knew for sure as the weathered front door began to open; a squeaking, creaking sound echoing around the otherwise silent environment. He scanned the canopy, spying the previously vocal ravens had become silent, yet many reflective eyes staring at and through him; hundreds of them; littering the branches, a watchful, feathered and silent army. He turned his attention to the property once more, unsure what to expect next when a voice beckoned him inside, a croaky, rasping yet inviting female voice. "

Enter..."

Upon hearing it Rapscallion back peddled nervously his senses issuing a clear warning. Regardless he dismounted, keeping hold of his sword in one hand while leading his steed to a lichen and cobweb covered tree with the other.

He secured the guide rope while uttering the following.

“Not to worry my friend. I’ll be back shortly. I hope.”

He approached the foot path, stopping metres from the entrance, scanned the area further, spying as he did a rake, hoe, pitchfork yet none long-since used. In moments, the voice sounded again.

“Come. Enter *if you dare.*”

He glanced at Rapscallion and prepared himself. He moved forward, treading carefully along the overgrown pathway before entering the property. He was caught off guard by the foul and pungent odour within, along with the condition of the house; it's walls dirty, mould infested. The few items of furniture cobweb covered, the floor filthy with mud, pieces of rotting vegetation, and dried blood stains. His eyes strained in the grim light; observing a discreet back room, barely furnished with a rusty chain and clasp hanging below a rear window.

He shook his head and felt if ever 'death' had a smell that would be it. He turned to his right; a flickering candlelight beckoning him onwards. He stepped cautiously into a second room. That was where he was supposed to be - the heart of a hag's hovel - for stood before him, dressed in a festering, hole-filled black shawl, her back turned was the thing he was supposed to meet – *the witch.*

He glanced around the room spying many upsetting sights; heaps of children's clothing including several pairs of shoes, toys and human bones scattered about the floor. Crude and deadly knives, implements used for torture perhaps. Gouges, hooks, saws; some wall-mounted with congealed blood and animal parts attached. Wooden ceiling beams bore more hooks and 'regular' cooking implements hanging loose. Even the 'classic' black pointed hat was there, left ready to wear upon a wooden side unit. His mind was in overdrive. Was it once a regular family home? An immense black cauldron was in the centre of the room, its bile green contents simmering and lit underneath by magical, conjured flames. His eyes narrowed, grip tightened upon the hilt of his sword, other hand quivering uncontrollably.

Detecting his presence the witch declared herself.

"Your weapon is useless, friend. You're in *my* territory now."

She turned to face him where he spied her for the first time, feeling instantly nauseous; had never-before witnessed such an ugly, disturbing, and repugnant sight. Her bloated skin was a wrinkled, putrid grey covered in pustules, tufts of wiry black hair, warts and blemishes. Her eyes were a bulbous, milky-white shade with thread-veins running through, her pupils large and black as the darkest night sky. As she opened her mouth to speak he observed her few remaining teeth were blackened, rotten and misshapen; lips cracked and dry.

"I've been expecting you."

He gathered his composure, steadied himself tried not to appear intimidated though he certainly was – *and* fearing for his life too. He replied, a false gruffness to his voice, a valiant attempt to disguise his fears.

"You must be Szrania?"

She cackled menacingly.

"Oh yes, that is I. Though to be clear: you are not welcome here. Other inhabitants want to kill you where you stand. My sister's included. Your reputation and reverence means nothing to them."

She coughed long and loud.

"So-called saviour of the lands. You are a necessary visitor this day. Others foolish enough to trespass die violently. If they knew you were present, Ms Green and Ms Grive would find you interesting company. They'd love nothing more but to 'entertain' you. And dear Margery, she'd give you one of her special hugs. But I'm sure you'd prefer to remove my head as well as theirs from our necks instead. But...it is in *both* our interests we form a truce, a temporary *alliance* if you will."

His eyes narrowed while she continued.

"I've no interest in murder at the moment. Instead I need you to capture something; a creation of mine and to return it to me."

He looked her up and down.

"The water creature."

She laughed, mocking his suggestion.

"Water creature? NO!"

She dipped a grubby hand into a bowl of dead spiders, grabbing a fistful and stuffing them into her mouth before offering a sample to him who leant away in disgust. She continued unoffended by the gesture knowing he'd never willingly accept such a 'treat'.

"No it isn't a 'water creature' but something far more dangerous – an experiment of mine. It prefers to hide there as it's able to move fast and free."

Then, and against all expectations and wondering how the witch knew he was headed there, felt at ease, the tension between the pair lessened. If slightly.

He raised his head, curious.

"How do I capture it, where do I begin?"

She shuffled towards the cauldron while he observed she were carrying a wand tucked discreetly in the cord around her waist. She peered into the mixture.

He followed suit, his curiosity getting the better of him and wished he hadn't as, amongst other things, observed floating eyeballs, small bones – some with flesh still attached as well as many other unidentifiable ingredients. He also spied several jars on the side, lids removed, ready to receive the same mixture perhaps.

With her back to him she continued causing renewed concern

"This wand? Curious are you? It is *mine* and

none of your business. Avert your eyes."

She grabbed a stirring stick and plunged it deep into the cauldron; closed her eyes while mumbling unintelligible words. He observed mesmerised and disgusted at the same time. Eventually she dipped two podgy fingers into it, grabbing a bone which she inspected before licking away the stewed morsels of flesh. She opened one eye – to observe his grimace – chuckling gleefully in response. A blatant attempt at provocation.

"Children. So innocent. So sweet..."

Hearing such caused him immense rage, but he had to suppress it. He knew he must remain calm no matter how much she taunted him; had to focus on the only reason he were there: to learn about the escaped creature and how to stop it.

He would never stoop to her level.

Sensing his objections she retrieved a second item – an eyeball – and bit into it. The object popped sending a greeny-yellow liquid spilling from her lips, cascading down her spotty chin. He averted his gaze, for if he hadn't would have vomited in disgust. Realising he'd never yield to her taunting; she chose to co-operate.

"Heh. You've a strong resolve which might have impressed some. But not I. Hmm, the creature you seek is known as *'Morgrae'* and it must be taken alive. Though to do so will put yourself at risk of death."

She laughed aloud.

"And you wouldn't want that would you?"

He didn't reply, maintained a firm gaze instead while she continued.

"Yes. There is an item you will need to ah, *'subdue'* the creature. Found deep within the caves at the Giants' Hills. Indeed, *those* Hills. You must venture there to retrieve a crystal which you'll need to form into a dagger. The same dagger will be used to pierce its skin thereby causing it to become temporarily afflicted and return to its small size and..."

He finished her sentence.

"Enabling me to put it back inside a vessel, right?"

She acknowledged they were finally in agreement.

"Yes. And crucially, alive."

She stirred the mixture further, made unnerving eye contact.

"And now...you will pay *me*. I have offered you this information. You must offer your own payment in return."

He turned away, clenched a fist in frustration; should have anticipated the request perhaps.

"Payment, what is it you ask?"

She moved in his direction her cruel gaze fixed on him, her mind whirring with wicked possibilities.

"A drop of your blood will suffice. Nothing more."

He recoiled, the hairs lifting upon the back of his neck, perspiration trickling down his temple.

"My blood! Why?"

"For insurance of course. To ensure you return it. You see if you choose to kill it or fail to keep your end of the bargain, *I will use it to...* No."

She took a lingering breath.

"I'll leave that to your imagination. Now what say you?"

He hesitated, became flustered even, but did his best to hide it. Meanwhile she wasn't in the mood for dithering.

"Choose quickly!"

His mind raced. Wouldn't that be selling his soul to the Demon King, something akin to that? She continued. Demanding of him.

"Make up your mind."

He refused to be intimidated; closed his

eyes, regulated his breathing. He knew it were essential to remain composed and in control of his emotions, Finally he replied, his voice slowed; the words measured.

"But if I agree, how do I know you'll keep to your end of the bargain?"

She tipped her head back and grinned.

"You'll have to *trust* me won't you!"

She pinched her thumb and forefinger close leaving only a small space between.

"I'll only need *this* much. Merely a drop."

His pulse raced, as did his imagination. He considered what terrible concoctions she might create while mixing his blood with substances of dark magic, as well as the potential consequences. For himself or the populace. He could run for it knowing he had the required intelligence, but that would be a cowardly and uncharacteristic act. Stand his ground and fight? Not in that squatty and infected environment. He considered what aid she might have to hand Others nearby waiting to pounce, or no one at all? He didn't know. Regardless, and after thinking of the greater good, he made a typically bold decision.

"It's a deal. I will return your creature and you WILL return my blood."

She rubbed her hands gleefully, the sound

akin to coarse sandpaper against woodgrain.

"Of course. You can use your dagger to create a wound, or I can use an implement of mine."

He was floored. His dagger was a discreet, last-ditch weapon hidden behind his belt. How did she know it were there? That concerned him further. Meanwhile she reached for one of her own rusty blades, which caused him to holler in response.

"Stop! I'll use mine. Bring me the vessel."

He retrieved his dagger while she grabbed a vial. He took his time, carefully sliced open the skin at the bottom of his right finger while she moved close to collect the specimen. It was then, with them yards apart, he experienced her true stench. Suffocating was one way to put it. His eyes watered; nostrils begged for mercy. He imagined her daily habits, food she ate, lack of hygiene, foul company or otherwise. How he didn't faint he'd never know. He took a step back as she pushed a cork stopper into place before holding the object close to her face.

"How are you finding my hospitality?"

He wiped his brow.

"This isn't a social call as you mentioned. I'm here for information only. We are different beasts your kind and mine."

She spat in revulsion.

"Your kind and mine? We are similar yet oh-so different my confused friend. There *can* be violence, but my sisters and I live mostly in harmony. Do your companions, the other humans, live the same way, I mean *truly* live in harmony?"

He considered his response.

"They don't. But we're a civilized and respectful species. We don't eat each other's kin."

She flung the stirring stick across the room and bellowed in response, spittle spraying in all directions, limbs animated, fists clenched.

She were livid.

"Civilised? Rubbish! I've witnessed humans fighting amongst themselves many times over. I've observed while family members murdered each other. Brothers. Sisters. Often over trivialities. And respect you say? Bah! Love thy neighbour? Hypocritical humans are. We wear our cold hearts on our sleeves, and never pretend otherwise. These Woods are sacred to the sisterhood. Mistress Mooney saw it so. So don't lecture me about morals. You were allowed safe passage into our domain. And you know this. Anyway, we are done talking. But before we part ways I wish you to inform the merchant I have something *special* planned for when he and I meet. The fool has failed me and must pay."

As her mood mellowed he inspected the incision upon his finger, sucked the residue away.

"I will."

She meanwhile considered the caves and perils within.

"Heh. Good luck with your search, Marchelle. You'll need it!"

She chuckled the beginnings of a frenzied, evil cackle, a lasting and mocking laugh. Hearing such he returned a spiteful grin but knew it the perfect time to depart. He exited the room stepping around and over the myriad of littered objects, sharp, infected, desperate to meet his flesh. He took one final glance around the hallway sensing for sure the house was once a family home but to whom, and what of their end? He entered the doorway observing other, previously missed rooms in a similar state. Then as he exited into the Woods, heard the loud and continuing maniacal laughter emanating from inside. That instigated a response from the ravens, they echoed her sentiments, commenced with a torturous ear-splitting chorus. Flitting from branch to branch, tree to tree. A mind-boggling frenzy of visual and aural activity. Regardless, he breathed an immense sigh of relief and muttered softly and deep into Rapscallion's ear, glad he'd remained loyally in place.

"I told you I wouldn't be long. Let's go."

He quickly untied and mounted his steed; headed in the direction from which they entered, frequently peering over his shoulder as they made progress. Then as they travelled onwards the witch's warning repeated itself, echoing inside his head.

'You are not welcome here. Others want to kill you.'

He maintained a decent pace, offering constant reassurance to his steed, and desperate to observe the Woods' exit and the sanctuary it would bring. Oh how he wanted free of the place. Then, above the thundering of hooves, and shrieking he heard another commotion; something was following them. Something had detected their scent. He glanced over his shoulder once more, catching sight of a most disconcerting of views; glowing eyes, large shapes, deformed shadows; all heading for them, their jumbled voices unintelligible yet threatening. He quickened his pace, begged for Rapscallion to move faster. The horse obliged, dug deep, knowing their lives were in the balance.

As they sped forward the ever-increasing mass became louder, ear-piercing in fact. He clenched his teeth, closed his eyes, begged for escape. Rapscallion dodged, leapt, avoided attacking branches; their tips failing to trip him. He dipped low, drew his sword in a last-ditch attempt to defend himself; swung the blade blindly, striking invisible enemies causing them to screech, howl, fall by the wayside. Then finally, and as all hope seemed lost Rapscallion's hooves touched down upon the lush grass at the woods' entrance.

They didn't stop though. Or look back. They pushed on desperate to create as much distance as they could between themselves and the apparitions, the notion of falling into their clutches unthinkable.

Then as they disappeared into the true night air and the safety it delivered, they failed to observe the manifestations stop at the Woods' boundaries cursing, screaming, and hate filled. Halted by an invisible and impenetrable barrier and furious their prey had escaped. The beasts fought and squabbled amongst themselves, razor-sharp claws thrusting back and forth, gnashing teeth biting furiously, their frustrations manifest by vicious infighting, their demonic screams horrific to behold.

The hero though, he felt the wind rushing through his hair and threw his head back in relief – punched the air in delight even. Rapscallion was in a celebratory mood too; he snorted aloud, with an extra skip in his step; for he, and his master, had made it.

By the skin of their teeth.

~ On the Hunt ~

It'd been two weeks since Maximus left the village. During that time Kieron had been transferred to a different town where his wounds could be treated properly. Bren, Charlie, Hawk and Grace had become closer and spending precious time together. Kapernicus was still present, initially an outcast but following news of him assisting the youngsters accepted in the village. But only just. He was still staying at the guesthouse though and 'paying' his way by working as the village dogsbody all the while suffering jibes, insults, stern looks from the locals, each one resentful of his presence.

Regarding the Morgrae, initial hysteria had subsided with many convinced Kieron was attacked by the infamous pike, and not by a 'deadly and magical serpent' as spoken by some. Bren and Grace were doubting themselves too even though they were there at the time of the attack. Kapernicus knew the truth of course but kept his views to himself for the sake of an easier life. A wise and sensible decision.

So early one afternoon four youngsters Bren, Charlie, Hawk and Grace were located upon the lush banks of the lake once more. The boys were equipped with their fishing gear and ready for another angling session while Grace had tagged along to mingle and kill time. Charlie was first to peer into the waters, staring long and hard while considering recent events, feeling the once calm nature had taken on a...*different,* and *choppier* appearance. He couldn't put his finger on it but after snapping back to reality and feeling of rational mind, opined.

"Are we *really* sure it's safe to be here?"

Bren replied, wondering why he felt the need to comment.

"Definitely. When was the last time anything odd happened? Apart from the attack on Kieron."

Before Charlie could reply Hawk interjected.

"Nothing. Nothing's happened to anybody."

Charlie continued regardless.

"Hm. I'm not so sure. There's a 'creepy' feeling in the air."

The others laughed in response while Grace commented, her tongue first to react.

"What, is the merchant nearby?"

More laughter ensued. However after minor hesitation she continued needing to prove a point; a remark destined for Bren's ears.

"You do realise he wasn't going to help that day don't you?"

"Uh, but he *did,*" replied her brother.

She snapped back.

"I KNOW he did, but he didn't want to. That's all I'm saying..."

"And all I'm saying is he DID help. So what's the problem?"

She glanced in Bren's direction which he observed.

"What? What do you want me to say?"

She continued, attempting to hammer home her point.

"Well YOU must know he wasn't going to help..."

He stared in bemusement.

"Um... I don't know. But he, uh, he *did* help."

She threw her hands in the air.

"Ugh. I'm *just saying* I don't like or trust him that's all."

Hawk replied, nonplussed. "

OK. We get it. You don't like him. Can we forget about him and get down to proper business?"

"Yes," finished Charlie, "by catching Lucifer. It's about time we did. There's so much negativity lately which isn't good for any of us. Besides, I've a good feeling about today."

A little later they were spread around the banks patiently awaiting their first bites. Grace was moving back and forth, checking up on them, imparting the odd 'pearl' of wisdom, while spouting her subjective opinions on, well, anything and everything really. She was in conversation with Bren, discussing the topic of the attack on Kieron.

"Would you have let him die; you know after all the torment he's caused you?"

He stared into the lake, reliving the event.

"Put it this way: if it were me in the same situation what would he have done? Think about that."

She did.

"I know what you mean. But..."

His gaze intensified.

"But what?" All I'm saying is he'd let me die. Then if I did, he'd..."

He hesitated, realising he could have said something he shouldn't have which would have been: 'he'd have you all to himself.'

Curious, she questioned him further.

"He'd what? What were you going to say?"

He refused to yield.

"It doesn't matter. He *was* saved. Though what kind of life he has now isn't much of one.

Imagine if you had to live the rest of your days with one hand and foot missing *and* your two front teeth. Oh and a father who hates you too – but with one foot missing himself. What kind of life is that?"

She replied after some thought.

"That isn't living, that's existing. I'd rather be dead."

He nodded in agreement.

"I suppose that'd be better."

Suddenly he spied something out in the lake, far out, and pointed in the same direction.

"Look. There!"

She peered into the distance but covered her eyes.

"Uh, I can't...what is it? Is it a person?"

Bren shielded his eyes from the glare too.

"It's two people."

He remembered something.

"Oh there was a sign on the noticeboard in the square. It said something about swimming practice, practice for the competition. I heard mister and missus Beech talking about it. They said they might be out today. It must be them."

"Ugh. Idiotic idea," shuddered the girl. "So much effort for what?"

"A trophy, that's why. Some people want to win stuff. And they must enjoy it," he retorted .

She maintained her stance.

"Pfft. Good luck to them. I'd rather not."

She diverted her gaze, spied Hawk's rod was curved over with a mild splashing in the water in front of him. She pointed in the same direction.

"Fish on!"

Bren dropped his gear and headed over while Grace followed. As they approached they saw he'd hooked a fish, though not big and certainly not Lucifer. Regardless Bren stepped eagerly forward, an excited grin upon his face.

"Do you want me to land it for you?"

Being of a slight frame, Hawk nodded gleefully.

"Please."

He crouched close to the waters' edge and

grabbed it beneath its gills. It was a pristine pike but no more than three pounds in weight. He rose to his feet, displaying the creature whilst removing the hooks. He presented it for its captor to marvel at.

"There you go. Good work."

Grace moved in, spying the myriad of razor-sharp teeth, imagined the damage a much larger specimen could cause. She remembered the open wounds over Kieron's body. The deep lacerations and seeping blood. Her fragile mind choosing an alternate scenario to the one witnessed.

"It must have been a pike that got Kieron. Look at those teeth."

Bren held it close, inspected the multiple rows of small yet deadly (for other fish) teeth.

"Hmm. You might be right."

They looked up as they heard another voice. It was Charlie. He'd arrived to witness the catch first-hand.

"Don't let it go. I want to see it."

He moved in and ran a forefinger along the flank marvelling at its piscine beauty'.

"Ooh. Slimy and cold. But I'm still the champion you know."

The others rolled their eyes; a statement they'd heard many times. It was then that Grace, after inspecting it further, asked a question – one she hoped they'd find interesting.

"Does anybody know the scientific name for pike, you know, the *correct* name?"

The boys exchanged curious glances before Charlie offered a wild first guess.

""I know. Isn't it *Pikeus fishus*?"

The group laughed in response with Grace eager to impart her knowledge.

"No, silly. But believe it or not the name you've given it is close. It's actually *Esox Lucius.*"

Gasps of delight followed with Hawk observing.

"Lucius…it…it sounds like Lucifer. Amazing!"

He turned to his two friends their joyous grins identical. It was then Bren stepped forward, pleased at her presence – and unafraid to show it.

"Thanks, Grace. That was really good. I never knew that. None of us did."

She grinned.

"If you read as much as I do, you might have known the answer. But thanks anyway."

However having been preoccupied with Hawk's catch as well as distracted with their conversation they'd failed to observe the commotion further out in the lake. Two swimmers were in serious trouble; their arms flailing while they dipped below the surface, their desperate cries for assistance failing to reach the youngster's ears. The unfortunate husband-and-wife team were being attacked by the Morgrae. And viciously so. Their meaty bodies were being plucked and pulled, bitten, and chewed, and it wasn't long before each had taken their final breath. An easy snack for the beast.

Meanwhile, safely on dry land Hawk had taken hold of his catch and in the process of returning it. He smiled feeling immensely proud, his eyes sparkling, gaze resting on it.

"Now be a good fishy and tell Lucifer I'm coming for him."

Several miles away Maximus and Rapscallion had stopped at a signpost near to the Catfish River. The chiselled lettering read: North/North-east – Western Plains/Giants' Hills, North-east – Oakdale Village, and South – Chidderton/Harpies' Crest. He stroked his chin, knowing the quest at the Hills wasn't likely to be easy or straightforward. He took a swig from his water container whilst stroking his animal.

"We made it again my friend. You and I. Let's hope our luck remains. Oh, and I saw you and the boy recently; letting him stroke your coat you were. Are you becoming soft in your old age?"

Rapscallion knew his master never missed a trick. He snorted, reared onto his back legs while Maximus tugged on the reins.

"I'm joking with you. Let's keep focussed."

He placed the container in a saddle bag then pointed ahead.

"Onwards to Oakdale!"

In moments all that remained was a cloud of dirt with the heroic duo heading eastwards, Maximus astride his best friend, who's hooves pounded the dirt.

***

Inside Szrania's hovel her podgy fingers caressed a crystal ball; smoky black in colour; her tool for remote communication. The object, the size of a watermelon was secreted in a back room, central upon on a stone plinth. She gazed at her familiar, walking in circles at her feet, its facial fur coated with a sticky red substance.

"Have you made a kill again, and where's my portion?"

The animal licked its lips while its gaze penetrated hers. She diverted her attention back to the ball.

"It doesn't matter. I've already eaten."

Her eyes rolled back in their sockets, she muttered under her breath.

"Distant hag come to me,

close your eyes and let us meet,

allow the mists to gently part,

a conversation we will start..."

A short silence followed before a shrill voice barked a response.

"Hello!"

Her jowls wobbled comically; the booming response having caught her off guard. She bellowed a frustrated retort.

"Always with the shouting. Do you do it on purpose?"

"Of course not," came the response. "It's how I always speak, so don't start. Anyway, how goes it?"

She observed as her familiar exited the room through an open window.

"My weekly communication is all. I'm eager for an update, my friend."

A gruff chuckle followed.

"You're going to enjoy this. But I've been a busy girl."

"In what way?"

"I've travelled here and there. Making new acquaintances. People in the royal residence, no less."

"The king's domain?"

"Oh, yes. Doors are being opened for me, if you know what I mean. New opportunities..."

She chuckled.

"Opportunities, eh?. What is it with you, why the fascination with the elite?"

"Because I hate him!" came the curt response. "I hate their kind. My mission is to destroy them all. Speaking of which, are you working on anything else?"

She gazed at a laden shelf, the same stocked with glass phials and other witchy paraphernalia.

"No. Too busy."

"Well, I'm expecting the shipment any day. My anticipation for your conjuring has me excited."

Her eyes widened, the fact the expected Morgrae delivery was never going to happen caused her anxiety. But opted to play dumb.

"But of course. It'll arrive soon. And though I never trialled it, I'm certain it'll satisfy your requirements."

"Heh. It will. And I'm looking forward to unleashing it...oh, wait a moment..."

A short silence followed before the voice continued.

"Ugh. I have to go. There's somebody at the door."

Szrania stepped away from the ball and returned to the cauldron room. She paced about the space, inspecting her collection of potions and knickknacks. Her gaze settled upon a row of larger jars; each one filled with liquid and containing a specimen of sorts. She grabbed one containing some small creatures, each one a different shade. She raised it to eye level and moved it to the cauldron's glow where it highlighted the contents: a trio of sleeping Morgrae. Each one two inches in length.

She offered the vessel a quick shake causing the beasts to react accordingly. They spun furiously this way and that while she maintained a firm grip, chuckling with delight.

"Enough, my children. Save your tempers for another day."

***

Returning to the banks of lake Dale, Alexandra received word Bren had ventured there and was fishing again. As expected, she was furious. She'd forbidden him from doing so. Told him time and again. But him being a typical teenager the temptation was too much. However, always worrying and protective, she'd joined him bankside to give him a piece of her mind – in front of his friends too.

"Well I've told you never to come here. And yet you have."

"But it's safe," protested the lad, aware of many eyes trained upon him.

"And how do you know that what makes you so sure?"

He gestured to his friends.

"Because look! They're all here. It's not the first time, and nothing bad has..."

He stopped mid-sentence, spied his father had arrived. Alexandra observed the fact too, turned to face him.

"See. I told you he'd ignore me. I should

have known."

Clayton gestured towards the youngsters and sighed.

"But he's right this time. Where's the danger, what's the problem? They love fishing and we know where they..."

He stopped mid-sentence too as something had caught his eye; the object having washed into the margins. All present followed his gaze as he stepped forward while a chill sensation travelled down his spine. A feeling of trepidation enveloping him. He hesitated, scanned the ripples.

"Everyone move away."

He shuffled towards the bank, moving cautiously, the feeling of morbid curiosity too much. Meanwhile the youths' own curiosity had gotten the better of them too. So ignoring his command they inched forward, their gazes fixed upon him.

Clayton reached the waters' edge first and what he observed caused him to gasp in horror for there, yards away was a lump of blood-covered flesh; unidentifiable yet floating amongst the weeds and other debris; bobbing calmly and at odds with its gruesome nature. Not only that but the top half of an exceptionally large pike was there, tragically at rest upon the shingle.

It were Lucifer's dismembered head.

Knowing his son's desperation to catch the beast, He realised he couldn't be allowed to see it. He had to believe it was out there still. Sensing their approach he gestured for everyone to halt their movements immediately. However they ignored his motion, instead edged closer. Then, upon spying the objects they gasped in collective in horror.

They swapped acknowledging glances having observed the predator's remains with accompanying – and unmissable scar upon its head. They realised Bren hadn't been lying. Yet had doubted him. Their stomachs felt hollow with Bren feeling the loss most. He bit his lip in frustration, knowing his fishy nemesis could never be caught.

A tragic end to a magnificent and worthy foe.

Meanwhile, Clayton diverted his attention to the mysterious lump of flesh. He could tell it was 'meat' of some variety. But sourced from where, and when? He craned his neck, sought more information, while sensing the youngsters' approach. He spun on the spot, pointing a damning finger.

"STOP! I TOLD YOU ALL TO…"

However he halted in his tracks as the nearby water erupted in a huge shower as a large and horrific shape emerged, a creature, a serpent-like manifestation crashed onto the grassy bank next to him. The manifestation was an olive-green shade approximately nine-foot-long though the rear portion was submerged below the water line. It had numerous arms along its segmented length, peppered in spiky hairs, each limb bearing long and vicious claws at the end. Its head covered in darker scales, rough in appearance, a bottle-green shade; It's eyes were crimson, angry; its appetite: famished. It stood on its tail, while its penetrating gaze switched between the six who had frozen in place.

It snaked slowly in, seeking a first target...

And then it lunged, biting Clayton in half, its eyes rolling back as it did. It chewed, crunched, and swallowed him, entrails draping from the side of its jaws while blood sprayed in abundance.

It diverted its attention to Alexandra, who was mortified. It hissed furiously while she stood rooted to the spot. The beast lunged and bit her top half away leaving the lower torso and legs. The youngsters watched in horror the as the remains crumpled to the floor, the amount of blood unimaginable in its content. The serpent threw its head back, choking temporarily; the body having lodged in its throat. Meanwhile the youngsters were dumbstruck. Minds blown with the events. The creature juddered, belched, regained its bearings and finished the carcass off before illustrating its dominance: it slid about the bank, making eye contact with each in turn; sending them a nightmarish warning should they attempt anything.

There was a sickening silence as everybody watched too terrified to move. And then, and as suddenly as it arrived, returned to the murky depths, only the resulting splash wave and blood-spattered bank indicating it were there at all.

Moments later hysterical screams emanated from the teens. They couldn't believe their eyes. That didn't include Bren. He knew what he'd witnessed. And had taken from him. An experience etched deep into his eyes, his soul; his existence altered in the most horrific and profound way. He collapsed onto his knees. Every pore, every part of his body distraught, agonised and empty. Meanwhile Grace, Charlie and Hawk were retching at the fact the victims' blood were covering them all; two horrific, unexpected yet brutal murders had occurred and were at a loss regarding how to react. None knew how to help. Where to go.

Or what to do next.

~ *A Hero's Welcome* ~

Several days later Maximus rode Rapscallion into the village square and though it were mid-afternoon, and the sun was out, was surprised by the fact there wasn't a soul about. Nobody. He looked to the public house, and playground. Nobody there either. The only sounds was that of starlings squabbling between themselves in a nearby tree. He glanced around further, spying a few cottages scattered about the area all with their front windows open. Intrigued he took a deep breath and stroked his steed's mane.

"Rapscallion…where can everyone be?"

He spied the guesthouse, its wooden sign stating vacancies.

"Hmm. Maybe the landlord can help."

He heard a door slam, followed by an angry female voice. He turned in the same direction. It came from the Community Centre where he spied a woman hurrying in his direction; she made eye contact.

"What you lookin' at? We don't like strangers no more."

She hurried on by while he adopted a beleaguered expression. He looked to his animal.

"Charming. If anyone deserves one of your bites, it's her, eh?"

Unsure what to do next he headed to the Community Centre to try and find somebody, *anybody* to converse with. As he approached the building, he heard jumbled voices with one speaking over the other and so on. He secured Rapscallion's guide rope to the post supporting the noticeboard, knowing that something must have occurred while he were away. He hoped it had nothing to do with the merchant or Morgrae. There was only one way to find out. He took an anticipatory breath then turned the door handle and pushed it gently, allowing the voices within to flood his senses.

The sight that greeted him were the backs of many villagers and judging by the amount of people in attendance and taking the size of the village into account, everyone. He breathed in the myriad of odours: ale, tobacco smoke, body odours. There was obviously a village meeting taking place, a rowdy one at that. He stood silent until Stanley Purser located at the front of the stage and the only person facing him observed his mysterious presence. He clapped his hands, gesturing for everyone to cease talking while he pointed in his direction.

"You, there, at the back. Who are you, and who invited you to this meeting?"

Maximus raised his palms indicating openness and he weren't there for trouble.

"A traveller, seeking the merchant."

As he finished speaking, he spied Kapernicus declaring his presence by waving gleefully. He called out, delight in his voice.

You've returned! Everyone – I told you he were here - that person is Maximus."

Murmuring followed while Stanley was first to opine, feeling none the wiser to the stranger's origins.

"Maximus? Maximus who?"

Kapernicus pushed his way through the crowd and took to the stage, his gaze upon the congregation.

"May I have your attention? That means *everybody*."

He gestured to Maximus, beckoned him over to the stage while he continued.

"Be nice everyone. He could be the saviour in your hour of need."

Stanley stepped forward, his gaze switching between Maximus, the merchant, and the attendees, a bewildered expression upon his face

"I say again: who is this, who are you?"

Maximus emitted a sigh. He snaked past the bodies. The observing faces were, without exception, eyeing him top to bottom. Meanwhile he motioned for everyone to remain calm and moved to Kapernicus' side.

"The reason I'm here is because of the monster residing in the lake – the serpent."

A voice shouted from the crowd.

"Well, who ARE you then?"

Kapernicus interjected.

"Ugh. How many times? He's Maximus, everybody. You know, THE Maximus. The Legendary monster slayer!"

Oohs, aahs and gasps followed, as did much muttering. Stanley narrowed his eyes suspiciously.

"Is this true, are you really him?"

He nodded in affirmation.

"I am. So let me speak."

Realising he *really* was the 'one' the congregation fell silent while the hero took a deep breath.

"I need your help. All of you. I must capture the beast and return it to its owner."

A voice sounded in return.

"Well, where *did* it come from?"

He turned to Kapernicus.

"He'll answer that. He brought it here."

Disgruntled murmuring followed while he scanned the audience.

"Let me finish before you cast more judgement. It is true. I *did* bring it here but not with the intent of releasing it. The blame lies on the shoulders of two locals. Two thieves."

Accusing voices called out.

"The bully and his sidekick!"

He nodded in affirmation.

"Correct. They stole it from my room at the guesthouse before releasing it into the lake."

Meanwhile in the crowd Albert's parents were in attendance. They exchanged furious glances, eager to return home while he continued.

"I made it clear to everyone it wasn't for sale."

He formed a tight fist.

"I made it *truly* clear. Yet the fools chose to...Bah. It's too late now..."

Maximus stepped forward, assuming control of the situation.

"Okay. The beast is on the loose and must be stopped. This much is clear. What's the current news, the latest happenings? I have been away; only returned today."

Stanley cleared his throat.

"This is where I step in. Tragically we have lost five villagers so far with the first confirmed victims being the parents of the teenager, Brenton."

Maximus' heart sunk, spun to face the speaker.

"What!? Did you say Brenton?"

He nodded in confirmation while an anguished expression appeared on Maximus' face. He grabbed a firm hold of him. Too firm in fact.

"Where is he now, is he safe? TELL ME!"

The gentleman squirmed uncomfortably, attempting to break free, but the grip was too strong. He blinked rapidly.

"Unhand me you cur. I... I don't know. Nobody knows."

Maximus cast him any icy glare; his head suddenly spinning, stomach in knots. He released his grip and turned to the crowd. The news had rocked him to the core. He called in desperation, pleading with them.

"This is a small village, one of you must know."

A voice returned a reply.

"His friends. Maybe speak to them."

He leapt from the stage and ran to the

villager in question.

"Their names, and where will I find them?"

"Uh, Charlie, Hawk," responded the individual. "And his girlfriend Grace."

He opened the door and gestured towards the lane.

"The cottage opposite the broken bench; that's where Charlie lives."

Maximus rushed from the building and to the property in question while Rapscallion observed, sensing his turmoil. He pounded a fist upon the front door, desperate for a rapid response. Fortunately, one came: Charlie's father, Benjamin. But having suffered the merchant's unwanted attention earlier he were none too pleased to observe another trespasser on his land.

"Can I help you?"

Maximus made eye contact.

"Does Charlie live here, friend of Brenton?"

Protective of his offspring, Benjamin questioned him.

"Who are you, and why are you asking about my child?"

He snapped a frustrated response.

"LISTEN. I must speak to your son. I *need* to ask if he knows of Brenton's whereabouts. I am concerned for his welfare."

Charlie appeared behind his father having heard the commotion. He declared his presence, curious regarding the stranger's identity.

"It's fine dad. He isn't a baddie." He looked to Maximus. "You're the person Bren spoke of..."

He nodded in acknowledgement.

"I am. It's imperative I find him."

The boy wracked his brain.

"Um, I haven't seen him for a while. He went to the lake a couple of days ago. Um, wanted to be on his own, he said."

Upon hearing so, Benjamin reeled in response. He knew nothing of that. He would have offered him accommodation if he did. He assumed he were safe elsewhere.

He turned to his son.

"A couple of days, you said, and you let him go? Why didn't I know about this?"

Charlie thrust his hands into the air.

"I wanted to help, but he said no. You might have said no too. And he's my best friend..."

Benjamin cast him a stern glare.

"What's got into you? Of course I wouldn't have."

Meanwhile Maximus had an idea where he

might find the teen, dashed away, neglecting to apologise for the intrusion. Then as father and son began a tense debate, the hero, astride his steed, headed hell-for-leather away from the village square.

***

Upon arrival at the lake, he spied smoke rising from his old campsite. So after dismounting crashed through the undergrowth observing Brenton in Grace's company, the two content but surprised by his intrusion. Maximus couldn't control himself; he rushed in and pulled him close with the intensity of the moment too much. Bren burst into floods of tears while his heart ached, weeks of pent-up emotions finally released. Grace rose to her feet and moved to a safe distance, an uncomfortable feeling washing over her. She'd never seen Maximus before; didn't know or recognise him. And with his unexpected arrival Bren hadn't the opportunity to introduce him either. None of that mattered to him, he were trying his utmost to comfort his pal. He wiped his eyes, sorrowful tears cascading down his cheeks. It was Grace who broke the silence.

"Um, do you want me to leave?"

Maximus didn't hear, while Bren muttered through the sobbing.

"N-no. Stay here please. This is Maximus. My friend..."

She nodded in acknowledgement; realising it was the individual who'd helped him with his bully troubles.

Maximus made eye contact with the forlorn youngster.

"I know you're hurting. And know any words cannot mend the pain you're feeling."

Bren nodded in agreement, sat next to the campfire, wiped his eyes, feeling vulnerable and awkward at the same time. He glanced to Grace, begging her.

"Please stay."

He gestured for her to retake her seat which she did. Maximus moved opposite and took a seat too. At the same time Rapscallion pushed through the hedge and into view, his white head and large eyes taking them by surprise, especially Grace who emitted an embarrassed yelp causing her to blush. She gathered her composure while the horse dipped its head in delight, appearing to relish the intrusion. Maximus smiled, considered what he might say next. It didn't matter though it was Grace who summoned the courage to speak.

"Are you really the um, monster fighter?"

He nodded, having heard the same question many times over.

"I am. And you are?"

"Grace, a friend of Bren's. I've been offering support."

Bren raised his head.

"Yes. She's been helping me."

He turned to Maximus.

"I've uh, got nowhere to go. My parents. They're gone."

Maximus took a deep breath.

"I'm here to help you, and I *can* help you. I'll do my best. But, uh…"

He considered his next question, wondered whether it were too soon to mention it but understood he needed urgent information about the serpent. Instead he turned his attention to the girl.

"May I ask you a few questions about the lake beast, what you know?"

She hesitated; gaze switched between the pair which Maximus acknowledged.

"But you don't have to. No pressure…"

She appeared as though she'd like to speak but was worried about upsetting her friend. Maximus gestured to their left.

"I see. We can go over there."

He glanced in Bren's direction who nodded the affirmative. The two moved to one side with the teen safely in their sights. Maximus placed a reassuring hand upon her forearm.

"I know you are not familiar with me, but I can help. I can help you rid the lake of this abomination. But to do so I need to gather as much information as I can about it first. Where it was last seen, how big it was, anything that might help."

She pointed a finger towards the lake.

"It was over there. By the fallen acorn tree. Er, the stony patch I mean. It was about er, ten feet long. I think. It had lots of arms along its body with er, sharp fingers. Oh, its mouth opened really wide, and it had red eyes and sharp teeth."

She became flustered the act of reliving the experience too much.

"It happened so quickly."

He returned a thankful smile.

"Thank you. You've been extremely helpful."

He glanced around the vicinity.

"This is a big lake, and it could appear any time, so the closer you are to the water the higher the chance of something happening..."

Ignoring the warning she replied, focussing on her friend.

"Bren said he doesn't care anymore. He has nobody."

He shook his head in disdain.

"Nonsense. In case you don't know he cares about you the most. Never underestimate the power of friendship. He needs company right now. If you can be there for him; put yourself in his shoes. Think how you would feel if the same happened to you. Who *you* might turn to, what *you* would do?"

His words caught her off guard, she didn't have an answer in mind. Instead she stared at the ground in silence. Maximus diverted his attention to Bren, the lad in a distracted daze. He opened his satchel and delved inside.

"Have you eaten recently?"

The teen looked away.

"Not hungry."

He knew better, retrieved a piece of bread, the morsel soft and tantalizing which he held aloft

"Herb bread. Tasty and nutritious and one of my favourite foods. It's yours if you want it... *or* I can feed it to them."

He tilted his head in the direction of two hungry mallard loitering nearby.

Bren spied the offering, battled his

stubbornness while Maximus wafted the object enticingly back and forth.

"Really? You'd rather I offer it to the waterfowl?"

Bren bit his lip, the food within his grasp. He spied the encroaching pair and wished he could share it with them. The fact is, he were hungry, and they'd need to look elsewhere. He hadn't considered sustenance until then; been wallowing in self-pit, as he were entitled to. Finally, he yielded and took hold of the offering causing Maximus to break into an overdue smile. In fact they both did, as did Grace. Further to that, with the first piece eaten, he AND Grace tucked into the hero's ration pack. They even shared some with the ducks. The teens wore satisfied grins as they filled their bellies with overdue nourishment, exchanged smiles even. A fact which pleased the hero. So much so in fact, he hadn't felt similar fulfilment in a long while.

All it took was patience, understanding and several pieces of oven-baked dough.

~ *Suspicious Minds* ~

Inside the walls of the community centre, Maximus' appearance was high on the agenda. That as well as a change of attitude with a suspicious mindset having consumed the congregation. Limbs were animated, while raucous voices echoed about the space. To say the atmosphere were tense would have been a huge understatement. Unrest was rife.

One villager asked: "Where the 'eck did he come from, I 'eard he was dead?"

Another enquired: "I think it's no coincidence he showed up at the same time as the monster."

Another spoke: "How can we be sure he really *is* the legendary monster slayer? How will we know?"

While another commented wryly. "What if the whole thing is a sham, they're workin' together to rip us off?"

Finally, having heard enough Kapernicus shouted above them all.

"Fools. He IS the true Maximus. I am familiar with his reputation and appearance. So instead of wondering whether he's an imposter or there's a conspiracy at work you should listen to him."

Another voice bellowed in response. Sarcastic but on point.

"Like we listened to you!"

A burly male grabbed the merchant by his collar before yanking him from the stage. The crowd parted, while a barrage of insults commenced, the sight of him being manhandled a welcome sight for the masses. He was shoved forcefully into the street, door slammed rudely in his face while he crashed to his knees. Reacting so he thrust his hands into the air in frustration while the sound of rapturous applause emanated from within. A reason for the villagers to celebrate at last.

Disgusted with the lot he dusted himself down and turned his back on the place.

"Idiots. All of you!"

He glanced around the village unsure what to do or where to go next, opted to return to the guesthouse. To seek respite from the building tension. But as he opened the front door was greeted by Ms Barnes and two snarling villagers, the trio 'happy' to see him. Usually so placid she took great took delight uttering the following words.

"You've overstayed your welcome, mister Weezle. So you've got two minutes to collect your belongings..."

The two males cracked their knuckles in anticipation while Kapernicus dashed to his quarters, thoughts of a pummelling putting the wind up him.

***

Returning to the camp Maximus had gotten Bren to open up. The pair were in conversation with the hero offering words of wisdom.

"I can never understand the pain you're feeling of course. However time has the capacity to heal, or at least lessen the feeling of hopelessness. But life ultimately leads to death. It's the journey to the grave that matters. Some folk live long lives while others are taken before their time." He shook his head disconsonant. "Some say everything happens for a reason, a rational response for many but I don't agree with that philosophy. For instance, a well-meaning soul who'd never think of harming someone could perish early while an underhanded and corrupt individual could last well into old age."

He clenched a tight fist. One of frustration while the boy listened intently.

"Basically I'm saying life isn't fair. And there is no justice merely what fate has in store."

Bren looked to Grace and smirked.

"But Kieron got his comeuppance at least."

She nodded in acknowledgement while

Maximus balked in confusion. He didn't know about the bully of course. So the teens regaled the events lakeside causing him to experience differing emotions. The first to grin in satisfaction, the second, sense there must have been a reason why he were a bully; and what might have caused him to become one. But to lift their spirits replied in a manner to aid their mood.

"Well I wouldn't consider myself as someone to wish ill upon another but in this instance I can make an exception."

They nodded in agreement, understanding his stance. They sensed he'd never wish suffering on somebody but believed in the notion of karma. The trio proceeded to finish the rations; their spirits well and truly lifted. It was then Maximus declared his next move, offering a proposal if you will. He began his pitch.

"So you know, I'll be travelling to the Giants' Hills soon..."

Curious as to why, Bren scratched at his scalp while he continued.

"I must retrieve a crystal there. One hidden within the caves."

The boy leant away, concerned for his welfare.

"You mean the Giant's Hills far away? But

aren't they guarded by giants, er, fierce ones?"

The hero's gaze switched between the two.

"There's only one Giants' Hills. And not anymore. I believe they've been slain."

"Oh," added the teen. "I guess you'd know."

The man stared into his eyes.

"What about you, are you staying with anybody?"

Grace replied on his behalf, biting her lip.

"No. He isn't. Charlie offered him to stay, and I offered him the same at mine, but he refused."

Maximus cast the lad a confused glare.

"Why? Why wouldn't you want sanctuary?"

Put on the spot he replied.

"I don't know buts that's how I felt at the time. Can I travel with you instead?"

Grace's jaw dropped.

"What, why would you want to go somewhere like that? You could die."

She gestured in Maximus' direction, a previously unheard passion in her voice.

"He's fine to go. He's a warrior. You're just..."

"A boy?" snapped Bren. "Is that what you

were going to say?"

She rose to her feet intent on fighting her corner.

"Yes. You're just a boy. You'll never return."

"Well maybe. But that doesn't matter. I've no family anymore and I want to go."

She adopted a beleaguered expression.

"What about me? I'm here for you. I offered to help. But no. You'd rather go to die instead."

She offered a stern look to Maximus before storming away from the clearing leaving the two bewildered. For once the hero hadn't the opportunity to retort and Bren were momentarily lost for words. So, having observed a side of her he never anticipated, Maximus placed a reassuring hand upon the boy's knee.

"Heh. I never saw that coming. She put me in my place for sure. And hopefully it proved she has feelings for you."

Bren looked submissively to the ground, conflict knotting his stomach.

"I suppose. When she gets angry like that she doesn't care who she's speaking to. But I need to leave."

Maximus rose to his feet and dusted himself down.

"She didn't like your decision because she

is afraid of losing you. That's why she stated her case so vehemently."

The words hit Bren hard, his naivety exposed.

"I um, have feelings for her too, which you know. But I want to travel with you, and I don't need anyone's permission. Er, anymore."

He hesitated, considered his friends, and their reactions should he abandon them, but realised if he were to stay he'll be haunted by gruesome memories.

"I must leave the village."

Suddenly they were alerted to a rustling in the nearby undergrowth causing Bren to call out.

"Is that you, Grace? I want to..."

The vegetation parted and Kapernicus appeared, taking them both by surprise. Maximus responded with an unwelcoming sneer.

"Why are you here, and where's the girl?"

He adopted a defensive attitude.

"Pfft. If you mean the angry one I passed, I'd say she's headed to the village. I'm here because I've nowhere else to go. And I saw the smoke rising."

Maximus approached him, crossed his arms. The merchant mimicked the posture while the hero vented.

"Lucky I suppose. As I was intending to look for you."

He gestured to himself and Bren in return.

"Because we're going somewhere, and whether you like it or not, you're coming too."

~ *Three's Company* ~

The residents at Oakdale were in turmoil; highly stressed, constantly bickering as well as becoming increasingly paranoid. Meanwhile Maximus, Bren and Kapernicus had left the village far behind. They were experiencing a forced change of scene, horseback and making their way to a new destination: The Giants' Hills. With Bren, after insisting he accompany them, seated upon the rear of Rapscallion. He wasn't given a choice as he had little experience with such animals, was advised he'd be passenger only and finding the ride uncomfortable. Still, he didn't care; he'd rather suffer a sore rump than spend another second in the village.

Maximus and Kapernicus were in conversation with the hero needing clarification about the Morgrae's history.

"So why *were* you travelling with the bottled monster, and where were you taking it?"

Finding the question unappealing, and wishing he were elsewhere, the merchant rubbed the back of his neck.

"Ugh. I'd been tasked with delivering it to somebody. A first transaction between myself and a new client. An individual based near Greenshire. I was paid well and in advance and knew the item in question was high-risk. Of substantial risk in fact."

He shook his head regretfully.

"But I should have never shown it off. It were stupid of me."

"So you made a mistake," replied the hero, "a big mistake sure, but everybody makes mistakes."

Kapernicus shook his head solemnly.

"Yes, but not like this. Not of this magnitude"

"Who were you delivering it to and why?, questioned the hero."

He pondered the question.

"An acquaintance of Szrania. Your foul friend from those Woods."

Maximus ignored the jibe instead his thoughts returned to the same destination.

"Pffft. Raven Woods. A hideous place."

Having been listening closely, Bren tapped him on the shoulder.

"Are the Woods really a place, and are they that bad?"

He turned to face him; expression solemn.

"It is. Hope you never need to go there. It's a dark place, a malevolent place. Things reside there that will eat you alive. A haven for all things sinister. They should stay there, eh Rapscallion?"

He caressed the steed's flank further recalling his experience.

"Indeed. He and I were lucky to escape at all. And my ears. They've recently stopped ringing. There's no such thing as peace under that canopy. Only torturous screeching."

Bren's eyes widened, realised there was a place even the mighty hero was afraid to travel to and regretted he'd asked such a question. He remembered a chant he'd heard several times. One uttered by the younger villagers; rhyming verse about a witch from the Woods with a particularly mean stare. He believed it were made up. Perhaps it were based on fact after all.

The hero continued, with a question aimed at Kapernicus.

"How do you know Szrania, do you typically consort with witches?"

He flared his nostrils.

"What? No, I don't know her. I met one of her...acquaintances at the boundary. An associate or something. She paid in gold pieces and informed me to take the Morgrae directly to the uh, the recipient. I've since forgotten the name. It was unusual, similar sounding to hers I believe. Still, I diverted from my set course.

Foolishly so, should never have stopped at all. Especially Oakdale. But I saw an opportunity…"

Maximus looked down his nose.

"For profit?"

"Yes. I saw an opportunity to make more coin."

Bren gestured towards him with a damning summary.

"And look what happened. My parents were killed because you did."

Kapernicus diverted his focus to him, attempting to sound sincere.

"I'm sorry to hear that. But though I brought the Morgrae to the village it wasn't I who released it. You realise that don't you?"

Maximus snapped at him, protective of the youngster.

"Leave him be!"

Bren shrugged in response, unperturbed by the remarks.

"It doesn't matter. I need to move on. I…I guess."

Maximus glared at the merchant, indicating he keep conversation with his charge to a minimum. He acknowledged, continued his conversation with him instead.

"I have no defence for my choice of profession and make no apologies either. I was born into this way of life. It's all I've known."

The hero narrowed his eyes.

"Hm. We all have to make a living. Some honest and some not so honest. I understand that but there are victims in all of this. Innocent victims…"

Kapernicus' jaw slackened.

"Innocent? How many innocents do you know? I'm talking about those who have never lied cheated, dodged the law or other issues in between. In my experience there's no such thing as an 'innocent'."

Bren disagreed, stating his point loud and clear.

"Babies and young children are innocent."

Maximus smiled, impressed by the witty (and accurate) response.

"Wise words."

Kapernicus' gaze switched between the pair.

"Ah, well…agreed. But for how long? The human race is corrupt, selfish, often self-serving. Akin to politicians I might add."

"True," opined Maximus. "But there *are* good people out there."

"Like my parents were," added Bren.

"Yes," agreed the hero who sensed Kapernicus had more to say. "Let's leave it there. This debate could run and run with resentment emerging victorious."

Several minutes' silence followed while they enjoyed the surroundings, the distant mountain tops, valleys, rolling hills and brilliant blue sky. Finally Kapernicus broke the tranquillity with a question for the hero.

"So, tell me. Why are we headed to the Giants' Hill's again?"

"We are to seek a crystal," replied the man, "according to the witch it can be found deep within the caves there."

"What about the giants, they've gone, haven't they?"

He nodded in affirmation.

"So I believe. And I plan to enter alone. I'm not expecting any resistance other than an unpleasant traipse through the darkness. However, one can never second guess risks within an unknown location. And caves of all places: they're naturally dark and mysterious among other variables."

"But what are *we* to do while you're in there?" remarked the merchant.

Before he could respond, Bren answered.

"I'll go in with you if that's all right. I'm not afraid. Especially with you by my side."

He hesitated, realising the only alternative was to leave him in the company of the merchant. An unsavoury proposition.

"Hm, that should be fine – as long as you follow my every instruction. And you know I can't guarantee your safety either."

Bren nodded enthusiastically.

"Of course."

"And me," enquired Kapernicus, "what shall I do?"

"Well," grinned the hero, "as one who entertains people for a living, entertain yourself for once. Practice your sales pitch to any insects you might discover."

Hearing such Bren giggled uncontrollably, while Kapernicus shook his head in disgust. He felt, yet again, the hero had made an unprovoked, and sarcastic remark. He could and maybe *should have* retorted but held his tongue. Instead he was making mental notes of everything. Each insult and putdown.

Every. Single. One of them.

***

A little later as the journey continued Kapernicus had dropped back a little, feeling sorry for himself and aggrieved he'd experienced humiliation in front of a teenager of all people. He believed he should be the one in control, the one to call the shots if you will. However since coming into contact with the hero had been put firmly in place; and felt, dare I say it, inadequate. Meanwhile, out in front Maximus and Bren were content and in conversation; the hero trying his best to keep the boy occupied with positive thoughts.

"So apart from hunting aquatic predators, what other hobbies do you enjoy?"

He pondered the question momentarily, reliving the image of Lucifer's severed head amongst the shallows.

"Hm. I really wanted to catch that fish. I wanted to show everyone I could do it. But now, he's uh…it's…it's *dead.*"

He looked to Maximus who nodded sympathetically before answering the question.

"So, uh, Oh, exploring new places I guess. I came to know everywhere in Oakdale; there was nothing to look forward to. Until you came along I mean."

Maximus offered a grateful smile in return.

"And this is the first time you've travelled far from the village?"

The teen looked to the horizon.

"Yes, I've never been this far before. I've always wanted to and knew I would one day. But not..."

Maximus finished the sentence.

"Under these circumstances?"

He nodded.

"Yes."

"Well young Brenton," continued the hero, "one thing's for sure: the kingdom is bigger than you, or I can imagine, with sights, sounds, people, and creatures far beyond your wildest dreams and imagination. Truly. There's a myriad of towns, villages occupied with hundreds of folk who we'll never see, let alone meet. We are all players in a huge and open world after all."

Following a minor pause while attempting to process his words Bren spoke once more.

"So you travel lots do you?"

He emitted a sigh.

"Yes. I've travelled aplenty. Typically not for pleasure or sight-seeing in mind but other reasons. Good deeds is one way to put it."

"Don't you have any family?"

Maximus saw visions of a loved one flash through his mind as well as an individual darker in nature.

"Not anymore. Not for a long while. She,

she was my world, while he..."

He froze mid-sentence, the memory quickly archived. And being of a young mind Bren didn't think to enquire further but changed the subject to something far more exciting instead, while Kapernicus remained ignorant, didn't care about the hero's past.

"How many creatures have you defeated; like monsters and stuff, do you remember?"

He tipped his head back, chuckled knowingly.

"Oh, my intimidating title and the stories of my exploits are just that – stories. But not always. I *have* killed many a foe. Beast AND man unfortunately...with the wonderful world we have it's a terrible shame - and fact - that people, human beings, we of a supposed, and higher intelligence, seek to destroy one another. The idealist in me wishes *all* people could get along. But that isn't the case, and never will be. Humans have fought amongst themselves since the dawn of time. Often over land, territory, love, as well as personal disagreements. The list goes on. A good soul is rare these days. If you find company of one whether it be man, woman, even animal, cherish it. Cherish them. For you would have struck gold indeed."

He took a deep breath, recalling Szrania's closing comments about humans and knew at the time she were talking sense. However, he couldn't let her know that.

He changed the subject.

"So, where do you see yourself in ten years' time, what would you wish to be doing?"

Having never expected such a probing question, the teen emitted a bemused sigh.

"I'm not sure. Part of me thinks why bother making plans when everything could be taken away so quickly."

"And unexpectedly," added Maximus. "Tomorrow's never guaranteed. For you, me, or anybody. So I understand why you said that. However strive to live each day as your best day; be thankful; kind and forgiving..."

He hesitated, considered the bully once more.

"Well, not to everyone. But *always* be you."

Bren smiled, pleased he was subject to words of wisdom from such a wise and respected individual, while, again, Kapernicus had nothing to add on the subject. His mind and focus was on more critical issues: his safety and long-term future. Regardless, he rode alongside with a question destined for the hero's ears.

"Either I missed something, or you never made it clear why you insisted I come on this expedition."

Maximus' jaw dropped, failing to comprehend the statement. He and Bren exchanged knowing glances.

"Expedition? Missed something, isn't it obvious?"

Kapernicus shook his head while the hero continued.

"So I can keep an eye on you of course. You still have a part to play with regards to the capture and containment of the Morgrae."

His gazed pierced the merchant's.

"You do realise that don't you?"

Kapernicus stared in silence while he continued.

"I've spoken this before but the reason the beast resides in the lake, winds all the way back to you; with *you* being the one who took it into the village in the first place. At the very least you're here to experience everything I, or *we* might suffer to fix the problem. Otherwise you'd be free to cause more chaos."

Kapernicus felt his stomach tie in knots, considered arguing back but sensibly changed his mind. Meanwhile Maximus winked at Bren which caused him to chuckle discreetly.

Soon they stopped at the crest of a grassy mound while Maximus pointed his sword.

"See that hill to the left, the one in shade?"

His companions stared in the same direction while he sheathed the weapon.

"Those are the Giants' Hills; the once *feared* Giants' Hills. We should be there by sundown if we continue, or we can set up camp here for the night. What say you both?"

Feeling hungry, tired, and filled with trepidation they agreed it better to hunker down and prepare themselves mentally with Bren imparting his wish.

"Make camp please."

***

A little later with everybody having laid out their pitch, Kapernicus positioned furthest away from Maximus yet closest to the campfire hogging as much heat as he could, and Bren located near to the hero they were settled having eaten their rations. Maximus was at ease in his surroundings, the merchant too with them both snoring softly. It was only Bren who was awake, and far too alert for his liking; with the night being one of the few times he'd camped under the stars. The trouble was apart from feeling chillier than he'd have liked there was the ever-present issue of strange noises surrounding them. He was unfamiliar with most of them. To an experienced outdoorsman of course they'd have known their fauna and accompanying calls etc. but with Bren being young, generally naïve and a lot less travelled was left feeling fearful. Way too fearful. He tried his utmost to close his eyes and drift into slumber but with thoughts of the Morgrae attacks and what dangers might await inside the Hills on his mind he envisioned all kinds of beasts in the vicinity; each one bloodthirsty; prowling, skulking; waiting for their moment to strike.

One thing, or should I say *person* who inspired confidence in his worrisome mind was the presence of Maximus. He never struggled with the notion he were in the company of a revered individual; somebody who until recently he hadn't believed existed; considered the odd tale he'd been privy to was just that – a made up story; told to entertain and nothing more. To him and his friends he was a mythical, invisible entity, existing elsewhere, and never to appear to his unworthy eyes. He always imagined if he were to have met him, been lucky enough that is, he would have become speechless. Tongue tied and lost for words. But no. Maximus, on the surface at least was a normal man like most others. However his wisdom was above all others he'd met as was his presence. In his experience the man was unshakeable, well, apart from his nightmare-inducing account of visiting Raven Woods. He wondered what made him turn out the way he was. What he'd experienced in his younger years and wished he'd probed further with his earlier questions. It were too late though. He'd need to try another time. He tossed and turned, eyed the two individuals, mulling over their unique personalities. Still in development emotionally he found it difficult to accept the merchant were a wily, untrustworthy sort, while opposite slept the hero: a shining beacon of honesty and integrity. He wondered what fate had in store for them all. Whether he'd or *they'd* return to Oakdale or whether the creepy caves might claim them. He pictured his parents' faces but during settled times. His father were a keen swimmer. Apart from being a fantastic role model he lived for the village swimming competition. An annual event held each spring. And his determination to have come first one day. He trained no matter the weather. But following his tragic end, that could never happen.

His thoughts returned to his mother during a typical summer afternoon, the woman content with chores. The simple task of hanging washing on the line would fill her with great satisfaction. He chuckled under his breath as her birthday were due in a fortnight, and for the first time he'd planned to help with the daily tasks. *Really* help. Maybe help cook dinner too. But not now. A gaping, unfillable hole had appeared in his life. He looked to the stars and hoped the two were smiling down at him, and he'd meet them again one day. Hopeful. But how, and where?

His eyes filled with tears; his nose became uncomfortably blocked. He stifled a frustrated scream, not wishing to disturb his companions. Even during torment he remained considerate of those around him. He rolled up a sleeve and inspected his left forearm, the urge to scratch it raw built inside; a powerful and intense desire to inflict pain upon himself but he remained strong. What good would that do? Nothing, that's what. It was then he considered Grace. He'd mulled over their squabbling. Why they did it, he had no idea. He endeavoured if he were to see her again he'd exercise patience. He'd listen to her ramblings and react like a grown-up might. Not a 'little boy' she'd sometimes accuse him of being.

Eventually however, accepting nothing was going to murder him in his sleep, he closed his eyes, his mind clearing of negative thoughts, the comforting crackle of firewood helping his cause immensely.

The next morning, following an uneventful night the trio were headed towards the Hills. As they made their way up a winding path Bren enquired about the unnerving sounds which had disturbed him throughout the night.

"Banshees? *Really?*"

"Yes. Really," replied Maximus. "Shapeshifters too."

He glanced at Kapernicus.

"Shapeshifters? What do they look like?"

He pointed to the hero.

"How would I know? You'll need to ask him."

Maximus hid a brewing chuckle.

"Oh, shapeshifters…that's the thing. They do as their name suggests: shift their shape."

Bren's eyes widened.

"So that means a shapeshifter could be anywhere, or anybody?"

"Uh-huh, anybody or anywhere."

He directed his gaze to the merchant who recoiled in horror.

"You don't think *I* am a shapeshifter, do you?"

He then switched his gaze to Maximus – for confirmation – but the hero didn't help matters.

"Him? No. But I could be!"

He wobbled precariously on the saddle; eyes widened in terror causing the hero to take drastic action.

"No. No. I was pulling your leg, my boy. Those noises last night? They were wild dogs; or muntjac deer. Nothing for you to worry about."

Hearing so he breathed a huge sigh of relief while Kapernicus chuckled under his breath, celebrating the supposition he, or in his view the young 'brat' had suffered a rough night.

"Heh. Toe rag."

***

The travellers were soon in sight of their destination where Maximus ordered them all to hold their positions. Which they did. Bren was happy to, but Kapernicus wasn't. He gestured towards the Hills, bewildered at the instruction.

"Why the hesitation? The cave entrance is *right* there."

He returned an icy glare.

"No. We watch and assess what's before us first. Until I see there are no threats only then will we advance."

He gripped the hilt of his sword, which caused the merchant to imagine a myriad of awaiting dangers.

"Or you can go on ahead, but *alone*."

Kapernicus realised he shouldn't have questioned the man and held his tongue further. However, after inspecting the space with his trusty spyglass it wasn't long before Maximus spied something unsettling. According to his observations there were signs of a giant's presence. An area of grass around the cave entrance was flat when it shouldn't have been. The remaining ashes of an unusually large campfire was visible too, as well as a scattering of fallen trees, all broken mid-trunk. Obvious warning signs. However with a clear line of sight between them and the cave entrance there was, bar a few scattered trees, no indication of a giant in residence. Or any living thing for that matter. Further to that there were no obvious hiding places, so a surprise attack was unlikely.

He stroked his chin contemplating their next move.

"We have an interesting scenario gentlemen: signs of giants' presence but all looking peaceful."

He pointed to the area of concern, explained the reasons also. His companions adopted nervous dispositions as neither had seen a giant in the flesh before, while the thought of meeting one filled them with dread. The trio observed patiently, while the noon breeze blew, cheerful birdsong their soundtrack. However it wasn't long before Maximus had chosen their next course of action, pointed to a clump of trees.

"We'll secure the horses over there and out of sight. We shall then proceed to the caves, using our torches to light the way once inside;

with all of us treading carefully and watching each other's backs. I repeat, watching each other's backs. Got that? Any questions?"

Bren had none, found the idea sensible while Kapernicus, as Maximus was growing accustomed to, did. But just the one.

"Are we likely to encounter any dangers inside?"

"Such as?"

"Um, apart from insects or uh, bats. Monsters, hazards. Issues like that," he replied, eager for reassurance.

Maximus looked over his shoulder to Bren, he finding the question valid too.

"I'm not sure, though darkness will be a major problem should our torches extinguish. But hazards, enemies? I don't know. We'll have to find that out as we go. Now, let's move."

~ Into the Unknown ~

They stopped at the caves' entrance with Maximus leading the way. Bren followed who was tailed by Kapernicus who'd opted to join them after all. Reluctantly but felt it the safer of the two options. The first thing they observed was the cooler temperature, pervading damp as well as musty odour. By their nature, spaces such as those are cold, dark and unwelcoming where any amount of hazards might be lurking.

He raised his torch and squinted into the gloom; made eye contact with the two in turn before urging them onwards and it wasn't long before Bren had a relevant question.

"Any idea where we'll find the crystal?"

Maximus waved his torch ahead. The flame illuminating little.

"Nope. We'll need to advance until something catches our eye for I have never set foot in here before; only heard things…"

He assessed what might lay before them but all he detected were rocks, covered with slippery fungus or crawling insects. A suitable habitat for a myriad of other living things, but certainly them travellers. Their torches flickered wildly; the feeling of claustrophobia ever present, and with it, occasional nervous glances, each thinking similar thoughts: fearful they might extinguish.

Of the three it was Kapernicus who was most afraid of losing his way. He was out of his comfort zone; in a place he'd never choose to venture. Missing the road, the towns, villages and awaiting victims, I mean *customers*. His thoughts were negative, that's' for sure, yet chose to remain quiet. Bren, though concerned for their collective safety, felt safe in the hero's company. Whereas Maximus? He wished for the whole affair to be over with as quickly as possible. He more than the others knew danger could be lurking anywhere. Whether that of living tissue and highly territorial, or those of naturally formed hazards.

Regardless all was going as planned until they reached a large gap in the rocks - a wide, and imposing chasm. Maximus stepped forward, lowered his torch into the void, reaching as far as he could before glancing to his companions.

He had no clue how far the drop would be if any were to fall as his 'observations' were, uh, peering into an empty void. Curious, Bren tossed a rock into the space; the object disappearing instantly.

It took several seconds before they heard it bounce far below, the resulting echo reverberating around them. The two exchanged concerned looks before their torchlight revealed

Kapernicus' fearful expression.

He fidgeted uncomfortably.

"What now, do we turn back?"

Maximus sighed.

"Of course not. But the fact is we don't know where we're heading other than deeper into the caves where anything could happen."

He waved the torch in front, the light still of little use.

"So you'll need to wait here while I jump across."

Bren pointed his torch to the opposite side of the chasm. His estimation was the gap was roughly the same length as his fishing rod; nine feet or so. Perhaps ten.

"But I can do it instead. Let me go first."

Maximus grabbed his forearm.

"No. It's too far and too risky. I won't allow it."

"But I've survived bigger gaps when jumping tree to tree near the lake," he protested. "Well, not as far, but I can."

Maximus hesitated, switching his gaze to the merchant who displayed his open palms.

"He's braver than I that's for sure."

He stroked his chin.

"Fine. But only if you're sure. And it'll be on your head if you fall. But I'll cross first."

Bren returned a look of steely determination.

"But all of my...er *most* of my friends could do it. It's only a long jump."

As much as his choice concerned the hero, he couldn't help but admire his bravery and adventurous spirit. He nodded in affirmation and focused on the task at hand. Then, after taking a deep, anticipatory breath he took the short run-up, leapt high into the air and landed safely on the far side. He rose to his feet, dusted himself down while his companions sighed with relief. He returned to the chasm' edge and spied the boy preparing his own run-up, had second thoughts about him attempting to do the same and outstretched a concerned palm.

"Listen now, are you sure..."

But before he could finish, observed he'd commenced his sprint. He stepped to one side, scanning the ground in anticipation, felt the distance was a tad too far. Regardless feet were in motion. The merchant's jaw dropped as the teen brushed past him, his facial expression one of intensity. He reached the edge, leapt with all his might and...crash landed in front of Maximus. Heavy, awkward and with a horrified grimace across his face. The hero sensed he'd landed too close to the edge so grabbed a firm hold of his wrist as he slid backwards. Bren however, had deemed he were destined to fall; emitted a shrill scream; his thoughts of instant regret.

"Help me!"

Maximus clenched his teeth as the tunic sleeve began to slip from his grasp. The teen reacted, grabbed hold of a clump of nettles which stung his hands, but it didn't matter – it was the nettles or potential death. Maximus crashed to his stomach and grabbed the waistband of his trousers. Their loose material stretched, threatened to tear but fortunately remained intact. While this was happening, the merchant was in turmoil. A part of him would love to have witnessed Bren's demise. Well, perhaps not. That'd be a step too far. But he were happy to observe him struggle. In his view he couldn't have assisted them if he wanted to. He were on the opposite side after all. Instead he offered the only 'assistance' he could, by shouting words of encouragement.

"Grab on. Pull yourself clear now!"

Finally the pair clambered to safety, regained their composure, and caught their breath. Maximus shook his head, feeling deep regret for he believed he'd misjudged the teen. Gave him far too much credit as well as too much freedom. A mistake he wasn't going to repeat. He imagined a scenario where he and the merchant were staring into a void with Bren nothing but a memory, only his final screams to remember him by. He made eye contact with the teen, in preparation of scolding him but amazingly he laughed, had found the entire event hilarious, and in turn caused him to become temporarily lost for words.

He looked to Kapernicus, then the boy, amazed at the lucky escape, while his voice echoed around the space.

"Well, you're fine and acting like that was a typical occurrence then."

Bren nodded in acknowledgement and shrugged.

"Um, because was. Kind of..."

The hero continued.

"Right then. Let's start as we mean to continue." He looked to the merchant. "Throw me our torches."

Kapernicus tossed them one each. Then as they turned their backs he called out.

"Uh, a question if you don't mind; but how long are you likely to be?"

Maximus shrugged indifferently.

"After that? I can't say. But it's best if you wait there."

Kapernicus took a step back, glanced to his left then waved his torch in the same direction.

"Maybe not…"

As they did he made his way gingerly towards the left-hand edge of the chasm, his torchlight essential in helping him safely along. Soon he stopped, scanned up, down, left, and right his eyes sparkling with delight.

"Well I'll be. Are these, are these steps? Surely not."

Maximus narrowed his eyes, held his torch low and moved in the same direction with Bren following close behind. In moments, the trio were within touching distance while Kapernicus wore an exaggerated *'aren't I great, look what I found'* expression upon his face.

There really were steps. Easy to miss. No, *incredibly* easy to miss. The two opposing edges of the rock face had gradually narrowed causing them to realise the dangerous leap across had been unnecessary. On top of that there was the merest hint of light below. A tiny speck and they weren't imagining it.

Maximus offered the merchant due praise.

"Well done. Well observed."

Bren glanced to Maximus then the merchant agreeing yet eager to continue.

"Shall I go first?"

Maximus raised a cautious hand.

"No. Wait..."

He sniffed the air as something had caught his attention. The other two followed suit with Kapernicus' eyes wide.

"How strange – there's a *pleasant* odour of all things and it's coming from that direction."

He gestured towards the pinprick of light.

Maximus and Bren echoed his sentiments the same sight cementing their decision to proceed. It had swayed Kapernicus too with all reasoning a pleasant smell should equal a pleasant experience, right? Maximus assumed control of the situation.

"I'll go first. So follow me but be careful, for the steps don't appear wide. Initially at least."

They began their descent with their noses and curiosity leading the way; all the while not a single word spoken with concentration being the name of the game. They sensed to slip could mean injury – or worse: death. As they did Maximus dug into past memories; recalling that over the years he'd heard stories about the caves with many untrue. Obviously so, and bizarre in nature, even to his well-travelled ears. But one, *ONE* tale remained forefront in his thoughts: the *'cave sprites'*. He'd heard on more than one occasion by persons unknowing of the other that there is a rarely seen/ encountered race of 'things' which dwell in the recesses there. Mysterious, intriguing creatures; their name unpronounceable to everyone but the most learned. He hesitated, considered declaring his suppositions but changed his mind. The other two sensed as such while Kapernicus commented, expecting a worst-case scenario.

"What is it? Did you see something, did you hear something?"

He cast him an icy stare.

"Why the constant drama? Calm down, man. Please. Just...just this once. Now, have you ever heard tales of this place, either of you?"

Bren returned a blank stare while Kapernicus replied.

"Only about the giants, why do you ask?"

He continued.

"I have. Many in fact. I've been informed there's a mysterious race of creatures present. Sprites they were referred to. Supposedly inhabiting these caves..."

Bren finished his sentence.

"If they are real, is that what you're wondering?"

He nodded in affirmation while Kapernicus, and true to form considered the worst.

“Monsters, are they monsters?”

He shook his head in disdain.

“No. Uh, possibly. Though rumours are they can be approachable. Under the right circumstances.”

“Right circumstances?” repeated the merchant. “What’s that supposed to mean?”

However before he could reply he lost his footing and slid onto his backside, his satchel spinning awkwardly around to his front, putting him off balance. His companions lunged instinctively forward – to stop him from tumbling off the edge. It didn’t matter though he’d managed to stop himself. But only just. He glanced gingerly over his shoulder, spying their relieved faces and offered an embarrassed response.

“Tread carefully, eh? Perhaps I should heed my own advice.”

The merchant smirked in amusement while Bren remained stone-faced. It went without saying from thereon in they planned to tread more carefully than ever.

However it wasn’t long before the merchant’s curiosity to know more revealed itself.

“So, the sprites you mentioned. What do

you know about them?"

He snapped a response.

"Ugh. I've told you all I know. Cave sprites that may or may not be friendly. Supposedly in here somewhere. There's nothing more to say at this time. So whatever happens hereafter we'll deal with on the fly, got it?"

Kapernicus nodded submissively, though his senses were on higher alert than usual. Meanwhile the other two moved forward, with the boy illustrating a high level of maturity under the circumstances.

A little later and to their collective glee they touched down onto firmer ground; formed a triangle of sorts, each holding their torch high in an attempt to find their bearings. All they could decipher though, was more darkness with the speck of light in the distance remaining just that – a distant speck of light. Regardless Maximus pointed ahead.

"Onwards gentlemen."

Bren looked to their rear, believing he could make out a passage, but wasn't sure. Kapernicus, his eyesight the weakest of the trio, relied on the hero's actions to determine his own so moved behind him leaving Bren at the rear which didn't bother him. A little later with the journey uneventful, and the echoed bootsteps tedious to their ears Maximus enquired further as to Kapernicus' history.

"Is it true what I hear about your type, the numbers many and increasing?"

He hesitated, unsure whether, or how, to respond. However Maximus held his gaze, prompting him to do so.

"Yes. We are many."

"How many, and are you based anywhere in particular?"

He squirmed uncomfortably in his winklepickers.

“As a matter of fact we hail from the north of the kingdom, with our numbers ever changing but capped.”

“Brayton, far north?” replied the hero, “or Somners Village?”

He shook his head.

“Not Somners, no. The nearby Brayton. That’s where our…er, headquarters are. Now I’d rather not speak about them.”

He sighed, regretting the fact he’d spilled the beans. Well, only a few. But still too many.

“Can we change the subject please?”

It goes without saying he were hesitant to talk about himself, personal information or otherwise as the less people knew about him the more mysterious he’d remain. The truth is he were a member of a shady organisation known as ‘The Dark Order of Merchants’ – or D.O.o.M for short. A collection of travelling, highly trained swindlers. Their existence as has become apparent – to make as much coin from as many persons as possible – no matter the status or circumstances. Maximus knew that but wanted to hear how much ‘inside’ info he could gain. Which was little more than he already he knew. So, realising his questions weren’t likely to bear further fruit, he turned to Bren for conversation.

“And what of you, do you…”

He diverted his gaze to his feet; his mood inexplicably altered.

"Did anyone else feel that?"

He held his torch low while the other two stopped in their tracks, Kapernicus on tenterhooks.

"What was it, should we be alarmed?"

He waved his torch about him.

"I don't know. But it felt like something ran over my boot."

Bren moved to his side, panic in his voice.

"What do you mean, don't know?"

In moments all three were holding their torches low, scanning, ears straining, senses on highest possible alert. It was Kapernicus who broke the silence, 'yelped' aloud, with something having spooked him.

"On the ground…there. Look!"

He waved his torch frantically then yelped again, kicking his left leg out.

"Argh! I've been bitten!"

Suddenly they were in disarray, shaking their limbs comically. Maximus called out fearing the worst.

"RUN – towards the light. As fast as you can!"

In seconds, they were sprinting for their lives, hurtling at break-neck speed along a dark passage. As they did Kapernicus offered an unwanted commentary.

"So many. Biting, scratching...run for your lives!"

Bren echoed his sentiments, calling in distress.

"They're on me too. Maximus - *help!"*

Hearing such Maximus screeched to a halt, lowered his torch and spied the culprits. For there in the torchlight were dozens, no many more, large insects, four to five inches in length and similar to what we'd consider an ant. But bigger. Much bigger in fact. And though it was hard to confirm in the artificial light of the torches' glow they were of a red shade – similar to our own red ants but of the mutant variety. Meaning bigger insects bore bigger fangs, or mandibles; and it were those the insects were using to bite, pinch, and nip the three intruders. The ground appeared to move, the mass akin to a rolling wave towards and around them all.

Maximus knew they had one option: to keep running, and if they stalled any longer they'd perish. He tugged Bren's forearm, gestured to the merchant.

"Keep running, both of you!"

As they did the distant speck of light grew larger while they felt the insects crunching beneath their boots, causing them to slip, slide, and nearly lose their footing such were the numbers. Then with them having been bitten from their ankles to their backs to their necks to their hands they finally reached sanctuary.

Maximus moved first, leaping into an apparent body of dark water. He was closely followed by Bren and trailing behind was Kapernicus – his unusual footwear and poor fitness levels having held him back. Regardless the three were soon treading water and coming to terms with the experience.

Having observed several dozen furious insects scrambling back and forth upon the floors' edge and inches from their faces; Maximus was first to regain his composure; fearful of their snapping jaws, the things desperate to experience yet more of their flesh.

"Try not to panic but keep treading water. We are safe for the moment."

Kapernicus bawled in return, his eyes tightly closed, arms thrashing about wildly while several of the offending creatures bobbed close to his face.

"But the pain! The pain!"

Ignoring them both was Bren. He'd spied a glimmer of light below and submerged to investigate. Seconds later having observed his absence Maximus called in alarm.

"Brenton! Where are you?"

~ An Underground Oasis ~

Silence. Nothing for several seconds before his head broke surface. His eyes sparkling.

"This way please."

He took a deep breath then submerged while the two observed in wonderment. Maximus was first to follow, then the merchant. They tracked the distorted silhouette forward, around and up before their heads broke surface, but into lighter conditions.

They gasped in relief while their lungs filled with cleaner, fresher air, their senses detecting the same pleasant odour they'd smelled way back. Then as their eyes became accustomed to the environment Maximus clawed free of the water first. In moments the three were standing beguiled, scanning their new environment for they were, for want of a better expression, in an open void of sorts.

There were colourful and mysterious shrubs; as well as plants of unusual shades: pinks, yellows, blues, the curved stones above them demonstrating a large yet unreachable hole with shafts of hazy sunlight streaming through. There were signs of new life, it's presence slight but noticeable. Airborne insects dancing in small 'clouds' while the never-before-heard croak of a frog-type reptile sounded, chirps of unseen birds, each call unique to their ears. The three were, however, unable to appreciate the sights as their clothes, hair and belongings were drenched; their footwear making the familiar 'squelching' sound. But it wasn't their attire causing most discomfort, no; their faces without exception were reddened, sore, peppered with bites, as were their arms, legs and rest of their bodies.

So with the adrenaline levels of the escape wearing off they experienced the *real* pain of their injuries; a stinging, burning sensation. Maximus, as leader, did his best to remain composed as did Bren, but it was hard, *incredibly* hard not to yield to it. It was Kapernicus who were most distressed failing to show any signs of coping; squealing, gyrating, irritated beyond belief.

Time slowed down as they suffered in their own way before a sudden 'something' caught Bren's eye. An intense light, airborne, miniscule yet flitting left then right and all around, its movements always unpredictable. So feeling he had nothing to lose, and perpetually curious he headed in its direction causing Maximus to follow. Bren observed in awe as the object commanded his attention; either that or he were imagining it. Maximus felt similar, observing the object in amazement before he spied Kapernicus, eyes wide, headed in their direction too.

They wound their way past and around ever more dense shrubs, their berries or 'fruits' enticingly fragrant. Each ignoring the urge to pick and eat one just in case, their real sights upon the ball of dancing light. In moments the 'ball' or sprite had ceased movement, actually flitted about but less so, more in a hovering motion. So being positioned closer to the object than the merchant, Maximus and Bren spied something wondrous dazzling below it; to all intents and purposes a fizzing, sparkling body of water located in a tall, conical mound. To be clear and to explain it better imagine a tube standing vertically but about four feet high and three feet wide but constructed of…hardened clay of a pale blue shade with the outside adorned with creeping pink vines and other assorted oddities, all enhancing its unique appearance.

Bren stepped forward transfixed, as the sprite, when close, measured approximately two inches round, and had since captured his attention. Soon he was positioned near to the object, its waters mesmerising, inviting to him. Witnessing such was Maximus but with Kapernicus creeping ever closer as his levels of curiosity were just as intense. Both men observed as the two appeared to be communicating, or 'speaking' to one another. To say the three were in a bad way was a huge understatement. Their wounds were inflamed; their faces bloated and reddened. In fact they looked like smudged caricatures of themselves. Without warning Bren removed his tunic and boots, kicked off his trousers, his socks, one landing on Kapernicus' sleeve, which annoyed him of course, while his gaze remained on the manifestation. Then in one smooth, uninterrupted motion he climbed into the waters. As he did he closed his eyes and submerged.

At that exact moment, they began fizzing, bubbling, spraying droplets high into the atmosphere while the sprite darted in all directions, unwilling to get wet. As it did it left behind a winding, iridescent trail which further enchanted the duo. However though witnessing the act Maximus knew not to interfere or try to stop it for he sensed the waters were of the boy's benefit. He was correct in his thinking. They were. They contained mysterious and magical chemicals belonging to, or administered, by the being.

After what seemed to be two to three minutes in the waters, submerging for several seconds at a time Bren looked in Maximus' direction, relief on his face.

"This...this is amazing. My...my wounds, my stings. They've stopped hurting".

He too was correct. As Both men observed they witnessed a change take place to his complexion. It cleared, the inflammation, the soreness dissipated; everything returned to normal in front of their eyes. All three observed in awe as the sprite changed position, hovering over Maximus' head instead, before moving to the waters and back again. They instinctively knew what it was trying to communicate. So again with nothing to lose or fear he undressed to his underwear before moving into position. He climbed in having waited for Bren to clamber free.

Then while he experienced the waters he was being closely watched by Kapernicus, himself eager no *desperate* to sample the delights. In no time at all and having fully recovered, Maximus climbed out of his own accord but interestingly the sprite remained distant of the merchant. Instead it hovered about the heads of Bren and himself, dancing whimsical, fairy-like. Regardless of that Kapernicus needed his wounds healed and was impatient. In his mind it was his turn.

He didn't *require* an invite. He was entering regardless.

In no time at all he was down to his underwear: tatty grey and holey underpants, his lily-white frame shivering. He moved to enter the waters, but the sprite changed direction and headed towards him, turning an angry red in the process. It bumped repeatedly into his head as if to tell him 'No'. Meanwhile he attempted to wave it away, furiously swinging his arms, but the sprite was speedy, dodging this way and that. Observing such Bren wiped himself down and gestured to it, catching its attention. It moved to him, then following a short silence with the two seemingly 'communicating' it 'stood down' as it were, returning to its usual, luminescent white, and allowing the merchant to utilise the waters and their magnificent benefits.

Maximus meanwhile stood mesmerised, observing every move, every detail. But not for threats but in sheer amazement. For if he hadn't witnessed them with his own eyes he would never have believed it. He'd heard tales of the 'caves' and their mysterious inhabitants but following a narrow escape from the vicious guardians he'd received confirmation the rumours of their existence were true, and following their dual experiences, in the most horrific yet best way possible. Their full recovery, because of the sprite's incredible hospitality, were miraculous in his view.

A little later with them dried, clothed and seated; their wounds distant memories they were in discussion with Bren, who entered the waters first, struggling to find the correct words to describe the experience.

"It... um, it was like I was in a dream. I closed my eyes and could see lots of different colours and shapes. All er, moving around and voices...strange voices speaking in a... er, different language. Oh, and the feeling when the bites were healing was like nothing I've ever..."

His words trailed off as he observed something else, a pair of sprites emerge from the mist and into view. Then another and another; all a glowing white and dancing hypnotically. They moved between himself and Maximus but kept a wide berth of the merchant which not only embarrassed him but caused instant resentment. Interrupting it all Maximus enquired as to his experience.

"How did it feel for you, the same as Bren?"

Now, though his wounds *were* healed in the same way as the other two his experience was vastly different. The waters though bubbling etc were cold and unpleasant as were his 'visions'. In his there were dark clouds and angry voices. Remaining low, jumbled, threatening. A pervading sense of *menace* to proceedings. However he replied not wishing for them to know the truth, regaling an inaccurate, made-up account of events instead.

"Oh yes. It was most wonderful. There were dancing fairies and joyous children. All singing, playing, having fun of course. Each and every one. There were fascinating colours too similar to those he mentioned; quite the experience I say."

He finished abruptly for a trickle of water had run down his wet hair and into one eye. It was then Bren's turn to speak. He questioned Maximus' experience who was happy to oblige.

"What about you?"

His eyes glazed over

"Hm. I saw everything in black and white. Well grey and white to be precise. I didn't hear any voices but saw shadows...or *shapes* of people, strange creatures; with most persons being of a light shade and all creatures being of a darker shade. And yes, the waters were warm and welcoming. I wonder what it all meant."

However something he never declared was the distorted form of an angry individual, the same pointing a threatening finger; a booming voice pummelling his senses. That in itself caused him to recoil uncomfortably, for the rest of his vision were pleasant.

Kapernicus grinned felt certain he'd figured

it out.

"It was all nonsense of course. Mere illusions of our time in the dark beforehand; strange gases messing with our minds. Things like that..."

Hearing such Maximus and Bren exchanged discreet glances, knew the merchant to be speaking nonsense for they both realised, independently of each other, there certainly *was* meaning to their visions. Precisely what those meanings were would be up for debate and for another time perhaps.

But gases, really?

Soon after, and feeling rested Maximus remembered the task at hand and its urgent nature. He spied an opening in the rocks beyond the healing waters, large enough for one person to squeeze through at a time and gestured in the same direction.

"I think we should consider ourselves fortunate gentlemen. But now we should continue onwards. We've a crystal still to find."

With his companions headed in the same direction Bren hesitated, remained in awe of the location. He could've explored the entirety of it if her were able. He observed yet more oddities: glowing caterpillar-type insects, the same littered upon spotted leaves the size of his head. To all intents and purposes winged worms.

Well, they certainly looked like it Instead he turned and took one final look around. It was then he spied several more sprites had appeared; congregated close to the healing waters. They flitted to and fro, here and there, but released as they moved, clouds of mysterious substances above and into the waters; a glowing, moving, airborne chain which illuminated the space; the sight incredible to behold.

He waved in return, knew exactly what they were doing and grateful for not only having the opportunity to experience their company but amazing hospitality too.

After negotiating a series of caverns they finally spied signs of more daylight: a brilliant shaft piercing a mound of boulders.

Bren were first to react.

“Look!”

He hurried into position, dropping to his knees and pushing his nose up against the objects. Peeking through his eyed widened in amazement before he turned to his companions, an elated expression lighting up his face.

“It’s a room full of jewels – and they’re glowing!”

Maximus peered through the opening too.

“Not quite jewels but crystals – the reason we’re here in fact!”

The boy assessed the area, his keen eyes darting back and forth.

“How do we get in there; how can we get one?”

Maximus wracked his brain while Kapernicus pondered the situation.

The area was curious indeed. For there were piles of rocks, imposing and weighing tonnes. Naturally formed? Probably. However, there was a potential and singular entry point but narrow in nature, and visible at ground level only. Teenager sized? Maybe. Regardless,

Maximus stood back and considered his options: he could move at least one of the boulders, *if* he were strong enough. But it'd only be a little and leave a gap too miniscule for either himself or the merchant to enter. But the boy? Probably. He crouched low, peering into the 'crystal room' scanning it as best he could for any potential threats or dangers; alternative ways in but spied none. Meanwhile, building inside the merchant's mind was the notion of vast riches, armfuls of valuable and hard-to-obtain crystals. He envisioned himself with fistfuls. His trolley laden down with them. He paced back and forth, desperate to spy an entry point. However Maximus stepped forward and issued a firm command.

"Stand back. I'll see what I can do."

He assumed position; sat upon his rump. And with legs bent, and a huge effort managed to push the boulder a few inches to the right; just wide enough for Bren to enter.

He gestured to the space, while the teen readied himself.

"Give it a go. But be careful."

He dropped onto his stomach then moved forward. But as he crawled through the opening had to shield his eyes as the incredible glow, in contrast to the darkness of the tunnels before, blinded him. He scrambled through; his hands, arms, and underside quickly becoming covered in slime. But as his sight accustomed to the conditions he savoured the amazing space. Magnificent was one way to put it. He'd never seen anything like it; as the entire area, other than the ground, really was covered in naturally formed crystals; their brilliance astonishing him. It were if he were standing amongst the stars; a behemoth reaching to the night sky; basking in their twinkling magnificence. Meanwhile, desperate to join him was Kapernicus. His hearing strained as the sounds of his wonderment drove him wild with jealousy. He paced impatiently back and forth, gaze directed to the ground, muttering angrily under his breath. He felt worse than a hungry toddler peering into the window of a closed sweetshop.

Then, as if from nowhere, one of the sprites appeared, moving close to his face, darting back and forth, causing him to stall.

He wondered if he should he take one or whether it was forbidden, He narrowed his eyes, glanced to the sprite then to the crystal and back again. Reacting to that the sprite sensed his intentions, moving from his hand to the crystals then back again, repeating the motion over and over, the same as it did within the previous void.

Moments later and snapping him out of the trance was Maximus. His hurried voice causing him mild alarm.

"Are you able to take one? The size doesn't matter. We just need a piece – a long, dagger-like piece if possible."

He returned to his senses. There WAS a piece, easily reachable too; hanging in front of his eyes, along with several others; all suspended like large icicles. He broke one off, the resulting 'crack' echoing around the space. He hesitated, broke off another in case they were to lose the first. Suddenly Kapernicus called out, pleading with him.

"Take as many as you can. Fill your pockets!"

However upon hearing such the sprite turned red once more causing him to understand it's change of attitude. He nodded politely in return, choosing to ignore the man causing him to call again but with renewed urgency.

"Did you hear me? Grab them while you can."

The sprite responded the same way while he dithered. There were many more of course. Hundreds available - all at his fingertips.

"Uh, yes. I heard you."

Failing to hear the tell-tale sound of a crystal being obtained, Kapernicus clenched a fist in frustration and gnawed at his knuckles.

He were raging inside. Meanwhile Maximus stood silent. He knew what was going on, and in turn furthered his attachment to the boy. He knew Bren respected the cave's hosts, and there was little chance he were going to yield to the merchant's demands. Confirming his suppositions Bren left the rest of the crystals hanging and offered a thankful smile in return. Following that he crawled back to the two, holding the objects up for them to observe, their brilliance reflecting in their eyes.

"That was easy. I got two."

"Good work," said the hero, "Let's go."

Kapernicus stepped forward, offered an outstretched hand.

"Is one of them for me?"

"No," returned the duo in tandem. "You can't have it."

Bren stowed the items in his tunic pocket while Maximus turned his attentions to the merchant.

"Forget about the crystals. Let him be."

He'd had his fill of the conditions while the merchant withdrew his appendage and was seething. In his view he'd been so close yet so far from untold riches. Riches he were forced to turn his back on. By a duo he was learning to despise. Brenton? He wished he'd left him lakeside with the bully. He'd never been a fan of children, and felt he knew how to rub him up the wrong way and enjoyed doing so. While he deemed the hero were dismissive and overflowing with disrespect for him. He was beyond furious. Following his experiences the caves had been a disastrous experience so far.

A dank spaces he'd happily leave and never return.

~ *Caught in the Act* -

The trio sensed a vague breeze and followed their noses, moving upwards and along winding, rocky steps similar to the ones they originally descended. But after a while with their legs heavy as well as the fact they hadn't a single torch to light the way; couldn't wait to be free of the environment. Tripping, stumbling and breathing in musty air, there was little conversation between them as one; Bren was mentally reliving the experience. Two: Maximus couldn't wait for daylight and fresh air once more. And three; Kapernicus was raging he'd missed out on a once-in-a-lifetime opportunity to become rich. That as well as feeling cold, hungry, AND unwelcomed by the sprites.

Soon enough they reached the top of the steps and were amazed to observe they'd returned to the original chasm. They exchanged silent, bewildered looks, as all felt, regardless of any previous beliefs, they were destined to. So after making their way carefully around the ledge, avoiding the dangerous drop they found themselves at the entrance once more.

They breathed in the fresh air and sense of open space; their expressions identical: blissful. However before they took another step , they heard a commotion in the distance. As expected it was the hero who responded first. Issuing a firm command.

"Wait here."

Bren and Kapernicus did as instructed as he moved behind a cluster of trees and bushes. He observed there were several strangers before him: three men and a woman. About thirty metres away and in the company of a raging giant.

The thing must have been nineteen feet tall, dressed in grey jodhpurs, long-sleeved green tunic and winklepicker type boots. Its face was wrinkled, its nose bulbous, filled with veins – appearing like a huge, and mutated strawberry. It's eyebrows were long and overgrown, same as its hair; while its eyes were wide due to the chaos taking place; people running here and there; the three horses still tethered to the trees, all in a distressed state.

Before he could move another muscle he was joined by his two companions. They peered around his shoulder and in the same direction causing them to gasp in horror. Kapernicus' jaw dropped while Bren stood rooted to the spot.

"It's a... a *GIANT! And look... look at our horses!"*

Feeling he'd assessed the situation the hero opined.

"Keep your voices down. Those people - I think they're thieves. Caught in the act I presume. Stay here and out of sight and we should be fine."

The sight before them was comedic. The giant was trying its best to grab one of the would-be thieves – any of them, all dressed in rag-tag attire, their hair long and unkempt. The group were dodging back and forth within the trees and bushes, tripping, stumbling yet managing to evade capture; all the while shouting a torrent of abuse.

The charade continued for a further minute or so while the trio observed bemused. Suddenly however, the situation took a turn for the worse as one of them stumbled allowing the giant to grab hold of him. It squeezed him tight, roaring furiously before tossing him into the air while his sword spun harmlessly away.

He crashed to the ground; the unmistakeable sound of breaking bones audible. That caused the other three to charge in, baying for revenge. The giant though was equal to the task, ready for all eventualities in fact.

It swung its strong arms, sending them flying. One crashed into a tree trunk with incredible force; surely a fatal occurrence; the others flung about the space; their limp bodies crashing to the ground akin to a series of ragdolls being dropped.

Moments later when they were out for the count, either unconscious or dead it grabbed two by the legs and placed them side-by-side. The third one? It stepped on him, pressing down hard, moving his boot from side to side, the sounds of crepitus, a nasty squishing sound which caused our protagonists to cover their ears and look away. It was ensuring a complete job done for that individual while Maximus and co. concluded he must have disliked him the most.

Witnessing such and unwilling to spy further violence Bren made an impulsive and potentially rash decision. He rushed into view and stood firm, ignoring his companions' hushed pleas to return.

"Over here!"

The giant spun in his direction and clenched its fists. Fearing the worst Maximus rushed to his side, sword drawn. The giant meanwhile gestured to the grounded individuals.

"Are you with these?"

He sensibly sheathed his sword indicating he weren't there for trouble.

"No sir we are merely travellers. We heard the commotion and came to investigate."

It marched in their direction which caused him to grab the hilt once more.

"Easy, big man. We are not here for trouble. Those thieves there – they were intending to steal our horses. They are *our* horses."

It stopped in its tracks; its expression changing from serious to something lighter.

"Oh, okay. So long as you're telling the truth, otherwise I'll have to beat you up too."

It's gaze switched between the three.

"Why *are* you here? There's nothing to do *or* see. This is *my* territory, and I don't like trespassers."

Without thinking Bren gestured over his shoulder.

"We came for a crystal in there. We uh, we needed one."

Hearing such its ears pricked up.

"A crystal, you say. Did you get one?"

Bren looked at Maximus who shook his head indicating he should say no. However, ignoring his mentor he questioned the giant.

"Why do you ask?"

"Because I've always wanted one, that's why."

His expression changed to one of curiosity.

"Why, why would you need a crystal?"

It shrugged in response.

"Because I've always wanted one. No other reason. I'm too big to fit in the caves so I live here with the hope that somebody someday will give me one. But no. They all come to fight me. EVERYONE comes to fight me. I've done nothing wrong."

Bren and Maximus look to the grounded bodies. The giant observed the same.

"THEY deserved it. THEY came into my territory to steal and attack me. Ruffians, vagabonds and ne'er do wells. Grah! All I've done is defend myself. Wouldn't you do the same?"

Hearing his side of the story Bren reached into his tunic pocket and pulled out a single crystal. He held it high, an offering if you will while his companions observed in stunned silence. Kapernicus saw wasted profit while Maximus witnessed a kind-hearted soul in action. The giant crouched, mindful of encroaching upon his personal space, while the expression of concentration on its face was hilarious; for it held thumb and forefinger together, tweezer style, in an attempt to take it carefully; huge and shaking appendages held mere feet from the teen's head, who smiled throughout, was unafraid and at ease, and certainly enjoying the experience. He made brief eye contact with his companions and offered the biggest of grins.

Finally, relieved to have taken ownership of the treasure the giant slumped to its knees while a tear rolled down its cheek.

A tear of joy, gratitude, and heartfelt emotion.

It held the crystal to its eye, the sunlight causing it to sparkle brilliantly. Bren too smiled, turned to Maximus who stood beside him feeling humbled and certainly the wiser following the experience. Only Kapernicus remained confused and annoyed as to why someone would 'be so foolish and give such a rare and valuable item away for free'.

To an abomination of all things!

Finally it was the giant who broke the silence. It offered a dirtied finger.

"Thank you, little man. You've made me so happy. You've given me something I've always wanted but never thought I'd get."

He bowed in response, 'shaking' the finger in the process. Maximus meanwhile was lost for words, astounded at what he'd witnessed.

Then as it sat pleased with its new toy Maximus had many questions for the youngster as they headed towards their steeds. With one in particular gnawing at him: something he'd been keen to ask.

"How were you communicating with the cave sprites? How did they know what you wanted and vice-versa?"

As the trio left the giant behind, with Kapernicus, feeling as jealous as he could ever be, he pondered the question momentarily before a crystal-like twinkle appeared in his eye.

"Easy. We just knew."

~ *Heading Back* ~

The trio were on the road and heading to the village, deep in discussion with Kapernicus unable to accept the fact that Bren gave away a 'rare and valuable' crystal; something he'd never consider doing himself.

"You do know you could have sold that – and many others - for a vast sum of money."

His companions shrugged indifferently while the boy replied.

"I got it for free and with little effort. Well, my tunic's really dirty now, but he wanted it more than me, so I gave it to him."

Kapernicus flapped his arms at the preposterousness of the gesture.

"But *I* would have given you gold coins for them. MANY of them!"

Maximus chuckled, enjoying his torment.

"It's too late. Have you heard of the expression 'What you give in this life you receive in the next?'

He shook his head defiantly.

"Bah! That notion's poppycock. Utter nonsense. I value the ownership of expensive trinkets and the like; valuable treasures I can lay my hands on."

"And there's the difference," scoffed the hero, "you're driven by greed; you value 'things' money, possessions above all else. Those can be lost, stolen, or taken away. Whereas a good heart, empathy, and kindness; those traits are inherent and indicative of the greatest of people. People like Brenton here and many others throughout these lands."

"Pfft. But what about the countless villains, the mean and crooked types throughout the land?" snapped the pedlar.

Maximus returned a nonchalant expression.

"Who cares? That isn't the kind of company I nor Bren wish to keep or consort with. Maybe that opinion speaks more about you as an individual. Have you considered *that* notion?"

He returned a derisory snort, needing final say on the subject.

"Well I expect *somebody somewhere* to eventually let me down and that's my outlook on life AND people and I'm sticking with it."

Maximus grinned before changing the subject, requesting to see the crystal. Bren handed it to him causing him to break into a smile. He observed the object at length: its natural beauty, its pointed tip, the potential for customisation.

"Splendid work. You did well. Fortunately I don't think it needs modifying or sharpening in any way. It should do the task as is...however, if we had more we could have one fashioned into a keepsake."

The boy felt meek while Kapernicus scowled.

"Oh no. Should I have kept the other one?"

He shook his head while the merchant hoped he were in for a telling off.

"Definitely not. You followed your heart. Never regret doing such things. My point was if we had more of them we might take one to a Jeweller. They could fashion a memento for us. A keepsake to remember this unique occasion."

"Memento?" enquired the merchant.

"Yes," confirmed the man. But only for he and I. There'd be no point in you having one – you'd sell it on for profit."

Bren chuckled while the merchant considered retorting, but knew he'd spoken the truth. He WOULD have sold it. In his greedy mind it would have been stupid no to.

Curious, Bren turned to the objects real purpose.

"How will it be used to stop the monster?"

Kapernicus replied instead his tone

condescending, words blunt.

"It's called 'Morgrae', child. That's its *name.*"

Bren ignored his rudeness, his attention with Maximus who replied.

"Good question. This thing will be used to pierce its skin. That's what the witch relayed to me. She said it will cause it to return to its original, smaller size but only briefly. We'll need to act quick and place it into a vessel with a secure stopper. It sounds easy saying so, but we have no idea what's been happening at the lake. It may have even moved on."

Kapernicus interrupted the speech.

"But it wouldn't have. It needs water to survive. It can only leave it for a few minutes at most. The geography of Oakdale and the lake means a suitable new home for it elsewhere isn't viable. The nearest body of water from there is at least a mile away. It would never make it. So knows it'll need to stay there."

Maximus grinned.

"That's one less concern. At least we know where it will be."

He hesitated, the cogs in his mind spinning.

"Come to think of it, how do you know so much about the thing, have you delivered others?"

He stuttered; knew he'd been asked a pertinent question.

"No. Only the one. And obvious I think. It's s reliant on water. Hence its watery prison. Would a fish," he directed his gaze to Bren, "survive long out of water, your "legendary" Lucifer for instance? No. It wouldn't have. So though I may be wrong with my assumption I presume it functions along the same lines. It would dry out and die. And when, and if, it's recaptured what then, are you going to return it to me?"

He held his gaze on the hero who cast him a stunned glare.

"Return to you? No. You cannot be trusted; you aren't capable of transporting such a thing. It will stay in my possession. *I'll* return it to its owner."

The merchant wobbled in the saddle; eyes bulged from their sockets.

"*SZRANIA!?* You're returning to those Woods? *Are you mad?"*

He snapped a response.

"You listen well, pedlar. The beast WILL be returned to the witch. That is certain. And another thing: YOU are going to accompany me there."

Hearing so caused Kapernicus to become enraged. There was no way he'd venture into the

Woods. *Ever*. He bawled a furious response.

"I will not. I will *never* go to Raven Woods – with you nor a hundred men!"

He dug his heels into his steed's side in an attempt to flee the pair. Responding similar Maximus looked to his young charge.

"Wait here."

The teen observed as a chase begun with the merchant leading the way. However, being an expert rider it wasn't long before the hero pulled alongside and yanked him from his horse. Following that he dismounted and grabbed him around the throat He moved in close, his blue eyes piercing his own whilst his iron grip illustrated superior strength.

"Listen *pedlar*: You WILL accompany me to Raven Woods. You WILL speak kindly to Bren. You WILL show me the respect I deserve. And you WILL help me to recapture the Morgrae. *Do you UNDERSTAND?"*

He nodded in submission, terrified of Maximus' threat who continued.

"Oh and another thing, I wasn't going to mention this, but now I will. The witch informed me she has something *'special'* planned next time you meet… and I'm sure you can guess what that means."

He dragged him to his feet while he

continued.

"I don't want to hear any more of your negativity either. If you do, you'll be sorry. Now climb back on your horse and re-join us. If Bren asks what happened here, inform him we had a misunderstanding that we've cleared up. He's been through enough and doesn't need anything else to worry about. Got it?"

He offered him a firm shove to the chest before remounting Rapscallion, his mood seething. Kapernicus meanwhile clambered onto his horse, a dazed almost shell-shocked expression upon his face.

~ *An Executive Decision* ~

Back at Oakdale the residents had concocted their own plan to ensnare the Morgrae. A fool proof one apparently. It was hatched during one of their protracted meetings and given final authorisation by Stanley. Their aim, as imagined by the Residents' Committee went something like this: one of the villagers would pretend to commence fishing by the water's edge. The resulting disturbance would attract the creature, thereby causing it to attack. That in turn would enable the numerous, armed villagers hiding nearby to pounce into action.

They'd use their spears, pitchforks and other weaponry to drag it from the water whereupon they'd kill it in the most brutal and spectacular manner. Once that was done its miserable corpse would be paraded through the village to allow the populace opportunity to celebrate, proving to themselves and everybody else how clever and brave they'd been.

Yes, a cunning plan to be executed by a formed committee, with the majority of members inexperienced with serious conflict.

So, gathered outside the village community centre were ten men of all shapes, sizes and abilities, dressed in their 'gardening' clothes so to speak – all volunteers confident in their roles and abilities. Stanley Purser was leading them, stood upon a pedestal issuing last-minute instructions as well as handing out various weapons to be used in the operation. He'd be supervising the event from a safe distance. Just in case. He had complete confidence in them. Total and utter confidence. He inspected the eager faces, adjusted his spectacles upon the end of his nose.

"Now everyone your safety is of utmost importance as is the slaying of the serpent. This plan has been discussed in detail, thought through and cannot fail. Will not fail. There will be tense moments of course but with our grit, determination and wills of iron we shall win the day. We will slay the menace and allow peace to return to the village. OUR village!"

A round of applause followed his words. He gestured in the lake's direction.

"Now let us head out and put an end to this menace."

As the men 'marched' away from the square their observing wives and children cheered with excitement, proud of their heroic kin. No, incredibly proud of them. All involved anticipated a swift and certain 'victory'. Meanwhile, the husbands, boyfriends, uncles etc, waved and blew kisses – each one looking forward to the action.

Soon enough the gaggle were poised, while

the angler or should we say 'bait' was in position. He held a rod and tried his utmost to appear as though he really was just a 'man out fishing'. Ironic as he'd never cast a line in his life. But he had played a leading role in one of the committee's plays once. Which afforded him the qualification. Anyway the minutes passed while he cast his line out before reeling in, cast his line, reeled it in. Cast out. Reeled in...

But it wasn't long before fatigue set in. A few of the nine, secreted in the surrounding vegetation, had become aggravated as the resident mosquitos were of nuisance. A few others complained of having to crouch for too long, their legs and lower backs aching. To make matters worse one was displeased because he'd stepped in animal faeces and didn't appreciate the lingering odour. Poor fellow. Meanwhile at a safe distance and observing via his trusty spyglass Stanley wasn't happy either. He was worried his dinner might be getting cold.

In short, the plan wasn't going as... planned. So following a few more minutes with nothing out of the ordinary occurring and as per previous instructions Stanley indicated to the 'angler' he should 'stand down' as it were. The individual emitted a delighted sigh as he threw down his rod while others emerged from their hiding places. They exchanged woes as their leader approached to - hopefully to put an end to their suffering – call it a day if you will.

Soon enough they were discussing the whys and wherefores and their what-to-do-next strategy. But as their conversation continued no one observed a *slimy, olive-green head with sinister red eyes* was watching from sanctuary of the lake. It were assessing them behind cover of a reed bed. Its eyes switched between the targets, seeking potential threats, but spied none. Following that the head disappeared below the surface readying itself. Then as they gesticulated and pontificated, a long, green speckled tail made its way up the bank, snaking its way through the vegetation in search of the first victim.

Oblivious the group complained, bellyached, even questioned its presence still; with a 50/50 split realised. However, refusing to dilly-dally was the thing, it savoured the calm before the ferocious storm. Homing in on the most vocal target.

Suddenly a panicked voiced interrupted them all.

"Look out – by your feet!"

But it was too late. The tail swiped hard and low, knocking several of them, including their illustrious leader, Stanley, to the ground. The remaining men reacted in one of two ways: fight or flight. But even then it was to no avail.

As some fled and others raised their weapons in readiness they were sent sprawling – the tail moving too fast to evade. Moments later a huge splash wave indicated something had emerged from the lake. The Morgrae had emerged, nine intimidating feet of it: crashing onto the bank mouth agape, jagged teeth showing...

The men screamed in collective terror desperate to keep it at bay, but it was hopeless. Only one individual lasted longest; the village tough guy; Greg. He'd always fancied himself as a fighter. He stood in place, pitchfork poised. The beast lunged while he dodged and swung the object but unfortunately the prongs became lodged in its crest. Reacting so it retorted, moving swift and bit off his forearms. He screamed in terror any future threat nullified.

His only option was to run away. But it were quicker. It leapt onto him from behind, it's heaving mass pinning him to the ground. It was then, at its leisure, and apparent enjoyment, it took leisurely bites until there was nothing left.

Indeed its speed and vicious nature ensured they were all silenced. Limbs were torn from bodies, intestines consumed, heads swallowed whole. None lived, none returned home to their wives, children or girlfriends.

A terrible price paid for their collective arrogance, with Stanley's hot pot dinner eventually thrown in the bin.

~ Shady Obstacles ~

Meanwhile the three travellers were still a day or so away from their destination: riding along the banks of the almighty Catfish River. Maximus' attention was on his young companion, gesturing to the vast area beside them.

"So you've never fished there?"

Bren shrugged indifferently.

"No. Is it good fishing?"

"Good fishing," chuckled the hero. "It's *marvellous* fishing. But you'll need the strongest tackle if you hook one of those monsters. Forget any challenge Lucifer might have offered. The catfish in those depths are the real deal. They've been known to pull a man into the water!"

"What? Really?" gasped the boy.

He returned a playful smirk.

"Yes, but I'm pulling your leg somewhat. The individual I witnessed being pulled in was a slight man, a short man; unprepared and distracted before he hooked one. I don't think a regular-sized and prepared chap would end up in the water at all."

Bren turned to the merchant.

"Do you fish at all?"

A worthless endeavour: for he wasn't interested in conversation as he was still licking his wounds following the recent tongue lashing but replied because he felt he should. Besides he'd been busy scheming.

"No. *It's a pointless and smelly pastime.* I'd rather cut a stranger's toenails. However, your horses, fans of fruit are they?"

His companions exchanged confused glances while he continued

"Ugh. I'm talking about those. *There!*"

He gestured to an apple tree at the side of the trail.

"I feel we've been neglecting our steeds and should offer them a treat."

The two smiled in response, their attitudes shifted towards him. Maximus nodded in affirmation.

"They do. As do we in fact. That's a jolly good idea."

In moments they were roadside picking apples. They each offered their steed one before Bren and Maximus witnessed a side of him they'd never expected: kindness. They observed as he paced contentedly from animal to animal feeding them whilst caressing their coats.

"Here you are horses. Eat up like good boys and girls."

The six, including horses, munched on the offerings while a pleasant mood prevailed. The sun shone and the breeze was warm. Any ill feelings forgotten about. Following that they picked a few extra for their ration packs before setting off, all in a positive frame of mind.

Maximus was content as was Bren. He were suitably distracted and sung to himself appreciating the surroundings while the hero's mind was on tackling the Morgrae. He knew it wouldn't be easy. But following their travels and joint efforts within the caves and dealing with the giant believed the tide was turning. Bren had been focused with the mission while the merchant, though often cold with his responses, had chosen to co-operate for once. Maximus observed discreetly while he stroked his steed. Something he never expected, and as a bonus were a joy to observe. Was there a hidden soft side to the pedlar, a 'human' side waiting to emerge? Time would tell he considered.

All was quiet for a while until Bren pointed to something unusual further ahead.

"Look. There!"

His companions peered into the distance while he continued.

"It's...it's somebody on the ground I think."

Maximus narrowed his eyes suspiciously, spied a dark mound by the side of the trail.

"I believe you're correct."

They approached the object while Maximus scanned the area. He identified it as being a large blanket or similar. Unexpected for sure but otherwise nothing out of the ordinary. Regardless, he were an experienced traveller. Expecting anything to happen at any time. On that basis he indicated the two keep their eyes peeled; causing Bren to feel uncertainty. Why would he request such a thing of him? He glanced to the merchant who shrugged in response, but Kapernicus, ever suspicious, dropped back a little, leaving the hero in front, followed by the boy with him last. Maximus dismounted, his plan to inspect the object. Perhaps it were a cover having fallen from the rear of a trader's wagon. He indicated his two companions to remain quiet while he drew his sword. As he approached the object he maintained vigilance but again, saw nothing unusual. Then, using the tip of his weapon, lifted the cover as his worst fears were realised; for there, waiting to pounce was a bearded individual.

Grinning, alert and dressed all in black.

He scrambled to his feet whilst clutching a short sword while Maximus gripped his own. Meanwhile the undergrowth parted as two more men emerged – armed with swords too.

It were an ambush.

In anticipation of their next move Maximus took a cautious step back while the three edged towards him.

Kapernicus called out to them.

"Gentlemen you might think twice about this."

The three grimaced in response while one barked a reply.

"WOT!? Maybe *you* should 'old your tongue mate. We're takin' any valuables you got and might even 'ave them 'orses of yours."

One of his comrades chimed in.

"And if 'yer cooperate, ya might keep your lives too."

Meanwhile Maximus were assessing the foes to see who the leader might be, the biggest threat even. Bren on the other hand wasn't sure how to react. His gaze switched back and forth unsure what to expect next. Maximus though had identified his first target - a burly, shaven-headed individual. He trained his gaze upon him.

"Okay gentlemen. Let's not make rash decisions here. There are three of you and..."

The individual, correctly identified by the hero returned a scornful response.

"That's right: *ONE* of you. The skinny bloke

and the kid don't count. We'll deal with you then sort them out after."

Maximus raised his eyebrows.

"Oh. Sort them out after? Are you sure about this? How about you leave us now, continue on your way and I'll forget this ever happened."

The three burst into mocking laughter.

He sheathed his sword, causing Bren to recoil in horror.

"So be it. One at a time or all at once? Your choice."

Expecting minimal resistance, the leader dashed towards him screaming furiously. However having anticipated such an attack he predicted the movements and dodged to one side. And as the attack missed he, in one swift motion, grabbed a hold of the man and twisted his sword arm behind his back: maintaining a firm grip. Following that he drew a dagger from his belt and positioned the blade close to his windpipe but stopped short of piercing the skin. The thug froze as his comrades closed in causing him to push the blade a touch deeper.

Fearing his demise the thug called out.

"All right, fellas. Stop."

The pair complied while Maximus addressed the individual .

"So what now? Do I kill you in front of your vagabond friends, or will common sense prevail?"

As he finished speaking, he pushed the blade a little deeper causing it to pierce the skin. But only just. The thug raised his palms in response.

"Alright. You win."

He gestured to his two allies.

"Lower your weapons and move back, yeah..."

They complied once more, but grudgingly so. Maximus meanwhile increased his grip on his sword arm causing him to drop the weapon before shoving him forcefully away; a hard push to the back causing his head to snap awkwardly backwards. He sneered cruelly in response.

Maximus stood poised.

"A wise decision at last. And you live to see another day. Though understand this: if we cross paths again, I will kill each and every one of you. This isn't an idle threat. This is fact."

The leader rubbed his throat, wiping away the small amount of blood, his facial expression a combination of embarrassment and rage. He never expected such an outcome; he'd been easily bested. And detested the feeling. He was desperate to retort but knew it'd be unwise, so spat at the ground in defiance. His comrades felt similar; they too humiliated, though their stern gazes towards their leader was one of disappointment.

Maximus drew his sword and pointed past them.

"We are headed in *that* direction, so I think it best you go the *opposite* way."

The leader nodded in acknowledgement while he climbed onto Rapscallion's back. Then as he, Bren and Kapernicus approached the would-be robbers, made one final comment.

"Remember this for today could have been the last day you drew breath. You might want to consider that next time you rob innocent folk."

The leader glanced to his two accomplices allowing them to observe his expression - one of unadulterated hate towards the hero, while Bren and the merchant had their own responses: Bren, bewilderment. Kapernicus: satisfaction. He smirked mockingly as he passed them, felt safe in the hero's company. And then, to add final humiliation, as Rapscallion drew level he emitted a cloud of stinky gas which, carried by the breeze, engulfed the villains, causing them to cover their mouths and noses in horror. The event caused Bren to burst into instant fits of giggles while Maximus scoffed heartily in response.

He glanced to Kapernicus.

"You fed him too many apples back there."

He patted the animal's mane in congratulation, while Kapernicus remained stone-faced but raging, as unfortunately for him, he caught a face full too.

***

A little later, with the robbers far behind, Maximus and Bren were in conversation with the hero offering words of wisdom.

"It's unfortunate you had to witness that, but this is the way of the world I'm afraid. There are people out there who will not only take your possessions but cause you harm in the process. Sometimes all it takes is to be in the wrong place at the wrong time; other times orchestrated ambushes like the one back there."

He absorbed every word of the advice.

"So it's best if I learn how to uh, defend myself. Learn to use a sword maybe?"

"Yes," agreed the hero. "Most certainly. Every man, or indeed woman, must have a defence against such people. I wish that weren't so, but my blade has aided me during many a dangerous situation. Maybe one day, if we get the time, I can show you some simple moves."

The teen gasped in response.

"You mean it? I'd...I'd like that very much."

Meanwhile Kapernicus who'd remained quiet for a period offered his take on the events.

"Those robbers – did you observe their black clothing?"

"Yes" replied the hero, "they all wore the same type."

"Their garb," continued the merchant, "their matching attire is indicative of the 'Slate Town Allegiance.' If you were to check their forearms you would have observed they were baring the 'crossed-dagger' mark – a crude tattoo, in other words, sign of their membership. I know of their type; their numbers are many; they are vengeful, unforgiving and violent folk."

Maximus nodded, grateful for the intelligence.

"Thanks. I'll bear that in mind."

~ *Civil Unrest* ~

The next morning the trio entered Oakdale. As they made their way into the village square, observed there wasn't a single soul in view. Not one. They observed all the windows in all the houses were closed too. They exchanged bemused glances before Maximus spied a hastily scrawled notice upon the community noticeboard.

He read it aloud.

"Due to the events at the lake today, a 5pm – 11am curfew is now in place. Everyone must stay indoors unless authorised by the town committee. For more information see Ms Barnes at the village guesthouse."

He glanced at his companions.

"I think we should speak to Ms Barnes immediately."

After knocking at the front door they spied her as she peered from an upstairs window. Which, initially they found amusing However she frowned before disappearing from sight which caused them to adjust their attitude. Moments later she opened the door, looking down her nose. Her tone one of sarcasm.

"What do you want, *more* bad news?"

Maximus replied on the trio's behalf, his feathers well and truly ruffled.

"Madam I have visited many towns during my travels but this one, this *tiny, and insignificant* village of Oakdale; the people here have a real chip on their shoulders – you included. Now listen well for I am here to assist with the serpent menace; and *not* come to interfere or cause harm. And if it weren't for the fact young Brenton here desperately needs my help I would gladly continue onwards while you deal with the problem yourselves."

He chose his next words carefully while the woman took stock of his outburst.

"So are you going to accommodate us or send us on our way? That one question is all I have."

She inspected the three, realized her attitude had been poor and downright rude.

"I apologise sincerely. You may come in."

She stepped to one side while they entered the building. They made their way along the corridor, while their boots left trails of unsightly dirt behind. Observing so, Bren chuckled under his breath, feeling his mother would have been furious if he'd done similar in his own home. But there? It didn't matter – sh'd had been rude, so was happy for her to clean it all up, especially as judging by the cleanliness of the surroundings, appeared to be an immensely houseproud individual.

A little later the three exited the property having been informed of the villagers' fate several days before. And though saddened by further losses of life, Bren was glad that none of his friends or their family had been harmed. Maximus meanwhile had planned to request a further committee meeting in the community hall; to discuss his own plan to capture the beast but been informed by the woman that *she* were the only surviving member of the committee, the rest having been eaten by the Morgrae.

***

The next morning rolled around, and Maximus, Kapernicus as well as several other folk were gathered in the village square, the numbers including Grace and Charlie's parents. Word had spread to the remaining villagers the hero had returned, so an impromptu meeting was organised. An essential face-to-face discussion regarding how to move forward. All youngsters were ordered to stay indoors while Bren was absent as he'd gone to check on his friends.

Maximus stood atop a wooden bench and scanned the gathering.

"I've been informed of your losses and unfortunately it was a foolhardy venture to try and kill the beast. For the creature residing in the lake is no ordinary foe. It's a conjured and malevolent manifestation – the work of a witch from Raven Woods."

Gasps were heard while he continued.

"As you know it was stolen from this merchant," he gestured towards Kapernicus, "and subsequently released into the lake; a terrible and stupid thing to have happened. However what's done is done. That cannot be changed. But now is the time for you to come together and support us in our attempts to defeat it and in turn reclaim your right to roam safe amongst your territories."

An exasperated, elderly woman responded.

"But that ain't the case. Everyone are at each other's throats now. Paranoia and panic is rife."

"But that's ridiculous," scoffed the hero, "instead of petty in-fighting you should be coming together. Can you not see the bigger picture? Your existence is at stake. Everyone will suffer."

He conducted a quick survey of those present.

"How many survivors are there, how many of you left, including children?"

Mumbling followed as each person scanned the area.

Finally, Grace's father, Joseph spoke.

"There are eleven of us here. My two children are at home along with Brenton. The guesthouse keeper is at her residence and the injured bully, and his father are recovering at their home again. A few families have fled the village having been scared off by the events. The Beeches haven't been seen since they went for a swim, so we'll assume they're dead too which leaves a total of sixteen," he gestured towards Maximus and Kapernicus, "not including you two."

Maximus pondered the statement, gestured towards the merchant.

"Well, he and I intend to remove the thing from the lake which won't be easy, but we've just returned from an important journey to the Giants' Hills where we retrieved a crystal needed to aid in its capture."

Hearing so one of the villagers bawled a furious response.

"Giants' Hills, and what crystal? After everything its done you want to take it *alive.* You should *kill* it!"

Maximus shook his head in resignation.

"If only. In order to acquire the knowledge to even attempt such a thing I had to venture deep into Raven Woods. It was there I struck a deal with a witch; a deal in exchange for the required information; which means I must return it alive to her."

He looked to the ground mournfully.

"Yes, the deal I made is a regrettable and personal one benefitting only her and yourselves. So I don't want to hear any questions regarding how it shall be dealt with. My say is final and non-negotiable. Now, I know some of you have lost loved ones but is anyone willing to step forward to help, anybody willing to rise to the occasion?"

No-one responded. Glances were exchanged while he waited patiently for a response.

He continued.

"You'll be assisting me under close supervision. And I'll do my utmost to protect you. But putting yourself at serious risk of harm is unavoidable and I shan't pretend otherwise."

Silence followed. Finally the peace was broken by a young voice; not from the congregation but from behind them all.

"We'll help you."

Everybody spun around. It was Bren, Grace and Hawk, with Bren stepping purposely forward.

"I'll help you, especially after all you've done for me..."

Grace followed suit.

"I'll help you however I can because you're Maximus – the legendary hero."

Then as Hawk opened his mouth to speak his mother, Ellie stopped him in his tracks.

"Oh no. You are not getting involved in this. You are both too young and will die!"

Joseph echoed her sentiments while the youngsters looked in Bren's direction. Maximus acknowledged their willingness to help but knew they were right.

"Agreed. It's too dangerous."

The pair exited the crowd and headed to their children while Joseph turned to the hero.

"You do know they can't help you, right?"

He acknowledged the sentiment.

"Of course."

"But I can't speak for Bren," continued Joseph, "He isn't my kin and can only advise him not to. As would my daughter."

Bren purposefully avoided Grace's glare and responded having made his one and final decision.

"And I choose to help him. That's my choice."

Maximus felt a pang of pride after hearing

such news while the four began home with Grace raging because she'd been rejected. Hawk, though feeling guilty he were unable to assist the heroes, knew it were the correct decision. He knew that he nor his sister would have been of use in a fight against the monster so to return home safely were their only option. He smiled at Bren who acknowledged him. Meanwhile Grace, after hearing of his decision, were desperate to offer him a piece of her mind but kept her gaze front, knowing it was neither the time *nor* place to do so.

The hero shook his head and looked to her, sensing her deep disappointment. She glanced at him in return and turned quickly away. He'd never allow her to risk her life in such a situation. She knew it too. She realised she were unsuitable for such a task but extremely precious to his young friend. She knew in her heart to put herself in danger would have been madness while the hero couldn't allow Bren to lose her. In his view her death might have pushed the boy over the edge.

His gaze swept the congregation.

"So nobody's going to come forward, to help save your own village, or does this fearless teenager represent the only courage to be found here?"

More silence followed as the assembly

avoided his gaze opting to stare at the ground instead. Then as it appeared nobody was coming forward Joseph turned tail.

"Fine. I'll help. But I wish I didn't have to as I'm terrified of dying. But this is *our* fight, *our* problem and I mustn't shy away from it."

Hearing such, Ellie rushed to his side while Hawk and Grace stood open-mouthed.

"I won't let you. You'll die!"

He ushered her away and cast her an icy glare.

"NO! Leave me be! I WILL help that man."

He pointed in Maximus' direction.

"We're fortunate he's even here. He was passing through our village. What are the chances of that? If he weren't, we'd have nobody; no-one to help us. Instead he's risking his life for a village full of rude and disrespectful… strangers!"

He gestured to the villagers, his expression one of desperation.

"Are you really too afraid to help?"

One of them raised his palms in surrender.

"I wish we *were* brave enough and had the skills, but we're not fighters. We don't know how to wield a sword or *any* weapon for that matter. You know that too well Joseph. And look what happened to the committee. Eaten alive. All of them!"

Maximus interrupted the individual having revised his plans as well as noted their concerns.

"It's okay. I don't need your help after all. With you," he pointed to Joseph, "Bren, Kapernicus and me we have enough. Of that I'm sure. Any more and we'd be compromised."

Hearing so Bren and Kapernicus stared at him with the merchant curious as to the sudden change of plan.

"What? Why so few, wouldn't more people increase our chances of success?"

"Not in this instance," replied the hero. "Not this time."

He directed his attention to Joseph.

"I appreciate your offer and will do my best to protect you. But for now return home with your family. I'll call for you *if* and when we need you."

Truth is there was no way he were going to request his help. He were a happily married and decent fellow with a wife and two wonderful children to care for. Regardless Joseph stepped forward and offered his hand which the hero shook firmly.

"Thank you."

He gestured towards the congregation.

"I can only apologise for their rudeness. It's just the way they are."

Maximus emitted a regretful sigh.

"You don't have to. The kingdom consists of many types. As you might have witnessed, I don't always receive a warm welcome."

~ *Heightened Emotions* ~

Following the meeting at the village square the trio had set up temporary camp and were sat comfortably around a campfire with Kapernicus' attentions on the hero.

"What I don't understand is the sudden change of mind. Why the need for so few to capture the Morgrae?"

Maximus nodded in acknowledgement.

"Fair question to ask, and at some point we might need extra hands. But as far as I'm concerned the more of us there are, the higher the chance of casualties; especially if those same hands are untrained in battle. To have useless support will only compromise us."

He emitted a sigh.

"First we must find out more information on the beast as we know very little. For instance how big it's grown, where in the lake it's most likely to be, and does it ever leave it to feed."

Kapernicus curled his top lip in disdain.

"But I've already told you it *cannot* leave the water for long as it would die."

"I know you've already said that" retorted the hero. "but the witch informed me otherwise. She said it *preferred* to remain there as it enables it to move fast, silent and discreet. And *not* that it's water-dependant as you insist."

He begged to differ, offering his own bizarre rationale.

"Fair enough. But what if she lied to you then?"

Maximus replied aghast.

"Nonsense. I've been tasked with capturing the beast so why would she lie? It doesn't make sense."

The merchant pushed his point.

"But what if she doesn't want you to capture it at all? What if she wants it to *kill* you instead? After all you are the only known threat to her kind. Have you considered that?"

Maximus poked the embers, affording himself thinking time.

"Fair point. But I know she was telling the truth because she could have killed me any time. We both knew that. I was in her domain and at her mercy."

He hesitated, reliving his foray into the Woods.

"I don't frighten easily as I've faced-down many a fearsome opponent, but this was different: there was an immense evil in situ; dark forces the likes I've never known. It's a shame you weren't there to witness it."

He observed Bren opposite, eyes wide and fearful so he directed his attention to him.

"Have my words frightened you?"

He nodded in affirmation.

"A bit. I've quite an imagination. I sometimes imagine things worse than they really are."

Maximus exhaled, the sound of the air pushing through his nostrils noticeable.

"Well as I mentioned previously and shall again; Those Woods and the fiends within are far worse than either you, I, Kapernicus or anybody else could imagine. Be under no illusion. Not just there, but this world too, the kingdom harbours creatures of such malicious intent, such evil purpose it defies all rational explanation. And to compound matters..."

He emitted a prolonged and heartfelt sigh.

"Often the cruellest villains wear human masks."

He directed his attentions to Kapernicus.

"You're a cynical type I know but what's the *real* story behind you transporting the Morgrae? Why choose to carry such dangerous cargo? Tell me in detail. Again."

He took a deep breath and considered the request. His beady eyes narrowing while his thoughts were of concocting a false response. There was a tense silence as his two companions stared at him. Feverishly awaiting a response. And in Maximus' eyes, after remembering his original version of events, curious to hear how good his memory was.

The fact is, he still planned to deliver the Morgrae. He was certain of that. Especially after hearing about Szrania's threat. We also know he had little respect for Maximus and next to no regard for Bren's welfare either. His ego had been bruised several times since they met and his thirst for revenge was growing stronger by the day. However he were wily enough to know he needed to 'play nice' for the time being. Or while it suited him at least.

He opened his mouth.

"Fine. As you request. This is all I remember so I'll tell you one more time. I was made an offer – when I was passing through Slate town. You know, where the bandits we encountered reside. I was approached by a strange woman, a street vendor. She enquired whether I was willing to deliver a top-secret commodity. She said other couriers refused to do it which I found unusual. Upon further investigation I discovered I'd be working for Szrania – a notoriously mean witch from Raven Woods – a rampant child-eater in fact. Of course I initially refused but when informed of the fee I changed my mind."

Bren leant forward, curious.

"You said you were offered lots of gold, right?"

He rubbed his palms together.

"Oh, yes. A worthwhile and lucrative endeavour: fifteen pieces of gold in fact. I needed the money as I was short of coin and of course who wouldn't want a fistful of gold?"

Maximus replied, unimpressed.

"I wouldn't."

He continued, uninterested in the comment.

"Well I did. I was told to travel to the entrance of the Woods whereby I would be met by an individual representing the witch. This I did too. The individual in question wore a hooded cloak, her face mysterious and obscured. Yet her hands were bony, even bonier than mine in fact and a curious shade of green. She entrusted to me a small, sealed wooden box, fifteen gold coins and simple instructions. Only three in fact."

1: Not to open the box.

2: Not to tell anyone who I was working for.

3: To go directly to the recipient.

Maximus enquired further.

"The recipient, who was it, do you

remember?"

He shook his head solemnly.

"Hmm The name I cannot remember still. But I assumed it was an acquaintance of Szrania. Cousin, friend, who knows? And I would have found them in an easily identifiable cottage north of Greenshire which I had directions to."

"But you broke all three of the instructions," returned the hero. "Why would you do that, bearing in mind the client was a ruthless witch?"

He took a deep breath before replying and for once speaking the truth.

"Because I was curious, naive and greedy – in that order. I delayed opening the box for several days, but my curiosity to know what were inside was too strong. So one morning, following breakfast I prised it open. It was lined with thick straw which upon removing I saw the contents for the first time; a smoky, ancient looking glass bottle, begging to be handled and admired. It was sealed tightly shut but contained the most intriguing of curiosities; a sleeping creature – a mini serpent if you will. I held the bottle up to the light, attempted to get a closer look but it was as if it had control of the fluid inside, like it could dictate the colour. Some days it would be an inky black, other times it would be an orange, honey-like hue. It was a remarkable sight to behold; as if it were teasing me; sometimes allowing me to catch a glimpse of its tiny scale pattern or beady eyes, other times refusing any kind of attention. Of course I realised as I'd broken one of the rules I might as well break another. I saw an opportunity to garner more business. So I strayed from my pre-determined route while using the newly acquired gold to purchase more items to fill my inventory. I stopped in the villages and towns peddling my wares and boasting of my unique stock, all the while concocting a fantastical origin story of the 'creature in the bottle'; a mystery for everyday folk to marvel at."

Maximus glanced at Bren, catching his eye. Both were unimpressed by the account in which, with each spoken sentence, he became more excitable. Maximus shook his head mournfully.

"So I'm unable say this without causing offence, but it was ultimately due to your own greed and arrogance this situation occurred?"

The pedlar hesitated; knew he were accurate with his observation but played along anyway.

"Yes. You are right. I am guilty. Guilty of stupidity, naivety and acting like a selfish fool for so long. But as you recently remarked: what's done is done. That cannot be changed. However I can help you in recapturing the thing – or try my best to do so. Now, where do we go from here, what's the plan?"

Maximus rose to his feet and stretched his limbs.

"I need to see it first-hand, to know exactly what we're dealing with. And for that I'd prefer it was done discreetly."

Bren opined, a rare smile upon his face

"I've an idea – the oaks at the waters' edge. We could climb one of those."

The hero placed a protective palm on his shoulder.

"Yes. I like the sound of that. Though you say 'we' it should be me alone. You can show me what you consider to be the most suitable one and I'll take it from there. You must be kept safe. No going near the water at this time. I can't have you taking unnecessary risks."

Observing impatiently, hands upon hips and feeling bemused, the merchant listened closely; his beady gaze switching between them. He emitted a forced cough, gaining their attention.

"But what about me, what should I do while you're away?"

Maximus replied, his attitude of thinly veiled indifference.

"Nothing. You'll stay here and keep the fire going."

Upon hearing such he was relieved yet offended by the instruction. On the one hand there was no way he wanted to be anywhere near danger, the other, being on the receiving end of more disrespect was beginning to grate. Regardless he received the comment without retort, feeling his time would come.

***

A little later Maximus and Bren were stood at the trunk of a large and imposing oak tree, the pair inspecting it top to bottom. Maximus imagined himself climbing it; nodded his approval.

"Good choice. Once I reach the top it should provide me with a wide view. You head back to camp – but keep your eyes on *him*. He's Weezle by name and weasel by nature, so inform me at once if he says or does anything you find suspicious or offensive."

The boy turned on his heels and headed away.

"OK. I will. But be careful. I might even be able to see you up there."

Minutes later Maximus were in place; straddled safe upon a branch overlooking the waters while the afternoon sun shone onto the surfacer; and fortunately, due to wind-free conditions, it was glass-like in appearance, increasing the chance of him spying anything untoward. It wasn't long before he observed signs of activity taking place below the surface. He witnessed as the occasional fish leapt into view, pursued by a hungry pike or perch perhaps. Or something much bigger. He drew his spyglass and scanned the expanse, knowing that such conditions harboured a monster unseen. He bit his lip in frustration, hoping to garner a glimpse of the monstrosity. If briefly. He knew eyes-on intelligence was the best from of intelligence. Hopeful, he continued his search.

Meanwhile Bren had returned to the camp and was pacing nervously back and forth. He'd since spied Maximus and they'd acknowledged each other. He felt uncomfortable alone with the merchant who'd detected his reservations. With that in mind he'd sought Rapscallion's company. He stroked his coat while he munched upon the grass. He'd paid close attention to Maximus' handling of the steed and was left impressed. Until recently such animals hadn't interested him. He'd considered their presence in the village as working creatures only. Suitable for laborious tasks as well as suitable transport for those needing to ride them. His recent experiences had caused his attitude to change.

He stared into his dark eyes.

“Hey, boy. You’re clever aren’t you? Are you really stubborn, because I don’t think you are. No wonder he chose you. I hope to get one like you one day too.”

Meanwhile Kapernicus had been watching closely; jealous of the steed as well as reliving the horrific events lakeside. He chuckled when thinking of Kieron and how a normal life was ruined; and how it might feel for Bren knowing he’d never see his parents again. Any other adult would have felt pity for the lad, but not him. He never knew his parents. So had no understanding of his loss. And in turn never felt the nurturing affection they might have provided. Something that gnawed away at his subconscious. And though sociable face-to-face he was very much a lone wolf. His sole mission was to provide a reliable service for the Order with an eventual aim of becoming immortal of sorts; for his striking visage to be immortalised in oils and reside forever upon the walls at their headquarters.

That matter withstanding he chose to instigate polite conversation, though his motives were far from honourable.

“So, I have to offer proper condolences for

the loss of your parents as I haven't done that yet. So I am sorry. Truly I am."

He nodded in acknowledgement while the merchant probed further.

"The crystal – where is it now, do you still have it?"

"Maximus has it," shrugged the teen. "He took it earlier."

Interestingly he did have it with him – tucked safely away in his satchel but knew to remain discreet.

Kapernicus hid his disappointment.

"Good. It must be kept safe of course. Now what are you intending to do once the Morgrae has been captured and he's moved on, any ideas?"

He stopped in his tracks.

"Um, I haven't thought about it too much. But I'm thinking of moving far away from here. I've heard Greenshire is a nice place to live. Er, busy but a nice place."

Kapernicus reminisced.

"Ah, Greenshire. I've been there on several occasions. It isn't just a busy town, it's a remarkably busy town. There's a large population present but with space for everyone. A myriad of folk. All of varying colours, creed and ideologies. However there's the cost of living to consider. A new arrival such as yourself would need to find work as well as accommodation. Have you considered that?"

He shook his head.

"Um, no. I've never needed to earn coin before. But I *could* find work and somewhere to live. I..I guess. Oh, have you met the king, doesn't he live there?"

He looked mournfully to the ground.

"Oh his poor, poor Majesty. He does. His residence is near the perimeter fence. But no. I've never met him and never will. Royalty doesn't mix with commoners like us, but I do know he's having an awful time. Such a good and honourable gentleman but with terrible fortune haunting him."

Having considered all royalty led pampered lives, and failing to understand the comment, the teen scratched at his scalp.

"What do you mean, haunting, like a ghost?"

"No," scoffed the pedlar. "I used 'haunting' in place of 'suffering'. Indeed the king has lost his wife *and* child in recent times. Queen Renee died not long after the birth of their only daughter, Princess Lucinda. She was said to have passed due to ongoing complications following childbirth but there are rumours it was due to something more sinister. Then only recently the Princess passed into the next world. It's said she fled the castle to commit suicide; with some claiming she tired of her father's overbearing nature, his unhealthy desire to keep her close instead. But even then, some have speculated she was led astray."

They suddenly heard the tell-tale sound of a twig snap. They directed their gazes in the same direction and reacting instinctively Kapernicus grabbed a length of branch while springing to his feet.

"Who goes there."

~ Turbulent Waters ~

Maximus' vigilance hadn't bore fruit as frustratingly there was still no sign of the Morgrae which didn't come as a surprise. Instead it illustrated it were smart, content to maintain a low profile, and revealing itself only when choosing to. However one area had caught his attention – a small island in the north-west corner of the lake. According to his keen eyes there were signs of recent habitation. The grass was flattened and muddied as was the shrubbery – indicators of activity. However the mass appeared difficult to reach so in order to investigate further he'd need to consider how to get there. He pondered the conundrum and stroked his chin. It was then he glanced in the direction of the camp. He spied Kapernicus sat fireside, but Bren was nowhere to be seen. He observed for several seconds longer, craning his neck. But saw nothing. That caused him immediate concern, so fearing the worst he returned to camp. He thundered in to the clearing and drew his sword which took the merchant by surprise.

"What have you done with him?"

Unperturbed he replied with sarcasm, gestured towards an area of bushes.

"Cease worrying Great One. He's behind

those."

Maximus glared in response, headed to the area in question then sighed with relief; for present and in the company of Grace was Bren, the two safe and sound. They were stood close and in intimate conversation which caused him to realise he were in ideal company under the circumstances.

Respectful of their privacy he retreated out of sight.

Grace had missed Bren while he was absent and did a great deal of soul searching. She'd let go his remark about helping to catch the monster, believed it excited bravado. She was the more mature of the two and had been considering the idea of mortality – whether her own or those around her; and with the terrible things she'd witnessed or heard about as well as the horrific manner in which an individuals' life could be taken her thoughts had had a profound effect on her. That along with the knowledge that he, a local boy she'd always had a soft spot for desperately needed someone to show him compassion.

She knew how much he were suffering and took hold of his quivering hand.

"I know we bicker too much. And for silly reasons. But...but I think you're really brave. The way you carry on after Kieron treats you so badly is a credit to you."

He averted his gaze, felt he struggled with the stress.

"Well. I, er, if you think so, that's good. And I like the way you're so clever. You say things that make sense. Like you're older than you really are."

He tugged his hand free and bit his lip as nervousness consumed him.

Um, you know, I *do* like Hawk, but I like seeing you more when I knock at your door."

She blushed, adjusted her mousey hair then hesitated; the sight before her – a boy, a young man lost and desperately in need of affection, required something to lift his spirits – if temporarily. Her heart raced; palms perspired. She edged forward, whispering nervously.

"Can I…um, do you need a hug?"

His bottom lip quivered before he burst into floods of tears – long overdue tears. They embraced, squeezing long and meaningfully. For her it was the first time she'd experienced the power of positive human contact with an unrelated other; affection desperately needed by them both in fact.

Their tears flowed; the sobbing seemed never ending. In response she pushed her head close while her tears intermingled with his. They held each other for what seemed an eternity while a caring bond began to form. A long, and overdue outpouring of intense emotion.

Meanwhile and only metres away Maximus and Kapernicus were having strong words again. Maximus didn't like the manner in which he'd responded to him moments before. He pointed a threatening finger.

"I'm telling you now. If you betray us both so help me, I'll make you pay. This… *this* whole situation leads back to your hands. YOUR crooked hands. I've had more than enough of your attitude. Stinks it does. You might not want to return to those Woods, but I'll do everything in my powers to take you there; I'll drag you screaming by your hair if I have to!"

Kapernicus leapt to his feet, consumed by a furious rage.

"But you accused me of harming the boy. You grabbed your sword ready to strike me down! And you were wrong. I know you don't like me, and I don't like you. But I'd never hurt him. And while we're being honest about our feelings, no, I will NOT go to Raven Woods. The witch will kill me!"

Maximus breached his personal space, prodded a finger hard into his chest.

"You've no say about this. You've caused this yourself and will have to pay the price!"

Kapernicus' eyes bulged in anger; plump veins rippled his skin. He were in an uncontrollable rage but observed the youngsters emerge from behind a bush so turned away. Maximus, meanwhile, spied them holding hands and adopted a calmer disposition, smiling in acknowledgement.

"Oh, Grace isn't it, what brings you here?"

She glanced at her companion.

"He brought me here. I was worried about him."

"Of course you were. He's in desperate need of a friendly face."

Meanwhile Kapernicus, wound tight as a coiled spring, walked away seething.

He invited the two closer

"Come. Sit near the fire. We can talk."

He gestured in the merchant's direction.

"He and I were having a disagreement. That's all. Now Grace I must say this, but you're aware you're putting yourself in danger coming here."

"I realise that."

"And your parents, do they approve?"

She nodded.

"Yes. Though I don't need their permission.

I'm here because I needed to be - to be here for Bren. I know he's safe in your company, but felt he needed me too."

She glanced at him and smiled, as did the hero, who knew his next remark was going to be unwelcome to at least one of them.

"Okay, regarding our next move I think you should both return to the village where you'll be safe. I don't want either of you at unnecessary risk."

Bren balked at the suggestion.

"But why? You've done so much for me. I must help. The Morgrae took my parents, and I want to see it captured."

Maximus sighed. The suggestion would have been foolhardy without context but justified on that occasion. His gaze switched between them.

"OK. But Grace, you must return to the village while we stay here. You being harmed isn't an option"

Her heckles rose, considered arguing back as she disagreed, but the serious tone in his voice caused her to think otherwise. He diverted his gaze to Bren and continued.

"Now hand me the crystal..."

Hearing such Kapernicus' rage intensified. He'd been lied to again and desperately wanted to scream in frustration. But knew no to. He observed discreetly as Bren handed the object to the hero who inspected it.

"Thank you. It's still sharp."

He placed it in his satchel for safekeeping before continuing.

"Now I'll give you a moment for farewells before we discuss the next move."

Having had a few seconds to devise a counter argument Grace made eye contact with Bren as they moved away from the camp.

"I think you should head back with me. Don't you agree?"

He took an instinctive step away.

"Uh, no. I'll walk you back to the village, but I need to be here with him."

She stopped in her tracks; unable to believe her ears.

"So you were serious after all? I thought… urgh. It doesn't matter. You clearly want to die like the others then?"

"No, but…"

She interrupted, her gaze penetrating his.

"After sharing our feelings like that, you're willing to risk your life?"

"But he's done so much for me. For the

village even. Who'll watch his back?"

"But he can take care of himself. He's THE Maximus. Not any old man."

He thrust his hands in the air, barked a frustrated response.

"I know. But if I leave, he's got to deal with the creature AND the merchant. That's too much to take on; even for him. He hates us both. I must watch his back."

Realising his fierce loyalty to the hero as well as his stubbornness she pushed him away.

"Watch his back? Ridiculous."

She took a few seconds to compose herself.

"All right. You win. I came here to help, and you choose death over me. Fine."

She sped away before he had chance to continue his case. Though try he did.

"But listen..."

She spun and bawled in his direction.

"No! What you're thinking is idiotic. What can you even do?"

He emitted a sigh; believing she were gone for good. He returned forlorn to the campsite to reflect in peace. Meanwhile busily sawing through a length of branch and having heard the argument Maximus made eye contact.

“That didn’t go well.”

He shrugged nonchalantly, an attempt to convince himself and the hero he weren’t bothered by the situation.

“Nope.”

Maximus knew otherwise.

“She’ll calm down eventually and forgive you. The fact she sought you out shows how much she cares. But now…now I’m afraid, she’ll need time, space and a lot of effort from you in return.”

He acknowledged then sat fireside.

“I guess. Oh, what are you making?”

Maximus raised the object to eye level and rotated it.

"As you can see this is a sturdy and suitably long branch. I'm going to split the end and fix the crystal in between. I'll bind it with cord to hold it firmly in place."

He peered down its length, pleased with his choice.

"This, my boy, this makeshift spear, will be our tool to subdue the Morgrae."

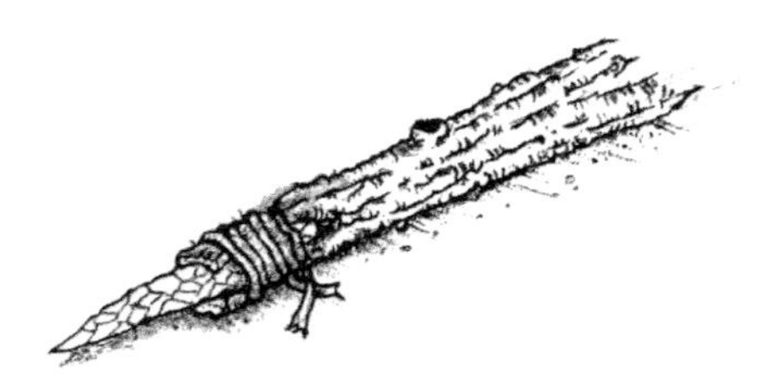

Bren attempted to visualise the finished article, which he did. He nodded in Kapernicus' direction causing Maximus to smirk in response, as it were clear he were sulking again.

***

The next morning rolled round and following an uneventful night, Kapernicus, who'd apparently calmed down, declared his intentions to go to the village for supplies while Maximus and friend scaled the branches of the lakeside oak for a second day of observation duties. The boy had convinced the hero he was competent in climbing trees and such acts were routine for him which were accepted as true. He considered while he were there a second pair of eyes might help in locating the beast so allowed him possession of the spyglass. He pointed to and fro, offering simple instructions.

"A little more to the left. You should spy an island a stone throw from the bank. Do you see it?"

He moved the spyglass into position.

"Oh, *that* island. I see it. And something HAS been there."

He handed the object back to Maximus who pocketed it.

"I'm glad you agree as I'm convinced it's the work of the Morgrae. Did you observe the area of flattened grass and muddy trail leading to the water?"

"Yes, something big definitely caused that. It had to be it. What shall we do?"

He mulled over available options.

"Hm. We still haven't caught sight of it. And we must as I need to assess the threat it poses as well as any potential weak spots. Hmm. I've an idea. Bait. If we use some form of bait to lure it from the water, we may be able to have a proper look."

The boy's eyes sparkled mischievously as he peered left then right.

"Couldn't we use Kapernicus as bait? You could tie him up near the bank. His screaming would make it appear."

Maximus chuckled in response.

"Ha. I'd like to but that isn't the way to deal with individuals like him. He'll receive his comeuppance eventually. So, the island, have you ever set foot on it?"

He responded eagerly.

"We all have. Well, Hawk hasn't. He's too afraid. And the water isn't deep on the far side. There's a slope we can walk down. It won't go higher than our chins I think."

Maximus remained steadfast.

"That's good to know, though you won't be crossing. That's something I alone will do. You'll be look-out instead."

***.

Meanwhile, at the village, Kapernicus was on a mission: a vengeful, hate-filled mission. He'd lied. Had no intention of shopping for sustenance. Instead he left with sinister intent; armed with a sharp and deadly dagger stolen from Maximus' own rucksack; his long in gestation plan finally being put in motion. As he strode into the square his heart raced while his clenched fists were those of wound-up fury. Overnight, instead of calming down as he stated, he'd worked himself into a mental frenzy. A raging bundle of bones and hatred. But being of thin build and lacking physical strength to tackle the hero head on, he realised to wreak revenge he'd require two weapons to inflict suffering: one of sharpened steel, and capable of piercing vital organs; the other a living entity, her welfare extremely precious to the duo.

In his warped mind the time for retribution had arrived.

~ *Raising the Stakes* ~

Kapernicus arrived at the guesthouse wearing his favourite mask; one of false concern for the people of Oakdale. He rapped his knuckles upon the front door, and it wasn't long before Ms Barnes answered. She were finally glad to see him, as the ongoing curfew had caused her a worrying amount of anxiety. So to see a friendly face was a cause of relief.

"Oh hello Mister Weezle. How may I help?"

He bowed in return.

"Ah, sorry to disturb you but I've been sent by Maximus with an important request. He's asked me to locate the girl, Grace, as it's vital he speaks with her. It's about young Brenton, you see, and urgent in nature. Could you tell me where she lives?"

She succumbed to his lie.

"Of course. But first I wish to apologise about the other day. Tensions were high as you know. For everyone in fact. But I've had a rethink: you may continue with your reservation if you like. I've changed the bedding in preparation."

He chewed on his lip as his mind went into overdrive.

"Sounds good. May I come in for a moment?"

She allowed him entry before closing the front door. He smiled.

"So, where might I find her?"

"Ah, yes," she answered. "Follow the road round to the right. The cottage with a pear tree in the front garden. Anything else?"

He moved in close, invading her personal space which caused her to backpedal.

"No, sir. I'm not interested in romance."

She stumbled backwards as he pulled a blade from within his jacket which he thrust deep into her chest. He gleefully twisted the handle while blood oozed from the resulting wound. Meanwhile her eyes rolled back into their sockets as her life ebbed quickly away.

He moved in closer and sneered, his pungent breath flooding her rapidly fading senses.

"Neither am I. And I'll be resting elsewhere this evening. However your hospitality has been exceptional."

Following that he bowed before exiting the property, an excited 'skip' in his step while her body slumped to the floor.

***

Lakeside Maximus and Bren had taken a wide berth around the bank and had stopped with the island ahead of them. The hero had assessed the distance, guessing it were forty to fifty yards out and, under typical circumstances, easy to reach. He muttered under his breath.

"Hmm. What to do now?"

He hesitated as they mulled the conundrum before hearing a sheep nearby. He winked knowingly at his accomplice.

"I know it's earlier than anticipated but we may have found our 'bait'. Help me to secure it in readiness."

Bren nodded in acknowledgement while he continued.

"Right. Follow me but keep low. We'll move behind and usher it towards the bank."

He placed the finished branch with attached crystal to one side while they moved stealthily through the undergrowth; They exchanged nervous glances before emerging near to several grazing sheep. Bren pointed to the closest one, the same looking in the opposite direction. However Maximus had spied an easier target: an aged looking animal. It's dishevelled state convincing him it'd be an easier catch.

He gestured to it, indicating it to be their target which the boy acknowledged. He advised him to move wide left as he crept to the right; a length of coiled rope retrieved from his satchel held in preparation. He gripped it in readiness and trod carefully. In moments they were in position. However, sensing their solitude had been interrupted the animals became agitated. They called nervously in response. The hero sensed they'd need to act fast if they wished to avoid a protracted chase so headed towards a different target. Responding so Bren moved to the rear of it, and in turn blocking a potential escape. Meanwhile the rest fled, scampering away to safety.

The pair dashed forward with the hero taking the lead. Spying a window of opportunity he lunged and wrestled the unlucky animal while the boy leapt in to assist and in in no time it had a makeshift collar and leash around its neck.

They sighed in tandem as they held it firmly in place while its protestations ceased. Maximus secured the rope around its neck whilst gesturing towards a pile of fallen branches.

"Grab me the one that looks like a shepherd's crook."

Bren handed him the object who secured it before pushing it deep into the soil. They stood proud as the sheep appeared unexpectedly compliant which unnerved the youngster.

"I hope the monster doesn't kill it."

Maximus placed a reassuring hand upon

his shoulder.

I'll do my best to keep it from harm, but it's the sheep or another human I'm afraid."

Bren pulled up his right trouser leg revealing an unsightly graze.

"And look. It stings. It scraped its hoof all the way down my shin!"

Maximus observed the affected and reddened area, chuckled in acknowledgement.

"At least you weren't bitten. Then you'd have reason to complain."

Suddenly they heard a familiar voice and looked up. It was Kapernicus but he wasn't alone. The fiend had Grace with him, whose hands, mouth and nose were tightly bound. She were his prisoner. With a knife held cruelly to her throat. However before Maximus could respond Bren, after spying the weapon, began in their direction causing him to holler in response.

"I'd stop there if I were you."

He pulled the girl close whilst positioning the blade closer to her skin. She squirmed uneasily while he bawled a raging retort.

"Let her go!"

Knowing the merchant were desperate Maximus caught up with his friend and grabbed him by the shoulders.

"Let him speak."

The boy struggled to escape the grip which caused him to tighten his hold.

"Let me go! Please."

Maximus understood his turmoil.

"I'm sorry. But attacking him won't help her. We must listen to his demands whether we like it or not."

Kapernicus called out once more while his gaze flitted between them.

"I am NOT going to Raven Woods with you and I'm NOT going to help capture the Morgrae either."

Maximus realised he'd need time to devise a counter strategy.

"Fine. But don't hurt her. Don't do anything you'll regret."

Bren called out, his gaze piercing the merchant's owns.

"Don't you dare. I'll kill you if you do."

He scowled in return.

"Shut it, child. This is between HIM and me."

The hero moved to the side of the teen.

"So, what now? Do you want to leave here, do you want to return the beast back to the witch?"

His's hands shook uncontrollably, his brow glistening with perspiration.

"I...I don't want to die. If I...if I run, you'll hunt me down. If I don't return the Morgrae Szrania will kill me. If I harm the girl, you'll kill me."

Maximus raised his hands into the air.

"So, what then? You're not really going to hurt her, are you?"

The man clenched a fist in frustration; hadn't thought that far ahead. However a sudden fearful expression spread across his face, indicating he'd seen something unnerving in the lake beyond. Maximus and Bren glanced in the same direction.

They spied a bow wave. Something was heading to the surface.

They knew what it was and at the worst possible time. Regardless Bren's priority were Grace. She too had detected its arrival by the sudden silence. In return she opted to fight the pedlar's clutches. Her rationale was if she were going to perish, she'd go down fighting. She twisted, turned and squirmed uncontrollably hoping if he intended to kill her he would have done so already.

Then as Maximus hoped, he pushed her

away which caused her to lose her balance. She stumbled precariously next to the waters' edge. Witnessing so Bren sprinted in her direction. He needed to be quick as she were heading towards the water. Maximus meanwhile had dashed in the opposite direction; his aim to retrieve the crystal embedded branch.

As Bren arrived on the scene Graced landed with a bump and slid headfirst towards the murk. He motioned into a diving lunge, grabbing a hold of her lower legs. As he did so the contents of his satchel spilled onto the ground, some items tumbling into the water, others amongst the long grass. He screamed in frustration as her head and face submerged, her hands bound infuriatingly behind her back.

She emitted muffled screams as he tried desperately to pull her onto dry land while tears of frustration ran down his cheeks. He was considering the possibility she might perish there and then. He screamed in desperation.

"Somebody help!"

Meanwhile the Morgrae had broken surface about twenty yards out causing an eruption of noise and spray. It screeched aloud, it's fiery gaze held in their direction.

***

While that was happening Kapernicus had fled the scene. He stumbled and clawed his way through and around the undergrowth intent on creating space between himself and all beyond. He muttered under his breath.

"Must escape..."

He arrived at the campsite and grabbed hold of his satchel. It was then he pulled out a sheet of notepaper and pencil before scrawling upon it. He scribbled away with the nearby commotion ringing in his hears before he dropped the letter to the ground. It was then he made eye contact with Rapscallion, the wary animal back peddling nervously.

"Now, now horsey. No need to be afraid."

He dug into his satchel and retrieved an apple – one of his favourites.

"How would you like this? Just for you."

Maximus meanwhile had retrieved the branch and spied Bren's predicament. He charged in and threw the object to one side, and together they began to pull Grace to safety, but the Morgrae had other ideas. It moved close causing him an instant dilemma; he needed to make a tough decision. He grudgingly let go of the girl causing her to slip back towards the water with Bren her only saviour. He knew he had to draw the monster away from them. If only to buy them time. He grabbed the first thing he saw - a rock and threw it. Fortunately his aim was good as it hit it on the head diverting its attention to himself who dashed away from the pair.

With a feisty new target the beast gave chase.

Since its last appearance it had grown even longer – its length being in the region of fifteen feet, it's girth thick, spiky; its multi-limbed appendages bearing sharp claws at the end. Its movements were rapid, splashing and hissing, desperate to eliminate the human threat. Maximus thought fast, intending by himself and young friends valuable time. There was a problem though: a BIG problem. He moved further away from the crystal embedded branch with each step taken.

The Morgrae crashed onto the bank as he forward rolled skilfully out of its way. Its arms desperate to find flesh. He withdrew the dagger from his belt and stabbed deep into one of the limbs and twisted the blade, felt the scraping of bone and snapping of sinew. He withdrew the weapon - the resulting blood splashing onto his skin, speckling it with its pungent odour.

The Morgrae was in pain and screeched furiously. It never expected such resistance. It rose high, readying its next attack; its gaze fixed upon its prey. He reacted accordingly, anticipated its move and leapt backwards as it slammed thunderously onto the grass beside him.

Further along the lake's edge Bren had managed to pull Grace to safety, though it had left him exhausted. Unfortunately for him the situation appeared grim as she wasn't breathing or responding. In his mind she'd been submerged for what felt like an eternity. He reached for the branch and using the crystal's sharp tip cut away her bonds, ripping away the sodden, weed-covered material from her head and observing her lifeless face beneath.

He muttered apologetic words under his breath.

"I'm…I'm sorry."

He raised his head, spied Maximus occupied with the Morgrae and unable to assist. In desperation he rolled her onto her back and commenced chest compressions. He wasn't sure if he were doing them correctly, but it didn't matter – it was better than doing nothing; and besides and he must *try* to revive her. He wracked his brain to recall his dad's emergency first aid advice. How he wished he paid more attention. He adjusted his position, placed hand over hand and pushed down, then up, down then up, his expression one of panicked desperation. He closed his eyes and visualised her lifeless face in an open casket and with him staring heartbroken; regretful tears cascading down his cheeks.

"You can't die. I won't let you..."

He looked to the skies, then back to her.

"I'm sorry. I...I love you but my urgh, my snot's dripping on your face."

He couldn't have felt guiltier if he tried. He were distraught. He doubled his efforts, gritted his teeth while saliva and mucus accumulated around his nose and mouth. Why him, why her, he thought. Had he been a horrible person in a past life, and paying the price in that one? He managed a quick glance sideways, to check on the hero's progress. He mustn't perish too. He hoped in his heart of hearts he were vanquishing the foe.

He couldn't have been more wrong. Maximus was in trouble and doubting his chances of surviving the encounter, feeling he might have finally met his match. He knew, regardless of the outcome he'd have taken on the beast even if he were passing-by; for him to defend the pair or any other innocent in need of help was, and would always be, key to his being. As a youngster he'd witnessed many ill doings first hand and endeavoured to live his life in a just fashion.

But as things stood it had proven it was strong, deadly *and* fast, its agenda being to kill him in as brutal manner as possible. He surveyed the area sought respite from the relentless assaults and spied a fallen tree several yards away, a rotting oak.

Maybe it would afford him temporary cover, a chance to gather his composure even.

He glanced up as it prepared for another attack and with perfect timing dove clear as it lunged – barely missing him. He felt the ground rumble as he reached the tree and clambered over its trunk. But it remained insistent. It smashed onto the wood causing splinters to fly in all directions. He covered his eyes from flying debris, keen to avoid injury. The Morgrae meanwhile thrashed around, its arms flailing wildly, its furious hiss pummelling his ringing ears.

With the creature grounded he seized an opportunity: dashed in once more, thrust his blade deep but this time into its flank. He gritted his teeth and ran the blade as far and for as long as he were able – creating an open wound some eighteen inches in length. It turned its head – its mouth agape; rows of needle-sharp teeth dripping with saliva, eager to bite down on him.

It was then he realised he were running out of options.

Meanwhile Bren's attempts to resuscitate Grace had proven successful. She opened her eyes, regurgitating dirty water and coughing violently. He scrambled close, held her tight while tears of relief flowed from them both. There was no time for reconciliation though as he remembered Maximus needed his help; and desperately so. He grabbed a hold of the crystal embedded branch and sprinted in his direction.

By then the hero was expecting to fall; was exhausted and out of arms; the dagger had been knocked from his grasp and fallen into the water. He closed his eyes ready for one last effort, one more chance even. And then when all hope seemed lost, he heard Bren's call, his voice rasping yet overflowing with heroic intent.

"Maximus! Over here!"

He glanced up as the Morgrae was poised to strike, witnessed his friend sprinting in his direction. He spied the branch and screamed at the top of his voice, pleading yet fearful for his welfare.

"Stay back and throw it to me!"

Bren drew back his arm before releasing the object which whistled through the air towards him who blinked rapidly; desperate to clear his blurred vision. At the same time, the Morgrae lunged, knocking him onto his back, severely winding him in the process. That caused him more suffering; felt certain his time was up. He shook his head rapidly, unable to catch his breath. It meanwhile spied an opportunity and dipped its head, jaws snapping open and closed, intent on finishing him off.

Having dropped to her knees and recovering Grace spied his predicament, which caused her gaze to switch to her pal instead. She screamed at the top of her lungs, the idea of the legend perishing before her eyes a devastating proposition.

"Help him!"

Meanwhile the branch had landed point-first into the soil, yet frustratingly inches from his grasp. So using his left arm and final reserves of strength he wrestled it, managing to keep its ferociously clawing nails and gnashing teeth at bay. Then with his right hand reached for the object - his fingers millimetres from retrieving the item. It sensed the danger and using it's immense weight: pushed him away from the object; its short arms also trying to grab the branch. He screamed in frustration, believing his demise was imminent.

All wasn't lost though. In a last-ditch show of bravery Bren lunged in to help but one of its arms grabbed him - its sharp claws easily piercing the skin of his left shoulder. He squealed in agony but remained undeterred and determined for he *needed* to help his friend. There was no other option.

So with blood oozing through his clothing, grabbed the branch and after negotiating the flailing limbs offered it forth. Maximus reached out and miraculously grabbed hold of the object before manoeuvring it into position. Meanwhile it had diverted its attention to the boy and sent him sprawling to the ground.

Then with a mighty, final effort he managed to pierce its tough yet slippery skin. The crystal penetrated deep and true. He withdrew it and stabbed once more but in another location, and even deeper. Its eyes rolled, its serpent tongue juddered back and forth, side to side; a loud and guttural hissing sound emanating from deep inside its throat. He rolled clear as it began to vibrate. He called out to the boy who'd scrambled to his feet.

"Move away. It's changing!"

They hurried backwards and observed as

it began to shrink, it's movements violent and unpredictable. In seconds, it had more than halved in size and were shrinking all the time. Reacting to that Maximus remembered the need for a container, looked to the teen.

"A vessel. We need a vessel!"

He remembered his satchel and the fact its contents had spilled onto the bank. He turned to Grace who were on her knees recovering.

"We need a vessel! Look around you!"

She bawled a confused response.

"You need a what?"

"No time to waste," pleaded the hero. "Look on the ground. Fetch us a bottle! Immediately!"

Hearing such she understood the question.

"Oh, a *BOTTLE!*"

She searched at her feet and spied what was required; grabbed one and headed towards them.

Meanwhile the Morgrae was even smaller and in the process of sliding back into the water. Maximus dropped to his knees and grabbed it. It was difficult to handle though, as its blood-covered form writhed around constantly, its bony arms sharp to the touch; and all the while trying its utmost to evade capture. He doubled his efforts, screaming in desperation.

"Hurry!"

The girl, meanwhile, was desperate to reach them but wasn't the fleetest of foot. They observed as it shrunk to its original size of two inches. The hero remained determined and held it securely between cupped hands but flinched in pain as its tiny teeth gnawed at his skin.

"It's biting me."

Bren raised his head and pleaded once more.

"It's hurting him!"

In seconds, she arrived and handed the bottle to him who removed the cork stopper. He dipped it into the margins collecting water as he did. He moved it into position allowing Maximus to part his hands slightly. They observed with relief as the mini beast plopped into the liquid and spiralled to the bottom, a trail of its oily blood leaking upwards.

He took the stopper and pushed it firmly into place before looking up to the youngsters. They breathed a huge sigh of relief while the wounded Morgrae spun around furiously, seething it had found itself imprisoned once more while the hero, exhausted, but oh so relieved stared into the container.

"This is staying with me now."

Bren scanned the vicinity, remembering another important fact.

"But what about the merchant?"

Maximus scrambled wearily to his feet.

"He's not getting away..."

His gaze switched between them.

"I'm going after him. You two stay here."

He shook his head, taking a moment to compose himself before dashing away while they observed in silence. They exchanged concerned glances as he stumbled precariously about, almost falling over in fact.

He entered the camp to observe Rapscallion was missing - Kapernicus must have stolen him! He scanned further and was surprised to see his gear was untouched. Even his precious sword; the merchant must have *really* been in a hurry. He wiped his brow, grabbed a few essentials including the sword and changed direction towards the village, a fierce determination in his stride.

***

Nearby, emotions were running high for the teens. They had freed the sheep from its rope allowing it to re-join its flock. And though her hair was matted and filthy, her youthful skin in desperate need of a wash; Grace's feelings for Bren and how to move forward were all over the place.

Yet he remained her priority. She inspected his shoulder, having observed the copious amounts of blood soaking his tunic. He, meanwhile, had a lump in his throat, attempting, and failing, to put on a brave face. Emotionally he were close to breaking point. After all he hadn't come to terms with his own parents demise, let alone began to process the events waterside.

Considering everything the two had witnessed it were a miracle they were functioning at all. Their resilience was remarkable for ones so young. Not only that but Bren had to deal with the fact Maximus had departed; he'd latched onto him and considered him a surrogate father of sorts. And to make matters worse he never had the opportunity to say goodbye. His mind was a fizzing cauldron of confusion as he turned to the girl.

"I think I'll never see him again."

She shook her head.

"But you don't know that. He said, 'stay here' that's all."

He gazed into the distance.

"But he's going after the merchant and then he's returning to Raven Woods. He'll never survive. Did you see how tired he was?"

She wasn't having any of it.

"What? He isn't any old man. He's the man other men wish to be."

Though her words rung true, Bren had a gut feeling the hero needed him. He pulled his tunic collar to one side revealing the gaping wound. It needed rapid treatment. That was certain. But it'd have to wait. He summoned his remaining courage and locked gazes with her.

"I'm going. He needs my help."

She recoiled in horror.

"Go? You don't even know where he's

headed."

He disagreed.

"But I think I know where the merchant's going. I'll inform him."

He dusted himself down and headed off which caused her to become enraged.

She screamed in defiance.

"You idiot. You'll NEVER find him, and you'll get yourself killed!"

But as he quickened the pace he called in response, a fierce determination in his voice.

"I WILL find him. And then I'll come back for you."

She had other ideas, bawled in return.

"No you won't. You should have left me to die. We're *finished!*"

***

Meanwhile Maximus was at the village square, knocking frantically upon residents' front doors. Nobody had answered though, the occupants too afraid or uninterested. He cursed under his breath before shouting in frustration.

"Come to your doors. Anybody. I need your help. The beast is no more."

For several seconds there was nothing. His ears twitched, hopeful. Finally a door opened across the way. Someone had been listening. A woman. She'd spied his dishevelled state from a ground floor window and beckoned him forward. Which he did.

She inspected him top to bottom.

"Did you say the serpent is gone?"

He wiped his brow then composed himself.

"Yes. But now I must find the merchant. He fled the village after taking Grace hostage."

The lady gasped in horror.

"Is she?"

"No. She's fine but a lot worse for wear. The same with young Brenton. Do you know where he might be, have you seen him at all?"

She wracked her brain.

"No. I haven't. But when he was at the community centre, he mentioned his next stop was east; er, Greenshire, I think."

Maximus thought he knew where. And it certainly wasn't Greenshire.

He believed he were heading to the Morgrae's original recipient - to clear his name. Regardless, he had to do something. He was also aware Greenshire was in the opposite direction of Raven Woods. So to commit himself was a high-risk strategy. If he got it wrong the merchant would never be caught. He turned to the woman, his expression pleading.

"I require a ride. Mine's been stolen. Do you know…"

She pointed over his shoulder and grinned. He spun around and spied Bren stood in the lane panting. He dashed over to him.

"What's happened, where's Grace?"

He stuttered an emotional response.

"I…I left her behind. She's safe and hates me now. But I don't care. I need to help you find Kapernicus. He must be brought to justice for everything he's caused, and I…I need to see it happen."

~ A Bad Harvest ~

As the dust settled Grace returned home to her parents' awaiting arms while Maximus and Bren trudged to camp. Following a rest and intake of sustenance they were on their feet and ready to move on. The hero had agreed to Bren's request to accompany him but only after promising he'd return to Oakdale following a successful capture of the merchant. With accommodation to be sought soon after. Regarding steeds they managed to acquire a horse each from one of the villagers – an offering of gratitude after Maximus informed the same of the Morgrae's capture.

They looked to the horizon, with Bren eager to proceed yet fearful of what might lie ahead.

"You'll protect me won't you?"

The hero draped an affectionate arm over his shoulders.

"Really? You think I'd abandon you?"

"Er, no. It's just…er, I'm about to leave the place I grew up. Will I need to mature quickly?"

"Quickly?" scoffed the hero. "Not at all. Always be you. Learn about the world at your leisure. Learn from your mistakes and follow your instincts. That said some of the harshest lessons are forced upon us."

He emitted a sigh, his thoughts turning to

his steed. He must locate him. He needed his friend back. Not only for a pleasant ride but as companion. He observed the two horses nearby then to his young friend sitting atop one. He raised a curious eyebrow as he struggled to take charge of it, sliding awkwardly about its back, keen to appear in control.

"Hm. You're not exactly experienced with horses, are you?"

He cringed.

"Is it obvious, because being on the back of Rapscallion was easy. Er, bumpy at times. But fun. I'll try to keep up, but you need to be patient..."

Maximus chuckled.

"Don't worry. There's no rush. We'll catch up with the merchant in due course. And hopefully by then you'll be experienced enough for a chase should one occur."

He hesitated, pondering his next question.

"So, regarding Grace...did you really part on bad terms?"

The teen nodded mournfully.

"Yes. She said we're finished again. She thinks I'm impulsive."

"Well, are you?"

"I don't know. If you mean do I rush into

things, then yes. I've always been like that. My dad did too. Until he met my mum. She, uh reined him in. Does that sound right? Calmed him down I guess."

Maximus patted him on the back.

"Yes, it is. And maybe you should follow their example. To rush in can lead to dire consequences. Especially if unprepared. I know that's easier said than done but try to heed that advice. You must consider consequences following your actions. Anticipate events if possible and devise a coping strategy. You may end up living longer."

He ended his monologue abruptly, realising he weren't ready for such advice. In turn Bren stared at the ground, taking a moment to himself. Observing so he changed the subject.

"You've done yourself proud, lad. You've made me proud and your parents proud. I'd even say you've done Grace proud. I hope you realise that. For someone so young you've coped incredibly well so far."

The boy nodded in acknowledgement while the hero continued.

"I believe your destiny is to be with that girl. She'll be good for you – and you for her. That said, and based on my experience, your relationship might be a tempestuous one."

Bren chuckled, believing the observation accurate.

"I suppose. I was never going to have a normal relationship anyway."

Maximus slowed the pace.

"Normal? It depends how you classify 'normal'. I'd question what a normal relationship is exactly. To me if a couple are happy regardless of the odd argument, I'd say their relationship is still classed as 'normal'. Maybe consider that."

Having heard enough wisdom Bren changed the subject.

"I forgot to mention but when we were eating those apples recently Kapernicus ate one with a maggot inside. He was looking away when he bit into it. It was funny because he didn't know."

Maximus chuckled heartily.

"Poor maggot. A terrible end."

Bren chuckled too before continuing.

"Are you going to kill him? I know I would."

The hero stared into the distance.

"That depends on him. Any patience I had is long gone. If he resists, I'll have no choice. He's made it clear of his intent to stay away from the Woods and I've made clear my intention he *will* accompany me there. He is underhanded and has committed various crimes; is despicable in fact. However we must locate him first. I'm sure Rapscallion knows his current rider isn't his true master and is hopefully making their time together difficult."

Bren stroked the mane of his own animal as they plodded onwards.

"Are you missing him?"

"Oh yes. He and I have been through much together. Good *and* bad times. He has even found cause to bite me on occasion. The menace. And I tell you now – it hurts. That said a steed isn't for life. They can sometimes be targeted for theft or assassination as I've experienced. But for now this girl will do."

He rubbed the animal's flank, the soft hairs comforting to his battle-worn fingertips. Having observed the exchange, Bren smiled before changing the subject.

"I'm missing my parents, my friends AND my old life."

Maximus halted his ride while his companion followed suit.

"You will. You'll never stop missing them. Especially after the way they were taken. Nobody should have to go that way – and with you witnessing it too. You have my deepest sympathies. Words cannot change or mend the tragedies you've experienced but they might help you cope"

He observed the teen staring into the distance, deep in thought.

"I've said this before, but a life lived ultimately leads to death. For you, me, everyone. But it's the nature and quality of one's life that's important. You must believe your parents are watching over you, looking out for you with your best interest at heart. Do your best to make them proud. I'm sure you did while they were alive. But now, with the knowledge they are watching over you, live your life to make their loss easier to bear. Give them reason to smile again. I know much of what I'm saying might not make sense right now but believe me when I say I have your welfare in mind. I really do. Speaking of which how is your shoulder?"

He flexed the area, winced in pain.

"Urgh. Really sore. The Morgrae's claws were sharp."

The hero inspected his own frontage.

"Indeed they were. And I still can't believe I escaped with nothing but bruises. But that will scar – leave a battle wound - something to impress your children. It hurts now and will for some time. But one day you'll be proud of it."

Bren replied unconvinced.

"Do you think so?"

Maximus nodded in affirmation while glancing skyward. He observed the sun had descended below the horizon and realised they wouldn't be able to locate the merchant in the darkness; instead figured it prudent to set up camp for the night. However before he could declare his intentions, heard a commotion in the distance. An eardrum-shattering cacophony.

The night air shuddered as the sound akin to a series of thunderclaps shocked their senses. Every creature in the vicinity scattered, birds, mammals, even the insects. Something terrible was enroute - it's arrival imminent. Both horses reared onto their hind legs in response. Maximus gripped the reins and remained firm, but the boy fell to the ground – his grip weaker. It was obvious something awful was about to appear. Maximus leapt from his steed, stood in front of the boy and drew his sword. He tightened his grip upon the hilt while searching the twilight. Bren Meanwhile regained his composure and scrambled close to him.

There followed a second sound, but closer and headed their way; that of hooves thundering along the dirt track, while a *desperate scream* reverberated about the space; becoming louder with each passing second. Their gazes switched to the curve ahead as all hell broke loose; a figure on horseback sped into view, swaying, cursing but most of all screaming in terror – it was *Kapernicus,* and he were astride *Rapscallion.*

They were being pursued.

By something horrid.

Maximus couldn't believe his luck but didn't want him to escape again. He stepped to one side and then, as the rider drew level yanked him from the steed. Bren meanwhile scrambled onto a grassy bank and safety.

Kapernicus however having been bundled forcefully to the ground called out in desperation – astonished as to what might have occurred. His destination was far from there and preferred to be astride Rapscallion's back; the horse though, he sped sensibly onwards. As did Bren and Maximus' new steeds. The hero maintained a firm grip on the merchant as he struggled to escape. However there was further movement, so he glanced skywards as *something* loomed into view.

It soon became clear what that 'something' was – a dark, airborne silhouette, cape flowing and straddling a broomstick. The shape manoeuvred into view, eyes wide and glistening, a long, pointed and filthy black hat atop her head – It was SZRANIA!

She were there!

She spied the trio as a wicked and satisfied

cackle filled the air. She couldn't believe her luck.

She had come for one - Kapernicus - but found three instead!

Maximus instinctively moved to Bren, to shield him all the while ensuring he kept a tight hold of the merchant. Szrania's laughter ceased, raised her wand and rotated her thick wrist as a penetrating light appeared – illuminating the entire area. Temporarily blinded the trio covered their eyes and for several seconds there was silence. Nothing. She watched, waited, savoured the moment. Finally she opened her mouth.

"Marvellous. Even I couldn't have predicted this: not only the merchant but the slayer AND a child!"

She burst into laughter once more which caused Bren to grip onto Maximus' leg - he were scared witless. She continued, her voice rasping, the words razor sharp.

"Where's my experiment, d*o you have it?*"

He lowered his forearm.

"I do. Right here."

"Give it to me *NOW!*" demanded the hag.

He dug into his satchel and retrieved the glass bottle which he held aloft.

Her eyes widened.

"Hand it over."

He shook his head in defiance.

"In exchange for my blood sample."

She diverted her gaze to Bren which caused him instant goosebumps. She then eyed Kapernicus who turned away with fear.

"And if I say no?"

"Then the creature perishes. We had a deal. You said I could trust you."

Aggrieved, the fiend growled .

"Hm. You were naive for trusting me. An unexpected chink in your armour."

Her gaze penetrated his, a momentary silence.

"You know how much I wish you dead. Yet fortunately I have it with me still. I never expected our paths to cross. I came searching for that one only. My friends and I wish to *'play'* with him."

She reached into her cloak whereupon Maximus spied a glimpse of her flesh underneath, scabby, repulsive and dotted with wiry black hairs. He grimaced while Kapernicus squirmed desperate to flee but too weak to do so; his fingers squeezed ever tighter into the merchant's upper arm.

Meanwhile she inspected the contents of the phial, muttering regretfully.

"The blood of 'he in denial'...a shame."

She directed her attention to the hero once more, he unaware of her utterings.

"Take it."

He grabbed a hold of the bottle and stuffed it into his tunic pocket. He then offered the bottle containing the Morgrae to her who snatched it from his grasp, holding it close to her face. Her eyes narrowed as she inspected the contents within. She observed it belly up with an open wound trailing tiny intestines. She rotated the object for a closer look and spied it in more detail: small fragments of skin and bone floating around it, the body limp. There was no doubt. It had perished.

She drew a deep breath as a frown formed upon her brow, casting him an icy glare.

"It isn't moving. It's *dead!*"

He snapped a reply.

"It was living when I captured it. Do you think it surrendered without a fight?"

Her nostrils flared; her lips turned to a sour grimace. She never expected that. A deal was struck.

"I expect compensation."

She glanced to Kapernicus then Bren in turn.

"I'll take the merchant AND the child instead."

Maximus drew his sword and screamed a furious reply.

"NEVER!"

He lunged forward at lightning speed where the blade stopped millimetres from her windpipe causing her to freeze. She cast him a contemptuous stare.

"HOW DARE YOU? How *dare* you threaten me?"

He stood firm. There was *no way* she were taking Bren. The blade's point touched her skin where she returned a seething, hate filled expression.

"You are mistaken. I take what I want. I *WILL* have him, and I *WILL* feast upon his flesh."

Maximus remained resolute; his posture that of a stone statue.

"Over my dead body. You will NEVER take him. The merchant fine. Do with him as you please. He deserves what's coming. This boy is innocent. I will come to Raven Woods and fight all to defend him. I will even fight you in the next life."

And then, unexpectedly she relaxed; had spied something in her nemesis' eyes; something she'd never anticipated. He a man of such renown and notoriety – even to those who reside in the shadows; putting his own life on the line for a child; one who wasn't of his own flesh and blood. She leant away from the blade while her expression softened. Slight but telling.

"Hm. I can see you care deeply for this one. I don't understand it. Why risk everything?"

He lowered his blade realizing 'civil' communications were to follow.

"Because we're different from you. And you from us. We normal humans have a trait you'll never understand: an instinctive need to protect the innocent. He is yet to find himself, has suffered great loss. Yet here he is. In many eyes he is weak, defenceless and at the mercy of those much stronger. But at the same time he's invincible. He may yet deserve a foul end but not now; time and his own actions shall decide his fate. Not you."

She leant forward to inspect him; her eyes never spying him for whom he really was, a caring innocent; no, she saw him as a potential meal only. Never anything more.

She barked a strict command

"Stand up. Show yourself."

Maximus nodded at the youngster, granting him permission to do so. He rose into the light as she inspected his thin frame.

"Look at you. Little meat anyway. Bah. I ask you this, will you *really* lead a pure life? Can you achieve what every other has failed to do?"

He didn't respond; didn't know how to.

"No. You will not. None ever will."

Her gaze switched to the hero.

"We exist because of your failures as human beings. We are what you deserve. No human *can* and *ever will* lead a pure existence. We feed on your weaknesses and sins; we have no remorse."

Maximus had his own point to make.

"Yet YOU feed on the *innocent*. How do you explain that?"

"We don't follow rules," chuntered the hag. "We run rampant; feed on whatever we choose. I have a sweet tooth and happen to like young meat."

She redirected her attention to Bren once more.

"We shall meet again child. It's only a matter of time."

She pointed a damning finger at the hero.

"And you, an accomplished performer I see. How long can you keep this up? Sooner or later you'll realise your true calling."

He sneered.

"Vile hag, you know nothing of me."

She spat at his feet.

"Wrong. Unfortunately for you I have fingers in many pies and know an uncomfortable amount about your past."

She peered over her right shoulder.

"Demons, seize him."

Suddenly several apparitions appeared, vaporous forms emerging from the darkness. They grabbed hold of Kapernicus by the wrists and yanked him free of Maximus' grip. He screamed in terror. His petrified gaze piercing Maximus' own. Meanwhile Bren closed his eyes, wishing he hadn't witnessed such a sight while Maximus didn't react. He didn't need to. It was the merchant's own doing.

In moments, his horrific screams were all that remained; fading screams from an individual scheduled to suffer; set for torture by claws of beings that existed only to cause pain and suffering.

He was reaping what he'd sown.

Szrania meanwhile began to chuckle. Slowly at first but then into a prolonged, and frenzied laugh. Bren moved behind the hero hoping to use him as a shield while she returned the wand to the folds of her cloak, causing darkness to envelop the pair. She rose further into the air, her festering cloak flapping in the breeze. Finally she tilted her head back and stared down her piggy nose, her words once more threatening.

"Keep away from my Woods, slayer. For you will not leave. And you child,"

She held Bren's gaze for an unnerving period of time, her thoughts pure evil, his mortification.

"Sleep tight and sweet dreams."

She turned and headed away from them in the direction from whence she came; to the foreboding sanctuary of the Woods, the sounds of her wicked laughter fading as she disappeared into the night.

With the witch gone Bren rose to his feet and gazed into Maximus' eyes, He felt punch drunk. His body quivering with fear, the experience scorched into his mind; adding to the other horrific events he'd witnessed.

"She looked into my soul and knows how scared I am. She's...she's going to eat me one day, isn't she?"

Maximus spat in the hag's direction.

"Not while I'm present. I'd say it's an empty threat. She had nothing else to say and wished to appear in control."

He peered into the darkness.

"She feeds on fear as well as children. Don't let threats her infest your thoughts."

He changed tact, wishing to lighten the mood.

"Besides she's a child-eater. You'll soon be a man. Your once 'sweet meat' will become unappetising."

He scanned the darkness, detecting the faintest of sounds nearby. Seconds later they heard the unmistakeable yet familiar sound of hooves approaching. They observed as Rapscallion raced into view heading towards them at great speed. They smiled in response so happy to see him return. They greeted him with a huge amount of affection, stroking, caressing his soft coat; making a grand old fuss, while he appreciated each moment of attention; the look in his eyes one of similar relief; with the trio incredibly fortunate to be reunited again.

~ A Tainted Sunrise ~

Soon enough the pair were astride his back with Maximus looking ahead, relief in his eyes.

"You've made me proud Rapscallion. I'd have kept running that's for sure!"

He glanced at his companion.

"Yes, my friend, he must be a glutton for punishment too, just like us!"

In a dour mood still Bren muttered under his breath.

"But I'm meant to suffer."

Crucially Maximus missed the remark, the hoot of an owl overshadowing it. Meanwhile he continued, adjusting his attitude and making a positive contribution.

"Your horse is amazing. I'd like a similar one someday."

The hero chuckled.

"Similar? Heh. Be glad there's only one of him. A stubborn steed such as this will run you ragged."

"Huh," he returned. "Really?"

"No." responded the hero. "My point is each animal is unique in character. Some placid, others stubborn for instance. You'll bond with your own steed eventually. Eventually you'll become an accomplished rider and appreciator of equines too. Make no mistake about that. I'm a rarity in the fact I believe the company of animals often outweigh that of humans."

"Bren processed the remark.

"Why is that?"

"Simple really. They're dependable; always there for us; keep the biggest of secrets and never complain."

Bren chuckled, realising he were talking from experience.

"Heh. You know best I suppose."

A little later and with dawn approaching; an unusual crimson glow bleeding into the horizon Maximus sensed Bren leant against him fast asleep, the sounds of his breathing indicating for the first time he were at peace. He took a moment to reflect, consider his own circumstances as well as his; with him not of an age for deep conversation proved he had a heart of gold. He thought back to when he was a passing traveller stopping for a few days at a random village and how, with fate's intervention, had become entwined in a deeply affecting tale of tragedy and loss; with Bren having transitioned from a curious teenager to having lost everything during an incredibly short period of time. He shook his head, wondering how the youngster was going to move forward, recover even. Would he want to return to Oakdale? Would anybody take him in? Those were questions he'd need answering.

One thing was certain; he'd protect him with his own life until they parted ways. Whenever that might be. More than anything he needed security, companionship, somebody to watch over him until he found his feet. If that were even possible. Another thing he intended to do was keep to his word and use the crystal to fashion a memorial, a keepsake for them each to wear; an object to remember their time together by, as well as something to cherish; and he were headed in the same direction of the craftsman qualified to complete the task.

Meanwhile back at lake Dale, under the last light of a fading moon, tranquillity had returned to its waters with barely a ripple upon its surface; recently polluted with so much blood, rage, and terrible loss, back to how they should have stayed; filled with life; that of its usual aquatic inhabitants.

Only those gifted by the hands of Mother Nature herself...

The adventures continue

While coming to terms with the horrific events at Lake Dale, Maximus and Bren are whisked away on another exciting adventure: in search of a cursed treasure secreted within the Jewelled Valley. An infamous and dangerous location abandoned by most. But after meeting a pair of new faces, events take a positive turn, with the teen looking forward to a brighter future. Meanwhile, separated from his young charge, and following a dangerously close call, the hero faces a foe unlike anything he'd encountered before, a terrifying manifestation which fears nothing or no one; with its threat of causing devastation for the populace rocking him to the core.

With that in mind, and a life-changing decision for Bren to consider, how far can the duo be pushed before they break?

And in the depths of Raven Woods, is Szrania placated following the capture of Kapernicus or is she planning further excursions into the human domain?

As far as she's concerned the fun has just begun.

Coming soon:

Book Two: Skelton's Horde

And soon after:

*Book Three: *Poison Hearts*

*Book Four: *The Allegiance*

*Book Five: *Fury of the Child Eater*

*Book Six: *Mooney's Legacy*

**not final*

About the Author

Ian A Taylor wrote his first story in 1987; a tribute to the books he used to read at the time. Fantasy-adventure. He was impressed by the illustrations found within, black and white, rich with detail which inspired him to do the same with his works. Aware of life's struggles, his characters run the gamut of emotions too, experiencing the highs of a deserved victory, and crushing lows of defeat.

A happy husband and father who is passionate about his stories and intends to write until he no longer can.

You can add your views on his Facebook page at: @Author.Olsentonbooks or Twitter: @IanTayl90927967

The author with his own prize Esox. Not a 'Lucifer', as those beasts are double the size. It was returned to swim free as always, but not before chomping his fingers first. Perhaps he should have followed Maximus' advice.

Finally, feel free to post an honest review. Your feedback means a lot to the author.

Sleeping Puppy Books 2023

Printed in Great Britain
by Amazon

19500498R00233